Novels by J.L. Weil

THE DIVISA SERIES
Losing Emma: A Divisa novella
Saving Angel
Hunting Angel
Breaking Emma: A Divisa novella
Chasing Angel
Loving Angel
Redeeming Angel

LUMINESCENCE TRILOGY
Luminescence
Amethyst Tears
Moondust

RAVEN SERIES
White Raven

SINGLE NOVELS
Starbound

It is bittersweet to end the series that is dear to my heart. This is for every person who stumbled across Saving Angel and ended up loving Chase and Angel as much as I do. This is for you. I can't thank you enough! You gave me courage to continue this crazy, fun, amazing, and rewarding job.

Redeeming Angel

J.L. Weil

Kindle Edition Copyright 2015
by J.L. Weil
http://jlweil.blogspot.com/
All rights reserved.
First Edition September 2015
ISBN-10:**1517499003**
ISBN-13:**9781517499006**

Edited by Kelly Hashway
Cover design by Jennifer Weil

Kindle Edition, License Notes

This eBook is licensed for your personal enjoyment only. This eBook may not be resold or given away to other people. If you would like to share this book with another person, please purchase an additional copy for each person. If you're reading this book and did not purchase it, or it was not purchased for your use only, then return it to Amazon.com and purchase your own copy. Thank you for respecting the hard work of this author.

This book is a work of fiction. Names, characters, places, and incidents are a product of the writer's imagination or have been used fictitiously and are not to be construed as real. Any resemblances to persons, living or dead, actual events, locales, or organizations is entirely coincidental.

All rights are reserved. No part of this may be used or reproduced in any manner whatsoever without written permission from the author.

A DIVISA NOVEL

BOOK 5

Part 1

Love is composed of a single soul inhabiting two bodies.

—Aristotle

Chapter 1

{Angel}

Like a kid who couldn't resist the last piece of chocolate, I wrapped my hand around the bars of my cage. *A freaking cage!* It only took a second for the searing pain to register—red-hot burning. I snatched my hand away, swallowing the scream at the back of my scratchy throat. Hours of screaming taught me two things. One: no one could hear me. The damn dungeon was probably soundproof. And two: it was entirely Chase's fault.

Bastard.

My hand was on fire. It felt like the flesh was literally melting off the bone. I glanced down to examine the extent of my injury, cursing Chase Winters to a hundred different kinds of hell. Redness bubbled along my slim fingers, the skin burning like a bitch. "Damn it," I hissed, cradling my hand. The upside, in an hour it would hardly be noticeable, just one of the many perks from being mutated by Chase Winters.

My egotistical, self-righteous, determined-to-make-me-miserable boyfriend, who also happened to be a half-demon.

Pain and anger whirled through me, a potent cocktail.

So many changes were reeling through my body. I didn't know exactly what was going on inside, but for once it didn't cause me physical pain. Oh, just the opposite. It was like an addict, begging and pleading for more, dying to be released.

Each bond Chase and I fortified had mutated the cells in my body. We hadn't known at the time what the outcome would be, and truthfully, I think we'd both been powerless to stop the forces of Hell. It was inevitable. Chase had saved my life, but by doing so, forged a link with my soul—a link that connected me not to just him, but to his bloodline—to Alastair—his demon father. My humanity had been pretty much doomed from that moment. The closer we got, the deeper our bonds and the darker my humanity became.

Man, I sure knew how to pick them.

A strangled laugh bubbled out. "Chase." His name echoed against the dirty gray concrete walls. The jerk was going to pay. Who did he think he was, locking me up like an animal? I was supposed to be the love of his life. What a freaking joke. Why did it matter that I suddenly embraced the dark side? Had I not accepted him as he was? All the flaws (not that there were many), all the danger, and the near death experiences. Now he just stopped caring.

Bull crap. I didn't buy it.

REDEEMING ANGEL

He was whipped and would do anything to save his precious Angel. It was the sole reason I was in this current predicament. Things had gotten…complicated. I wasn't precisely sure how things had gotten so out of hand. There were dark patches in my memories, but really, why did I care about the how? It was where I was going that mattered. And I had a purpose. Being contained in a demon version of Alcatraz was not how I envisioned spending my first year of college.

Plopping down on a small bed in the corner, the lumpy mattress dug into my butt. I squirmed, trying to find a comfortable position, and finally gave up. No amount of wiggling was going to make this sad excuse of a bed comfortable. I guess I should have been thankful he didn't make me sleep on the floor.

There had to be a way to get to him. I just needed to appeal to his sappy side, because I didn't see another way out of this godforsaken contraption the hunters had constructed. Leave it to a bunch of whacked-out-of-your-mind demon hunters to possess advanced yet archaic torture chambers.

The metal was a blend of titanium and amber. At least I thought it was amber. The flecks of gold reminded me of Chase when his demon prevailed his humanity. I eyed the perimeter with my newly enhanced eyeballs, desperate for a small crack in its defense, and to my utter dismay, I found nothing. Nada. Zilch. Zippo.

I was so screwed.

Rage boiled up inside of me. Hot, scolding, and fierce. There was no fear, grief, or panic…only power.

It crackled, radiating in the tiny box, and if it wasn't being snuffed out by this prison, its destruction would have been catastrophic. This harboring of hate inside me was easily evoked and took nothing more than a flick of a switch. Keeping it controlled and reining it in was an entirely different problem I had yet to master.

Dampness gathered on my cheeks.

And then it struck me.

They were tears, I realized slowly.

I swiped at my cheeks, disgusted *I* was crying. Weakness wasn't something I could afford, not when I had a task set before me. Failing wasn't an option, but there were these moments, these little breakdowns, where my humanity peeked through. Good and bad. Light and darkness. Human and demon. They resided inside me, but the want for power was resilient. Luckily, the new and improved me was stronger, able to keep my humanity at bay.

Yet, I knew there was one very determined, fearless, and

ruthless obstacle in my way. He was going to be the key to getting out of this dump, considering he was the only person who actually came down here. Not that I cared one way or the other. It was the good thing about losing your humanity; you no longer gave a rat's ass about feelings. You didn't care your friends left you here to rot. I only had one purpose now. Like a crackhead looking for their next fix, it was all I thought about.

I sat in the middle of the bed, back rigid, and stared between the bars. The memories, they were the kicker, flashes of my former life. My childhood. Mom. And even Dad. Moving to Spring Valley where my life changed. Even then, I was happy, so happy it made me sick. The first day in hickville and meeting Lexi. But it was always the memories of Chase Winters that did something funky inside me.

From falling in love to thinking he was the biggest douche in the world. There wasn't a whole lot to do trapped underground, so my mind drifted, and I'd relived those moments over and over again. It was maddening. The memories actually hurt more than the damn demon-proofed bars.

But the absolute worst were the memories of thinking I'd lost him. That was a torture I'd rather not relive, and it shot a different kind of pain down my body, curling my toes. Both physically and emotionally, it sucked. Knowing I couldn't survive without him—the bonds made sure of it and even the power rippling through my veins knew it.

I blinked at the harsh lights shining down at me, the only light in the entire dingy room. No windows. Not that I needed the light or glow of the sun. My eyes saw perfectly in the dark, a new side effect from being the keystone.

Also, my very attuned hearing picked up the approaching footsteps before I saw a face. I didn't need any special abilities to tell me who it was. The tingle that spread throughout was a foolproof detector. My body went haywire when Chase was near.

So annoying.

It was the times when *he* came to see me that were challenging. The good girl inside me fought tooth and nail to the surface, clawing and scratching just to give *him* false hope I could be saved. There was no saving me. The darkness was too strong.

But the other part of me, she was relentless, screaming his name. I knew he was suspicious, but that was about to change.

I had a plan.

A dirty, no-good plan.

{Chase}

REDEEMING ANGEL

When I met Angel, I never imagined we'd end up here. Back in my pre-Angel days, I had a plan. It involved me on a crusade, traveling across the country, blaring the Eagles greatest hits, and killing as many demons as possible. A lonely road. Life rarely turns out as we expect.

Meeting Angel changed everything.

The good, the bad, and Hell.

How many other guys could say their girlfriend commanded a demon army? None. That's how many. In a twisted way, it was kind of hot, until she went all Terminator on me, glowing red eyes and all.

Bitter anger surged through me. It was an emotion Angel and I shared more and more lately. It coated my insides like battery acid as I picked up speed, darting and weaving past the college row houses, making a beeline toward the trees surrounding campus. It was early or late depending on how you looked at it. A streak of whitish-yellow crested on the horizon, overriding the dark blue sky dotted with tiki torch stars that would have made an astrologist geek-out.

When I wasn't with Angel all I could do was think about being with her. Part of that might have been our bond, but ninety-five percent of it was just my wanting to be near her. Each time I saw her, my heart splintered, more painful than any knife to the gut. Seeing her locked in a cell no bigger than a cabin pissed me off. Knowing I was the one responsible for putting her there really pissed me off. The guilt was ridiculous.

Not everyone agreed with my methods. It was no surprise Emma fully supported caging Angel. Lexi, on the other hand, lost her shit. Angel was her best friend, her first real friend who wasn't a half-demon. I knew how much she cared for Angel, and not letting Lexi see her was a battle I thought I would lose some days. But I knew once Lexi got a glimpse of Angel behind bars, she would crack—and in a not-so-pretty way. Like Hello Kitty crossed with the Hulk.

It was a shuddering thought.

The speed of the brisk wind washed over my face as I ran, trekking up rocky hills, catapulting over fallen trees, and dodging anything in my path. I was impatient to see her, needing to know she was still safe, that she hadn't found a way to escape and unleash Hell on Earth. Good times.

Not even halfway there, I felt the familiar prickle of disorder. Lower-demon would be my guess.

Oh goodie. Just want I needed—a punching bag to release all my rage and frustration.

The bastard was coming straight for me, and with the way I was feeling right now, my anticipation grew. Skidding to a halt, the not-so-bright demon zoomed right past me. *Dumbass*. I whirled around, fists curled.

Realizing his blunder, he circled back toward me, a ball of blazing darkness. In the shadows of the tall evergreens and the thick maples, his eyes glowed like hot ambers, charcoal oily skin flickering as he ran. Demons without a human suit were ugly mofos.

A split-second before he reached me, I lunged, choke-slamming the slimy prick to the ground. A pile of pine needles embedded into his flesh in what I considered icing on the cake.

"I hope that hurt," I sneered, my fingers squeezing.

His black lips pulled back, and he hissed, "Where is ssshe?"

I titled my head to the side, pressing my thumb into his windpipe. "Who?" I countered, playing ignorant. They were more fun when provoked, and so was I.

"You can't hide her forever."

I had a mammoth-sized bone to pick with Alastair, and his minions were just a means to an end. "It's killing you, isn't it? Knowing I have what every demon in Hell desires. The key to your freedom."

He hissed, his tongue—the color of tar and forking like a serpent—catching between his jagged fangs. "Tell me where the keyssstone isss."

I glared. "I just bet you would love to know."

Shooting daggers, his eyes got brighter. "Then you die."

I cracked my neck. "Bring it."

There was no hesitation.

Not from me. Not from him.

Launching to the side, the lower-demon shot forward, a blur of dark limbs. I ducked, his swing whizzing over my head, and sprung up behind him. The heel of my foot slammed into the bow of his back and down he went. I welcomed the physicality of fighting. Fist against flesh. Knuckles cracking bone. I poured every bit of fury, worry, and aggravation into each punch, each kick.

No sooner did he hit the ground was he back on his feet. I leapt backward, but not before he was able to clip the side of my jaw in a brain-rattling hit. I spit blood from the corner of my mouth, thriving on the pain that erupted from the side of my face. It fueled my hate.

So the bastard wants to play that way, does he?

This time when he came at me, I grabbed him and spun, tossing his ass straight into a tree. Bark splintered, flying up into the air around his grotesque face. I charged, the ground trembling under my feet. The demon met me halfway in a thundering clash, both of us taking pot shots at the other in punches so fast you felt them before you saw them coming.

My knuckles were bleeding, but the pain was irrelevant. I didn't feel it. All I saw was Angel's face with crimson eyes—demon eyes. I pounded and pounded, dipping and dodging as many blows as I could foresee. Time ceased. We could have been going at each other for a minute or an hour. Mostly, I was mocking him. Holding back, to drag out the fight.

And then he took me by surprise, landing a blow that stunned me for a fraction of a second, but that was all a demon needed. His hand went straight for my life source, latching on with his claws on my heart. I guess he wasn't joking about killing me. Too bad today wasn't my day. I had a mission, which didn't include dying.

It was time for the stupid SOB to go home. Wiggling my right hand behind me, I inched my fingers to the hilt of the blade tucked into my pants. He was too busy basking in what he thought was surely a victory to notice the glint in my eyes. Doing what I could probably do blindfolded, I sent the blade into the dead center of his chest.

Let it rain demon ash.

His eyes went wide right before I was covered from head to toe in smoky powder. I sat up, shaking the dust from my hair. What a way to ruin a perfectly awesome T-shirt, but there was no time to waste.

A cold wind moved down my spine. I jumped to my feet, pivoting, and took off through the trees, racing toward Angel. My brain was churning. They were looking for her. Of course, I hadn't thought Hell would just forget about its secret weapon, but I'd really banked on having more time to figure shit out. I didn't have much of a plan. Nothing concrete, really only consisting of a few things: Save Angel. Destroy Alastair. Don't die.

As I crested the grassy hill, I looked over my shoulder, listening. It would do none of us any good if I were being followed. Hunter or demon, I had to make sure neither of them found Angel.

I knew the risks of what I was doing, hiding her. So many people could get hurt. People I loved, but *I* had brought Angel so deep into my world. If only I had stayed away from her… But I hadn't, and look where that had gotten her. I owed it to Angel to pull her out of the fiery depths of Hell.

If anyone should be sucked down into the clutches of the underworld, it should be me. Never Angel.

A whoosh of air left my lungs, and I shot down the hill, breaking into the clearing lit by the golden streaks of sunlight. With a heavy heart, the old barn-like door creaked as I pulled it open and let it close behind me, shutting out all the glorious light. This place gave me the creeps, and it was no place for Angel.

I cursed under my breath, swiping a cobweb from above my head. This had to end. I wasn't sure how much longer my resolve could last. Seeing her trapped here was wearing on me. I had to work harder and faster at finding the answers. I would not rest.

Taking the rickety concrete stairs down into an abandoned cellar, I felt the familiar tingles. Even though the circumstances were grim, it didn't stop the excitement from fluttering inside my belly or the hope I might get a glimpse of the girl I loved.

Chapter 2

{Chase}

My heart stopped.

Curled in a corner, her dark hair curtained her face. She didn't move at my approach, yet I knew she felt my presence. I heard her heart kick up, beating in an identical rhythm to mine. It was the same each time. Our separation, whether it was hours or days, caused amplified reactions between us.

I paused at the bottom of the steps. If I closed my eyes, I could see Angel coming out of her house, the sunlight streaming through her hair and picking up the red highlights. And she'd be wearing those little shorts she loved. I might have loved them more. They did crazy things to her sun-kissed legs, which did crazy things to me. There were a number of things about her that caused my belly to turn inside out.

Her scent. Her smile. Her laugh. Her sharp tongue.

The usual icy guilt drenched my insides. I had to fight every basic instinct to zap across the room, throw open the door, swoop her up in my arms, and take her far, far away from here.

My fists balled at my sides and a shudder rolled through me.

Then her head lifted. Letting out a shaky breath, I walked toward the bars of her confinement, careful not to get too close. "You're awake."

She stared right through me.

No life glittered in her eyes. She was just an empty shell with no one home.

My stomach knotted.

I'd come to expect the crimson glares, so to see her blue eyes made me a little dizzy. "Angel," I called softly.

"Chase?" Her voice was hoarse and confusion clouded in her expression. Slowly, her eyes traveled over the room, and I felt her blood pressure rise.

This was only the second time I'd seen the clarity in her eyes since that night she'd killed her father. I was suddenly afraid this moment was going to slip away before I had the chance to savor it, because who knew how long it would be until the next time? I could only hope it would be sooner rather than later.

My thrill at seeing her overrode my common sense. Before I processed what I was doing, I moved, shutting myself inside with Angel. It was only a blink, and the only reasonable explanation for my stupidity was she made me do stupid things.

"I can't believe it's you," I said, framing her pale face.

"Who else would it be?" The hoarseness in her voice caused a twinge in my chest, for I knew it was from screaming.

Her beauty struck me hard, like a bolt of lightning. She was the most beautiful creature I'd ever seen. As soon as I touched her face, I knew I was in trouble. My heart hammered inside my chest. *Thump. Thump. Thump. Thump.* It felt as if it had been a lifetime since I'd been able to feel her skin. It was still as soft as I remembered.

Then I was kissing her.

My lips were fastened to hers in a hard, desperate kiss. I pulled her close, not thinking. In seconds we were wrapped up in each other, the gloomy room disappearing, which tended to happen when we kissed. Her arms secured around me, fingers running along the back of my neck and leaving scorching tingles trailing from her touch.

Deep down, I knew everything wasn't hunky-dory. She wasn't magically better, but how convenient the mind worked to get what it really wanted.

And oh, I wanted her.

There was no denying that every fiber of my body wanted this. It had been weeks since my lips had touched hers, and the hunger came on swift and strong. I ached inside. Ached for the physical touch of her skin, of her soft, berry-flavored lips.

Using my tongue, I parted her lips and plunged, deepening the kiss. A thousand fires ignited inside me, joining into one flame I couldn't contain. I was drowning in the sweetest fire. My hands inched under her shirt, splaying over her lower back. The world didn't seem so screwed up when Angel was kissing my brains out. It was the greatest buzz.

She pulled back just slightly, her eyes capturing mine, and then she cupped the back of my neck, reclaiming the distance. Damn. She kissed me in a way that put all others to shame. It would have made the Angel I loved blush. There was nothing innocent or sweet as she nipped my lower lip, and I swore I tasted blood.

Her breathy moan nearly undid me, yet it was the wiggling of her hips that sent me over the edge. Our hearts sped up. I totally took the kiss there, throwing every worry and fear into it. It was then I felt the sudden change in her, but I was powerless to pull away. My demon was screaming, "Yes, yes, yes!" He loved the darker side of Angel, and it was tearing me in two. The struggle between my demon and me was the hardest I'd ever had to deal with.

I gripped her hips and pushed back. Her eyes. They were dark in the shadowy light, but the glimmer of red was undeniable.

They were wrong. So very wrong.

My stomach sunk in what felt like a swift kick to the gonads. Having my emotions plunge from one extreme to another left me slightly off-kilter, and after the intimacy we'd shared, I was torn in half. Remorse ate away at me.

It was a splash of cold water thrown in my face. Shell-shocked, some part of my brain thought I'd been struck by lightning. It only took a moment of sanity to bring me back to Earth. I flashed to the other side of the bars, slamming the door shut with a clatter of metal. So many things could have gone wrong. What had I'd been thinking, and that was the problem. I hadn't been thinking. Too much time had gone by without seeing her blue eyes that I lost it, which could have led to a catastrophe. I couldn't allow for mistakes or let my emotions get the best of me.

I released a long, deep sigh, instead of thumping my forehead on the nearest wall like I wanted.

Control. It had always been a struggle, and I spent my life exercising power over my demon. All it had taken was one look from Angel to shatter a lifetime of discipline.

I scowled darkly over my shoulder, and she gave a sultry, devious laugh. "If you let me out of here, we can go for round two."

My face remained motionless. "Do you still want to open a portal to between Hell and Earth?"

Silence.

"That's what I thought."

"Are you sure?" She tucked her hair back. "Because your body definitely wants more."

I took a step forward, a storm swirling inside me. "Maybe. But I've spent my life battling my demon. I think I can handle other parts of my body."

She choked out a laugh. "The notorious Chase Winters. Heartbroken. She's never coming back, you know."

Folding my arms, I showed no emotion. Perhaps I'd grown used to her intimidations over the last week. "Guess what? I won't give up. And you know when I want something, I don't stop."

Frustration rolled off her. "God, you're such a sucker. I twitch my ass and bat my eyes, and you're drooling all over me. Typical male."

I exhaled roughly, sparing her a brief glance. "You and I both know there is nothing typical about me."

She lowered her head. "I've accepted that, accepted you for who you are"—emotion clogged her vocal cords—"but why is it so hard for you to accept me? That I've changed?" Her long lashes blinked back tears.

A muscle popped along my jawline. Her high and low tactics wreaked havoc on my sanity. My body went rigid.

Her lower lip quivered. "Why are you treating me like this? How can you claim to love me? This isn't love." Her eyes were shining with dampness.

Like a hamster wheel, this topic of conversation was going nowhere and was a waste. The fact she could doubt my love only reinforced how much of a hold the darkness had on Angel. Our bond made it impossible to question the depth of my feelings. "Here." I tossed one of her favorite gamer shirts and a pair of lounge pants through the bars. "I brought you some clean clothes."

She caught them midair, causing her rumpled shirt to inch up. My eyes were drawn to the exposed skin. It was still a rush, seeing my marks on her. They trailed up her side, identical to mine, a reminder of our connection. Soul. Heart. Body.

Every second. Every minute. Every goddamn hour that ticked by with her sealed away drove my insane, because I was no closer to finding a way to cure her. *If* she could be cured.

It wasn't like she was ill. This wasn't a cold or the flu. I couldn't give her a pill or a dose of medicine and expect her to be fine in twenty-four hours.

"I've got to go," I said. If my calculations were correct, she was about to activate her rage tactic. I'd rather avoid that today. She'd already gotten to me.

{Angel}

I felt sorry for the lab rats. Being caged sucked. Being tormented by Chase's forlorn eyes and grim scowls was downright depressing.

I was a menace. Dangerous. The darkness Hell trapped inside me was pissed, and it was time Chase saw me for who I was. If I had accepted his demon, then why couldn't he accept mine? "You're a hypocrite, you know that?" I yelled at his back. "When I get out of here, I'm going to rip the flesh from your bones."

He halted, placing a palm on the wall.

"They're coming for me," I informed. I was stalling, because even though his smirks and frowns were irritating, it beat being alone. There was something almost fun about mincing words with him and making him suffer.

"They'll never find you." His voice was low.

It was cocky conviction in his tone that pushed me to my boiling point. "Shut up," I spat.

He finally spun around and faced me. "But *I'll* find them. In fact, I met one of your groupies on the way here."

The knowledge of what he said sparked, caught fire, and spread through my veins. "Shut up!"

His nostrils flared, sexy if you were into that kind of thing and apparently I was. "He sends his regards. I think his last words were *I'll be back*. Cheesy, if you ask me, embodying Arnold Schwarzenegger."

"Shut. *Shut*. Shut!" *Kill him*. The words whispered through my mind. I couldn't have cared less where the voice came from. *Off with his head*.

Caution crept into his eyes. "Whoa. I think someone needs a tranq or some happy pills."

Anger gnawed at me. Red flames moved through my blood, and it felt as if I would spontaneously combust if I didn't hurl the fire building inside me.

It gave me a high, and I wanted more. I wanted to hurt him. But mostly, I wanted out of this prison. There was this deep yearning in the pit of my stomach, a calling from Hell. It was time for drastic measures.

I clenched the titanium bars, and even as my skin sizzled, the pain making my eyes water, I hung on. The metal might neutralize my newly discovered abilities, but it didn't stop me from harming myself. One way or another, I was getting out of this hellhole.

"No!" he shouted, moving so fast he startled me. His hands shot through the bars, clasping my wrists and physically removing them from the bars.

I wasn't a match for his strength, especially after the amount of agony radiating down my arms. I went still, suddenly feeling weird, and backed away from Chase. My back hit the wall.

"Angel," he called, frantic.

Time seemed to slow, and the world around me began to darken until a sheet of blackness engulfed me. Sound faded from my ears. *Well, that might have been a bad idea.*

Chapter 3

{Angel}

I blinked my eyes open and realized I couldn't breathe. Why couldn't I catch my breath? There was air. My lungs were working, yet I felt like I was suffocating. Unfortunately, this was a feeling I was quite familiar with. As ridiculous as it sounded, I'd thought these new abilities that had awakened inside me would make me…I don't know…invincible to such fears.

Rising to my feet, I swayed unnaturally to the left and my hand flew out to steady myself on the wall. It was then I noticed my pitiful attire. My clothes were torn and I had dark black spots on the front of my shirt that looked eerily like blood.

Oh God.

I was betting it was *my* blood…or so I hoped, because the alternative meant I'd hurt someone. In shock, my entire body was trembling as if I'd run a marathon—uphill.

I bit my lip and—

Sweet baby Jesus.

My lips were swollen, but that wasn't what made my knees buckle. I could taste Chase. His brand of flavor was one I'd never forget. It was permanently etched into my taste buds.

He'd been here.

And he'd left me.

In a cage!

Why?

Dust bunnies lingered, floating in the stale and musky air. Snapshots of images flashed behind my eyes, making my brain hurt. Everything was so foggy. I winced, fingers pressing into my temples. It felt like my head was splitting in two, and there was a golf ball-sized lump on the back of my scalp.

Eyes cast downward, a pop of blue caught my gaze. A pair of yoga pants and one of my favorite T-shirts lay on the cold, concrete floor. At the sight of clean clothes, I forgot about my fuzzy head and quickly stripped, slipping on the soft fabric. Burrowing my nose into the material at my shoulder, I inhaled.

It smelled of laundry detergent and faintly of a woodsy scent. It smelled of home.

Pangs twanged around my heart.

I wanted to go home. I wanted to see my mom. I desperately wanted to see Chase.

My hands dropped to my sides, horror rolling through me as

I realized I might never leave this place. This might be it. These titanium bars and the windowless room might be the last things I see before I leave this earth. Depressing and utterly messed up.

As my lower lip started to tremble, I tipped my chin up, refusing to let Hell break me. I wouldn't give them the satisfaction. It was bad enough there were gapping black spots in my memory, but to travel down the lonely road of self-pity wasn't going to help me survive. And I was damn determined to live.

Mom needed me. But Chase needed me more. Our lives were intertwined. If anything happened to me, he would be doomed. My last breath would be his last breath. That thought alone was enough to make my spine a little straighter. Hell was not going to use me. Whatever mutations were going on inside me, I needed to find a way to stay *me*, a way to stop the darkness. I wasn't utterly clueless. I knew something was very wrong with me. The blackouts, they weren't normal, not even by Divisa standards. I was close to freaking out.

This wasn't the first time I'd been held captive. How many eighteen-year-olds could say that? Not that I was bragging, just the opposite. It was completely messed up, just like my life.

So I made myself concentrate on the small things, like clean clothes. It was little, but when you'd been wearing the same clothes for a week, it was an indulgence taken for granted. The only thing that would top clean clothes would be a foaming bubble bath. All I had was a lukewarm shower in a refrigerator-sized box.

Dear God, I would give my left boob for a hot bath and a bubble bar from Lush.

I sighed.

Chase forbad me even the simplest luxury. It was a flitting thought, but like a twig, something inside me snapped. Gone was the confusion and murkiness, and in its place was a fire that crackled and popped. Everything became clear again, my purpose, who my real enemies were. Chase Winters was going to regret ever sticking me behind bars.

{Chase}

I woke up alone and drenched in sweat and ready to kick some serious ass. My body was tight, prepared for a fight, but unless I was going to be duking it out with my shadow, there was no need for my demon to be on edge. Yet he was.

Sitting up, I ran a hand through a very bad case of bedhead and looked toward the window. I blinked. I didn't have a normal sleep schedule, not like the rest of the world. Nowadays, it was hard for me to tell whether it was night or day without peering outside or at my phone.

My vision didn't need to adjust to the dark room, a demon perk. There were many perks—treacherous demon DNA—but none of my abilities could help Angel. As unearthly as my skills were, I didn't have the power to sever the cursed connection Hell had over her.

So, of course, I acted like a class act jerk and taunted her, because God knows that was totally going to cure her. In my self-defense, that dirty and sensual stunt she pulled scrambled my logic and control.

If I was being real, Angel and I thrived on riling each other in what was a twisted form of foreplay. It was how we met, how we fell in love, how we ended up here.

Control.

I was beginning to hate the word.

Gazing up at the ceiling, I secured my arm behind my head and stared at the water spot that stood out against the stark white paint. My thoughts turned, mulling over an absurd plan I'd formulated during my run back to campus. The ludicrousness of it was what I liked. In my head, the less likely my survival rate, the greater my chances of success.

An inside look at just how warped my mind really was.

I listened to the wind whistling outside the slightly cracked window, to the crickets rubbing their wings together, and to all the other little critters that prowled at night. The breeze that blew through the room was neither too hot nor too cold. I imagined this would be my last moment of calmness for some time.

Leave it to Lexi to ruin my last five minutes of peace and solitude.

"I need to see her!" she demanded for the millionth time as she burst through my door. Her ivory skin was flushed, and unless I was mistaken, she was trying to kill me with a dirty look.

Shaking my head, I scrubbed my hands over my eyes. "Privacy? Is that too much to ask for?"

Lexi drifted right into the center of the room, not giving a second thought to my state of attire or possible lack of. "This is college. There is no such thing."

I groaned, closing my eyes and hoping she would disappear.

"Did you hear me?" she added coolly.

I opened one eye, gazing up. Ugh. She was still here, hovering over my bed and glaring down at me with impatient, bright aqua eyes. Her wheat-colored hair was pulled back into a ponytail, emphasizing the dark shadows under her eyes and the gauntness of her cheeks. She was worrying herself sick.

Pressing my lips together, I asked, "Shouldn't you be at class or studying something? Don't you have a boyfriend?"

"It's almost ten o'clock. *At night*," she added helpfully, in case I was confused what time of day she was referring to. "And Colin is studying if you must know." Feet planted, she crossed her arms over the pink sweatshirt that hung off one shoulder. "I'm not leaving until you take me to see her."

Just what I needed—a sit-in taking place in my room. Scooting up, I pressed my back against the headboard, tugging down my worn gray T-shirt. "We've been over this," I mumbled.

"I know. And I still don't understand why I can't see my best friend." Her lips turned downward.

"Lex," I growled, not wanting to rehash the same old argument. "My answer is the same. No." I held my ground.

She looked around the room and then yelled, "Emma!" My cousin turned her pouty plea on the hunter as she darkened my doorway.

My jaw hardened. "Jesus. Why not make this a party?"

Emma stood against the door, ankles crossed in her usual black jeans and tank. "Oh, someone is feeling prickly this evening. Did the big, bad wolf have a rough day?"

I struggled for patience, the vein in my neck throbbing.

"Kiss ass, Emma."

The redheaded Lara Croft wannabe absently spun a pen between her fingers. "Don't make me dot your eye."

I snorted. Emma and I could exchange insults all day. I never comprehended the term frenemy until Emma.

Lexi's hands went to her hips. "You don't scare me, Chase Winters."

Courtesy of Travis and me, Lexi had been sheltered, protected, and indulged, which I was now regretting. Shifting, the mattress groaned under my weight. I rested my wrists on top of my knees.

"Fine," she said spinning, her blonde hair flying in the air. "Emma will take me."

Emma grimaced. "Uh-uh. Don't drag me into this. I'm not willing to risk the mongrel's wrath. No thanks. I'm saving my strength for when the world goes to shit."

I frowned. It's not like I hadn't been called worse, but on the flipside, at least she recognized my skills and agreed not to help Lexi. It still blew my mind that Emma and I could agree on anything. Not long ago, she'd been hell-bent on carving out my heart. I had committed some pretty unforgivable acts.

Lexi's lip started to quiver.

Oh dear God. Not tears. I couldn't handle another bout of

tears, not from Lexi and certainly not from Angel. Emma…? I no longer thought she was capable of deep emotions.

"I have a plan," I quickly rushed before a single drop made its way down Lex's cheek.

Searching my face, she narrowed her eyes. "Why do I suddenly have a bad feeling about what you're going to tell me?"

I gave her a look.

"Chase," she drew out my name. "I know that face. Tell me you're not thinking of doing something that demented?"

All I could do was clear my throat and stare at the empty spot between her ear and shoulder.

"Chase! You can't. Not after spending so much time controlling it. Not after everything you went through." She looked crestfallen.

"Will someone please tell me what the hell we are talking about?" Emma demanded, her golden retriever ears perking up and the hunter in her sniffing out trouble.

I ignored her. "I will do whatever it takes to get her back, Lex. Even if it means sacrificing parts of me."

"I want her back as much as you do, but I can't lose you both. There has to be another way." Her eyes began to well with tears.

It hadn't been my intention to hurt Lexi, but I also hadn't intended to fall in love. Shit happens. "There might be, but I don't have time to waste chasing after possibilities. This is the fastest way to get the answers I need. You know it is."

"That doesn't mean I like it." A tinge of yellow flashed in her irises as she rubbed her hands down her arms like she was brushing off a chill. "Putting yourself in that kind of situation is something you might not recover from. It can change you. Would Angel want that?"

"Someone better tell me what is going on, or I'm going to start cracking skulls," Emma badgered.

I flashed my demon eyes before turning back to Lexi. "The reverse psychology bullshit you're learning in class won't work on me. It doesn't matter anyway. My mind is made up. What matters is Angel is alive and that I find a way to bring her back. Her safety is more important than my black soul."

"Fine, d-bag. Have it your way, but I'm coming with you. Someone has to keep you from going AWOL."

"No."

"Chase," she whined. "If you won't let me see Angel, then at least let me help you. I can't sit here day and night, pretending everything is okay. Nothing is okay."

She didn't have to tell me. My whole world was turned

upside down. "I'm going alone."

"Alone?" She started to pace the floor, and I didn't like the way her eyes began to glow. She was supposed to be the one with all the self-control, and here she was on the verge of letting her demon take possession.

This was bad.

And only explained how much Angel's betrayal affected her. Lexi was far from okay.

"Oh boy. Now you've done it, Deputy Dipshit," Emma said, leaning a shoulder on the doorframe.

I frowned. "Travis!" I roared.

A second later he popped his head into the room, chomping on a mouthful of a monster-sized turkey club clutched in one hand. "What?" he mumbled, crumbs covering his 'I don't need to get a life. I'm a gamer. I have lots of lives!' T-shirt. He had taken up wearing them in Angel's honor.

Seeing the ridiculous shirt squeezed my heart. *Will I ever get her back?* I let out a heavy sigh. "It's your turn. Lexi's throwing a tantrum."

"Again?" He ran his free hand through his tousled sandy hair. "Christ."

Lexi's sea-green eyes went from me to Travis and back to me. She shook her head. "You're all idiots." Then she was gone as stealthily as she had arrived.

"Umm, that went well half-breed," Emma commented. "Now, are you going to tell me what is going on? Where are you going?"

An awkward silence descended in the room. Travis inhaled another bite of his sandwich, dropping more bread bits on my floor. I sighed. "Three's a crowd, don't you think?" *Hint. Hint.* I wanted to be left alone. "Someone should probably check on Lexi and make sure she doesn't break a nail."

"On it," Travis said, turning to leave.

I cleared my throat. "Take your girlfriend with you."

"Winters, I have a right to know what you're planning. It's my duty to protect humankind. If you're about to—"

Travis scooped Emma off her feet, tossing her over his shoulder as she gave a little shriek of displeasure. I didn't know a guy on campus who would envy Travis right now. Two extremely pissed off extraordinary females that could give him one heck of a fight—he was going to have his hands full. Hopefully, he didn't come away with too many cuts and bruises.

I waited until the door closed behind them, listening to Emma bitch and moan to Travis about how she was going to pull his balls out from his throat. Sinking against the wall, I let my back hit the drywall. There was only one more person I needed to see before I hit the road.

Chapter 4

{Chase}

No matter how long I stood under the steaming hot spray, I didn't feel cleansed, and the growth on my face was out of control. After a quick shave, I put on black sweats and a white shirt that was identical to the fifty others I had. I could have gotten dressed in the dark and my look would have been similar. My wardrobe was simple. Jeans. T-shirts. Comfy clothes.

I hadn't even left the house and already I felt tainted—the demon slowly shadowing my humanity. My gut twisted as I stared at my reflection, the silver in my eyes glossed by an uncanny gold.

Before Angel, I had traveled down a dark path. There were many moments in my life I wasn't proud of, but there were some choices I wish I could whiteout, obliterate from existence. Angel didn't know of my less than stellar past, other than I had one. I didn't want to talk about it or think about it.

That person no longer existed.

The pain I'd caused my family was unredeemable, and I'd

taken a vow to never go back. At that time I'd meant it with my last dying breath…until Angel.

She had no idea how much she'd saved me. How much light she'd offered me at a time in my life when I was emerging from such blackness. Knowing I was about to enter a past I swore to leave behind was chilling, but for Angel, I would walk through Hell. Nothing in the world was going to stop me.

And if it came down to it, I would choose her over family, over life, over death.

There was no doubt in my mind I would help. No matter what condition she was in when this was over, I could handle it—we could handle it. I just hoped I was in a state of mind to see her through the worst of it.

Plucking a set of keys off the dresser, I turned to leave, kicking a discarded bottle of some kind of carbonated drink. I swore and took a good look around my room. Christ, was I in desperate need of a maid. Everything had gone down the shitpot, including my necessity for tidiness.

Closing the door behind me, the house was silent as I moved through it toward the front door. No one tried to stop me. I didn't know if I was relieved or disappointed, not that it mattered. My mind was made up.

Slipping behind the wheel of my newly-acquired sports car,

REDEEMING ANGEL

I revved the engine a few times, eyes glancing in the rearview mirror. This was it. Do or die. My foot slammed on the gas. The wheels spun for traction a moment before lurching forward and shooting down the road like a bullet.

I had a thing for fast cars. I also had a thing for crashing fast cars. In my defense, four out of five of those had not been my fault. Demons materializing out of nowhere, while cruising at speeds nearing seventy miles an hour equaled big crashes. Angel unfortunately had a front row seat in one of those famous wrecks.

The drive to nowhere was only about twenty minutes from the college, but the way I drove, I could do it in half the time, except my paranoia was real. I spent more time staring in my rearview mirror than I did on the road in front of me. Not a damn thing happened the entire drive. Sand and gravel kicked up from the tread of the tires as I came to a stop.

What was down in the cellar wasn't really Angel—not the girl I loved with every breath I took. And she wasn't in control of herself or her abilities. It was only a matter of time before she hurt someone or worse…herself.

The idea of what I was about to do screamed wrong on every level, but there was no other choice. I had to do this.

As I stepped out of the car, a dry heat more suitable for

Arizona washed over me. Even the climate was feeling the heat of Hell. There had been little butterflies in my stomach the closer I got, but as I pulled open the hidden door, a warm tingle shimmied down the base of my neck that had nothing to do with the sun.

I couldn't wait until I never had to see this dump again. Titanium and whatever other twisted crap the hunters used to secure this place fucked with my mojo. And no one messed with my mojo, not unless they wanted to die.

I zapped down the stairs, anxious. Whether she was snarling at me or threatening to kill me, it didn't matter. I only wanted to see her face one last time before I walked into Lucifer's den.

She lay on a bed of blankets, her hair spilling over the gray material, eyes closed. Approaching the bars, I slipped a hand through, my fingers brushing aside the tangled mess of auburn hair. She could pretend all she wanted, but with me, it was pointless. The quickening of her heart gave her away.

{Angel}

The sound of footsteps neared, and I cracked my eyelids. A face, tilted sideways, came into view, blocking the measly amount of light. Fabulous. It was my not-so-better half.

The skin around his eyes crinkled as his brows knitted

together. "Good. You're awake."

My body locked up at the sound of that particular male voice. Jaw clenched, I tried to look away. "Duh. You try sleeping on a slab of metal."

"Guess I don't need to ask how you're feeling today," he said in a level voice.

I spit in his face.

The bastard laughed. "Spunky." He swiped the back of his hand across his face. "I'd say that's progress. I'm getting to you. I can feel it."

Pushing up on the bed, I sung my feet over the side. "The only thing you are feeling is my bitter hatred emitting through our despicable bond."

Backing up, he propped a shoulder on the concrete wall, all while keeping those silvery eyes glued to my face like he was memorizing every detail.

"Take a picture, it lasts longer."

A lazy smirk crossed his lips. Amusing him was not what I wanted to do. "Ah, there she is."

"You're demented, you know that? I *will* destroy you."

"Angel, I know you're in there. I would not be standing here if you were truly gone. Our connection wouldn't be just as strong if a piece of you weren't still alive. I know you."

I wiped at the corner of my eye, swiping an invisible tear. "Isn't that just too sweet. Go suck a lemon."

Chase. The nicest jerk I'd ever met. He made sure I had everything I needed to survive in my little jail cell. There was a small bathroom off the back left side of the cage. A metal bed was bolted to the floor with a lumpy mattress, but at least the sheets were clean. And each time he came, he brought me fresh clothes and food.

Today it was a chicken salad.

"Eat," he demanded, staring at the untouched plastic bowl. "You need to eat if you plan to take over the world, Angel Eyes."

Unfurling my legs, I flashed to my feet, standing as close to the metal as I could without getting fried. "Don't call me that. I'm not your Angel anything anymore."

He blinked.

"What? No plans of salvation?" I pushed out the words, feeling the anger grow inside me. I angled my head. "Did you finally come to your demon senses?"

"Actually, it's why I'm here."

I slid my gaze to him, one side of my lip tipped up. "About damn time. We can make such a great team, you and I. Nothing will be able to stop us."

"That's true," he agreed.

"Then what are you waiting for? Let me out of here."

"Sorry, toots. That's not on the agenda for what I have in mind."

"Grr," I growled, hands clenching at my sides. I pulled back my lip, letting out an eerie, real-sounding hiss. "Why are you wasting so much time on something you can't change?"

"Because you're worth it. You're everything."

I smiled. "I hate you." Then I hurled the plastic bowl directly at where he sat. Lettuce, shredded cheese, and pieces of chicken, flew through the air and crashed against the bars before clattering on the floor. Salad dressing and some other gunk splattered on his shirt and cheek.

He crinkled his brow, face strained. "I just took a shower. And that's not true. You love me. You just need to look deep enough. It's there."

I lifted my head, eyes blazing. "Go away."

He rubbed the heel of his palm over his heart. "Never. I'll be back. You can bet your freedom on it."

A dull ache pressed against my ribs. I stamped it out. Soft, love-sick Angel was not going to make an appearance today. "So you're just going to leave me here to starve to death?"

He snorted. "I'm not that cruel. Travis and Emma will make

sure you're taken care of."

I hated that my eyes were drawn to his lips, unable to control the attraction between us— although wanting to kiss him and choke him in the same moment wasn't a foreign feeling. "Oh goodie. Let me try to contain my excitement," I said dryly. "You better hope the hunter doesn't shank me in my sleep."

Chase's shoulders stiffened, the lines around his face hardening. "She won't touch a hair on your head," he promised.

"Why? Because you trust her?"

His eyes narrowed, turning all amber as he stared at me. "No, because I'd kill her."

I grinned. Finally, he was speaking my language. "That's more like it."

He rolled his eyes, his tight shoulders relaxing a fraction of an inch. "Now who's demented?"

I took a step back from the titanium, not willing to risk singeing my eyebrows. Already my skin was feverish, but oddly it wasn't the heat that bothered me. It was the nonstop tingles that flittered up and down my body. "Whatever. Are you at least going to tell me what shenanigans you have planned?"

"Funny," he said flatly, pushing at a strand of hair that fell over his right eye. "On the very slim, and I mean minuscule, so tiny it can't be seen by the human eye—"

"I get it. I'm stuck here, but do you have a plan?" I asked, interrupting.

"If you let me finish," he said, drawing out the words.

I folded my arms, leaned my weight on one foot, and waited.

He shot me a look. "On the chance you do manage to get out of here, I think it's better for everyone if you don't know."

I frowned. "Why do I remember you being more fun?"

With a half grin on his lips, he started toward me. "You want some fun? Here." He pulled a small device from the back pocket of his pants and slipped it through the bars. "I brought you something to pass the time."

I stared down at the electronic handheld video game unit. "What the hell am I supposed to do with this? Try to beat some nerd's highest score in Pac-Man?"

A crestfallen expression crossed his face, and he was quick to hide it behind a sinister smirk, but not before I caught a glimpse. "Hang on, Angel. When I come back, this will all be a bad dream."

"I don't plan on being here when you get back," I yelled, but it was useless. He was already gone.

Bastard.

The hope in his eyes made me sick. Pacing, I kicked the

stupid gaming device with my foot, watching it skid across the hard, cold floor. I couldn't just sit here, waiting for him to take away what I had just gained. Power.

Why does he get all the demon benefits?

Even if he managed to save me, I could never forgive him for locking me away. How could I? I had no idea if I'd been here for days or weeks. Hell, a year. Days and nights were nothing but a blur of rage and bitterness.

Chapter 5

{Chase}

I had a full tank of gas, a half-eaten package of Red Vines on the passenger seat, and the classic rock station pumping through the car speakers—all the good road trip essentials. If only this was a vacation and not a death sentence.

The black leather interior warmed the car from the sun beating down above. I'd been on the road for ten hours, only halfway to my destination. It would have been much faster to fly, but I didn't trust myself thirty-five thousand feet in the air, going over five hundred miles an hour sealed in a pressurized containment.

Disaster in the making.

Not that what I was doing was exactly smart, but there was little choice in the matter. The kind of information I needed came only from a certain breed. Demons. And the best place to seek out a great deal of demons was the City of Sin, obviously. I was never a fan of the hot, dry heat of Nevada, but demons gravitated to it like flies on shit. What better place to conduct sordid dealings than right here in Las Vegas? Demons fit right in, and it didn't matter what kind of suit they wore. There were a hundred different kinds of weird walking around. They loved the chaos of the nightlife. The sex, the lies, the gambling, the splash of lights…

Demons thrived in Vegas, surrounded by willing participants ready to trade just about anything, even their souls. And oh, how Hell's hierarchy loved the taste of human souls. My soul, however, was the cream of the crop.

Half-breeds like me avoided this place. The overwhelming presence of so many demons did strange things to us, in a not good way. Many Divisa considered coming here a death sentence, but because I was linked to Angel, it didn't matter. Either way our time was ticking. If the demons uncovered my weakness, I was as good as dead. If I didn't save Angel, she was as good as dead. Options were limited.

Surprisingly, there were demons who didn't want to make corpses out of us at first glance—a rare commodity, but they existed, and I was banking on one of them helping me.

First, I had to find one without having my head decapitated or my heart carved out.

I rolled down the strip at about noon, and although I should have been calculating a plan, the only thing I could think about was catching a few hours of Zs. After being cramped in the same position for twenty-plus hours, I wanted to stretch out. There was a motel not far, just outside the city limits, where questions weren't asked, exactly what I needed. It wasn't the Bates Motel, but damn was it close.

I swung the car into a near-empty parking lot. Overhead a neon sign glowed *ACANCY* in a dim red. The *V* had burned out. Classy. I was too tired to even muster a chuckle. "This should be fun." My muscles were tight as I unfolded my body from the car.

I wanted to stay off the map. This place couldn't get any more secluded. As I walked the distance across the road toward the lobby, not a single car drove by. No shocker. It was the kind of place people avoided, unless they were looking to get high or hang themselves.

The building was a ranch-style, one floor with the lobby at the far end of the *L* shape. A little bell dinged as I pushed open the door and entered. The air smelled of cigarette smoke and apple spice freshener, doing nothing to mask the pungent stench. If anything, it magnified the cheapness.

An older woman drooped behind the counter, everything about her sagged. Her eyes. Her skin. Her tits. The source of the clogged air and clover-spice stank hung from the side of her lips. "Hey, handsome," she greeted, eyes roaming over my physique. "Need a room?" She made it sound like an invitation.

Gag me.

I approached the counter. "Yeah. Got any available?"

"For you, sugar, I think we can make room. You looking for a few hours or overnight?"

"Possibly a night or two." This was going to be a short visit. I was optimistic—about myself *and* my ability to kick major demon ass.

"You can stay as long as you like."

Normally, I creep people out, but this lady with her sea-green eye shadow was starting to give me the heebie-jeebies. "I'll let you know."

"How about you pay for the night and we'll see where things go?" She turned around, plucking a single key from the rack.

"Sounds good to me." I dug into my back pocket and pulled out my wallet. "Cash okay?"

Her eyes lit up. "You're speaking my language, honey."

I was pretty sure she and I would never speak the same language.

"That'll be eighty-nine for the night."

I handed over a crisp hundred dollar bill. "Keep the

change."

After safely tucking the money in between her airbag-sized boobs, she dangled the key from her lengthy nails, leaning forward on the counter. "You just let Sasha know if you require any service." Then she winked, part of her false eyelash getting stuck on her lid.

I thought I'd just been propositioned for sex or something. The need to shower was overwhelming. Nodding, I took the key to the room, and because I didn't want any unexpected visitors showing up in my bed, my silver eyes flashed gold and I said, "Make sure I'm not disturbed."

Sasha only nodded, her eyes glossy under the flickering florescent lights. I backed out of the room, glancing at the number on the tag dangling from the key ring. Room eleven.

The space could have been worse. There was a double bed in the center, sheets turned down. Across from the bed was a console with a TV that looked like it still needed to be adjusted by an antenna. A nightstand sat on the left side of the bed. Dropping the key next to the alarm clock, I crawled into the bed, fully clothed. My face planted on the fresh linen pillow. It was a welcome scent. Fishing out my phone from my pocket, I set the alarm for midnight.

Then I dozed.

.*.*.*.

Buzz. Buzz. Buzz. My hand shot out across the bed, landing on my discarded phone. If the noise didn't stop now, I was going to Hulk smash it. My eyes snapped open, lighting up the dark room. I clutched the device in my fist, swiping across the screen angrily until the constant buzz ceased.

I turned on my side, spying the clock.

Midnight.

Nothing good ever happened after midnight. That was Devin's motto. And he was right. Back in Spring Valley it was my favorite time of day. Then again, I'd been on my turf. At home I took care of business. I protected my family. Now I was outnumbered, out powered, but never outwitted.

It was go time.

Less than a half hour later, I was stashing my car behind a rundown convenient store on the strip. A circus of colors buzzed with live energy in the city that never sleeps. This place had a vibe about it—an ill effect on me, and on them, and an even nastier one on my demon. It wormed its way inside me, snaking around my humanity and threatening to smother it. Something in the air amplified the darker side of me, and I knew it was only a matter of time before I would no longer be in control.

REDEEMING ANGEL

It wouldn't be the first time I'd lost myself.

I shuddered.

Unfolding my tourist guide I'd picked up from the motel, I scanned the list of bars. There was one that literally jumped from the page. Demon's Breath.

Now that was my kind of establishment.

The last thing I wanted was for *them* to know I was coming. I wanted the element of surprise on my side. I was sort of counting on it, really.

I took off down the alley, weeding in and out between businesses, staying in the shadows. The trickiest part was keeping my demon at bay. Bloody bastard was being persistent. If anything were going to give me away, it would be the eyes.

Bright moonlight filtered in between the alleyways, and the balmy evening air rushed over my face as I moved over the uneven ground. Minutes later, I was standing outside the backdoor to what had to be the seediest joint in town.

I mean it reeked of dirty deeds, among other things. There was a distinct smell of smoke and alcohol in the air. Vines so thickly covered the side of the building that it resembled a tree.

Placing my hands on the steel door, I gave a push, expecting to find it locked. Not that a locked door was going to keep me out, on the contrary, but as luck would have it, there was no need for forced entry. The door squeaked as I quickly eased it open and stepped into a dark hallway, bathrooms on either side. Sticking to the shades of blackness, I hugged the wall, my eyes flitting down the corridor leading into the lobby.

Jaw clenched tightly, I stepped out into the main room. I was used to drawing attention, so when no one bothered to so much as glance at me, I raised my brows and looked around. Nothing special, a few pool tables, scantily dressed servers, and plenty of dim lighting. As my eyes roamed the room, I counted at least a handful of demons. Not unreasonable, I should be able to hold my own.

It was in that moment one of them noticed me. I leaned my hip against one of those cigarette vending machines, waiting to see what would happen next. Eyes void of color met mine. My nostrils flared. I was about two seconds away from snapping someone's neck. Anyone would do. I wasn't feeling picky.

Smiling coldly, I let my demon encompass me, flaring to the surface. This was where things could have gotten hairy, and I needed to tread carefully. If I didn't, my biggest problem wouldn't be a demon brawl. It would be the internal battle with my temperamental other half.

The demon looked me over and I was sure he was going to fly out of his human suit, coming straight for my heart, but he only turned back toward the bartender and downed the tumbler of whiskey.

Feeling I'd dodged a bullet, I continued my perusal, seeking out a demon who looked like he wasn't dumb as rocks. Big Boy and his buddy at the bar were nothing but lower demons. I needed someone higher on the food chain. Good lord, this better not be a bust. I couldn't afford to waste a single second. Already, I was beginning to feel the first inklings of being apart from Angel. In twenty-four hours, I'd be lucky to throw a worthy punch.

Then I saw her across the bar. Instinctually, I wanted to dagger her.

Demon. Male or female, my instincts didn't discriminate.

Curious, I stayed where I was, waiting for... Actually, I didn't have a clue, but as I stood there she leaned over the pool table and expertly sunk the nine ball into the left corner pocket.

Dropping the end of the cue stick to the floor, her cherry lips curled in a satisfied grin. She was dressed from head to toe in black leather that fit like second skin. Great. A demon hustler and a temptress.

With a sinister sparkle in her unusual eyes, her bold lips puckered as she spun to face the two pathetic suckers. There was something about her that struck a chord of familiarity. *Had we fought before? Was she one of the countless demons I'd sent back to Hell?*

I shook my head. It didn't really matter. She was only the means to get what I wanted.

One of the guys she'd been playing went for his wallet, but Duck Lips put her index finger in the air, waving the blood red nail from side to side. "I'm not interested in your money, boys." I heard her say. She ran the tip of her nail down his shirt. "You've got something else I want."

"Oh yeah," the scruffier one replied, intrigue lacing his tone.

What a fool.

I knew exactly what she was looking for, and it was most definitely not what this imbecile was thinking. No one was going to get lucky tonight. Not even the platinum-haired seductress. I was about to ruin everyone's good time.

Hey, I was just that type of guy.

Letting my eyes rim in gold, I stepped out of the shadows and intercepted. This wasn't me being a nice guy; it was me being selfish. My wants and needs came first. "Let me do you both a favor," I said, catching them each in my gaze. The ability to force my will on humans was second nature. I'd been doing it for far too long. "Scram. You don't want to get on my ugly side."

Their eyes went glassy, and it wasn't from the booze. Another few seconds went by as my compulsion worked its way into their tiny brains. The tension in the air went up several hundred degrees. *Shit. Nothing like pissing off an entire bar of demons.* I positioned myself between her and the two jokers stumbling toward the exit.

She spun on the spike of her heel, facing me. "Now, that wasn't nice." She drifted toward me. "You owe me a soul. Two actually, Halfling."

My nostrils flared. "By the end of the night, it's going to be you who owes me."

She looked me up and down. "Intrigued. Take a seat. I'll let you buy me a drink."

Chapter 6

{Chase}

The high-handedness of demons drove me nutty. Sure, I could be a pompous ass when I wanted to be, but it was different. I slid into one of the round barstools, dark shadows drifting over my face. "My name's—"

"I know who you are, Chase Winters, son of Alastair," she said, slinking into the seat beside me. A subtle scent of jasmine and something a tad bit tangy followed her.

I made an ugly face. "Well that's unfair. I know nothing about you."

"Kira." She smiled.

"Cute. Is that what they call you in Hell?" I couldn't keep the judgment from my tone, and why should I?

"I'll hand it to you. It takes a lot of balls showing your face in this town."

"That's me. I've got kahunas of steel."

She let out a husky laugh, her slim fingers wrapping around a glass half filled with a pink drink.

"I didn't come here to amuse," I stated flatly.

"You do know that Daddy has sent out an amber alert on your girlfriend and a wanted bounty on you. Dead or alive."

"What's new? I've spent my life sending his devoted kiss-ass puppets back to Hell."

"But I'd bet my soul you're here more out of desperation."

She was toying with me, and the knowledge made my blood pressure spike. "Tell me what you know about why I'm here," I grated out. I was grabbing at brittle straws, but it was better than doing nothing. That nearly drove me over the edge.

She put her lips to the rim of the glass, taking a sip and leaving behind a perfect imprint of her mouth. "You have something Hell would destroy for, *will* destroy for. You've been lucky up until now."

I snorted. "Obviously, you haven't heard the best thing about me." I leaned over and whispered, "I don't give a flying feather about the wants of Hell."

"And that will be your fatal flaw. Like father, like son."

My voice dipped into frozen tundra levels. "Don't ever compare me to that bastard."

"I guess I don't have to ask how you feel about Alastair."

"Oh, and you're a saint?"

"We've both done things. It's in our nature." She plucked

the spear from her drink, twirling the cherry at the end. "But believe it or not, we do have a few things in common."

"How about we cut the crap? I didn't come here to bond over Dirty Shirley's and chitchat about whose killed more people. If you know who I am and why I'm here, why haven't you taken my soul? Why haven't you turned me into the a-hole who condemned me?"

Crossing her legs, she sat back in her chair. "Good question. I'm still considering it, but I believe we can help each other."

I snorted. "What could you possibly want from me besides my life source? I'm sure it's almost run dry." I'd challenged the lines of life and death one too many times.

"The strength of your soul is not in question. What I need to know is just how far you're willing to go to save the girl you love."

I cast a dark look. "Tell me how to save her."

"Who said she could be—?"

Determination burned through me like a righteous fire. "Don't say it. I refused to believe she is lost to me. Let's get that clear right now. Got it?"

There was a pause. "If you say so. Doesn't change that I can't help you."

My fist came down on the bar top, splashing her drink over

the rim of her glass. "I have a lot of pent-up anger I'm just dying to take out on someone. Don't push me."

Her scarlet eyes moved from her glass to me. "Duly noted, but don't forget what I am, halfling."

"As if I could. The stench in this place is sickening."

"Boys," Kira said, sliding off her chair. "I think the halfling has overstayed his welcome."

Chairs scraped against the sticky wood floors, but I wasn't the least bit concerned. "I'm not leaving until you give me what I want."

The short-fused demon who had earlier given me the stink eye took a step forward. "You think you can take me, hybrid?" he spat.

"Why don't we find out?" I scoffed, cracking my neck. A hot rush of rage twisted my insides into giant knots. Whipping around, I let out a deep roar just as a demon shot across the bar, heading straight for me. *So much for escaping without a fight.*

We slammed into each other like a crashing avalanche. Everything in our path was destroyed. The impact shook the walls, knocking over bottles and glasses. Gripping onto his forearms, I spun around, pinning his back to the wall. Plaster cracked and paint chips sprayed the air, but I hung on.

"You should have listened to me," Kira said.

The strong SOB swept his arms up, looping them in a circle that forced me to lose my grip. His shadowy arm coiling out, aiming right for the center of my life source. I was pretty keen about keeping my soul intact, whatever I had left at least.

Darting to the side, I threw my fist into his beer belly. "You should really lay off the spirits, old man."

The demon hissed.

"Boys. Boys. Boys! Cut the shit, before you piss me off," Kira warned, sounding more than a bit miffed. She strutted between us, putting a palm on either side of our chests, separating us. "I'm in no mood to clean house." Kira's frown grew into a menacing scowl. "You were leaving if I'm not mistaken."

My head snapped up, eyes narrowing. "I was, but I'll be back. Every. Damn. Day. Until I get what I want. This isn't the last you'll see of me."

She angled her head, a glint in her red eyes. "Oh, I'm counting on it."

{Angel}

Huddled into a corner on the bed, I stared at the crisp apple, ignoring the hunger pains. *I'm not going to eat that apple,* I repeated like I was Snow White and Emma was the evil Queen.

Huh. In reality, Emma was kind of an evil bitch.

As long as they kept me prisoner, I was going to do every tactic my devious mind could come up with, including starvation.

It was a lot harder than it sounded.

Travis paced back and forth on the cold, splotchy gray floors, his cell phone pressed to his ear. I was really hoping the darker stains weren't blood. As dark as it was, probably demon blood. Ew. The thought of hunters torturing demons down here started a campfire of rage in my belly.

"She's not eating," Travis said to Chase on the other end of the phone. He'd called to check up on me. How sweet. It made me want to barf. "And I doubt she's even sleeping," he added.

Give that half-demon a gold star. What had started out as an experiment, turned into another way to manipulate my newly assigned babysitters. I discovered my body no longer needed as much rest. A few hours here and there were just enough to function.

While Travis was busy discussing my eating habits with Chase, I figured this was an excellent opportunity I shouldn't waste. "Hey, Legolas. If I throw a stick, will you leave?"

Silence.

There was nothing more grating than someone not

participating when you were trying to provoke them. And provoke her I wanted. Emma was quick-tempered, and I needed that hot head of hers to make a mistake—one that would get me out of here. "Cat got your tongue?"

Her emerald eyes turned to slits. "No. I'm just visualizing duct taping your mouth."

I gave her credit. She was creative. "Shockingly, you aren't the first person to say that to me, but what a good idea. Why don't you open this cage?"

"Why don't you go fly a kite? Oh wait. You can't."

I grabbed the bars with both hands, closing the distance between us, intending to get in her face and forgetting the bars were not my friends. I hissed as the metal seared my fingers. The air permeated with the fowl scent of melting flesh. I growled in frustration. Control was not one of my stronger character traits it seemed.

Emma laughed.

It sounded like acid to my ears. "When I get out of here, your little sister and mom are chop suey," I said between clenched teeth.

Emma shook her strawberry blonde ponytail. I wanted to yank it through the bars and play tug of war. "Ah. That never gets old," she said with too much enjoyment for my liking.

"You wouldn't be so full of yourself and righteous if I wasn't locked up like an animal. I would love to see your bravado face-to-face, hunter," I spat.

She pressed her face to the titanium. "Those demon eyes don't scare me. Threaten my family again and this little hideout is going to be nothing compared to what I will do to you. Is that clear she-devil?"

"You're not going to harm Angel," Chase's voice snarled through the speakerphone. "Not one hair on her head. Do you understand me?"

My lips twitched. "If I'm still here," I muttered, knowing damn well he could hear me.

Emma shot me with a legion of dirty looks. "Jeesh. We know you love her, but Earth's—"

"You don't know shit," Chase cut in. "If you did, then you would know the lengths I'm willing to take to protect her, including taking you out."

"Oh, I know you're absolutely insane and extremely dangerous. I just didn't know you where stupid as shit too!" Emma ranted like the lunatic she was.

Travis frowned at the phone, his fingers squeezing. A small crack splintered across the screen. "Chase," he warned, his sea-green eyes being overrun by glowing amber.

Very little, if anything at all, intimidated Chase Winters. "And if that means killing those who get in my way, I won't hesitate," he roared.

I had to admit I kind of enjoyed listening to them go at each other. The angst of it all invigorated the darkness spreading inside me.

Emma and Travis shared a look, right before Travis exhaled roughly. "Honestly man, I think you're what's keeping her alive—your connection. Without it, I think she would be worse." Travis's eyes wandered toward me. "Way worse," he added woefully.

I glared, knowing what he said was probably true, and I sharpened my listening skills.

"I know, dammit," Chase swore. "I need another day. Two at the most." I could hear the urgency in his voice, along with heavy doses of frustration—seemed to be a theme. That's what the occasional shooting pangs in my chest were—his extreme frustration.

Travis stared down at me, expression pinched. "She might only have a few more days before we lose her for good. She needs you, Chase. You're the only one who can get through to her. If Angel is in there, I haven't gotten a glimpse."

I smirked, leaning a shoulder against the back wall.

A tormented sigh came through the other end of the phone. "You have no idea how much I hate being away from her while she is suffering. It's tearing me up."

"Suffering?" I choked. How could they be so dimwitted? I was alive for the first time. I had power. I had purpose.

Shortly after that, the conversation ended and I knew it wasn't long before I was left alone again. Just me. The voices. My thoughts. And the mice. "He's not telling you something," I blurted.

"What did you say?" Emma asked, eyes narrowing.

"Chase. He has a secret."

"How would you know?"

I gave the hunter the stink eye.

"Right. Dumb question. Of course *you* of all people would know. So what is it?"

"You really aren't the brightest bulb in the shed. The bond doesn't work that way. I can tell he is hiding something, but I'm just as clueless as you are. If he wanted me to know, he'd share."

"Can't you…I don't know…make him tell you? Use your bond?"

"I could…*if* my abilities weren't being snuffed by this prison."

She eyed me for a moment. Girl to girl, we both knew what I was doing, taking an opportunity to gain my freedom, including using every situation to my advantage.

Travis ruined it. "Nice try, Angel. If Chase isn't telling us something, then he has his reasons."

"So trusting. Do you really believe he is going to be so forthcoming?"

Silence.

"Let's cut the bull. We all know he would let the world burn if that was what it took to save his precious Angel," I prattled.

Travis's mouth opened and I saw him form words, but I couldn't hear what he was saying. My palm sprung out, flattening on the cold wall. Black dots circled behind my eyes, and I knew what was about to happen next. I was going to hit the floor. I heard a gasp as I went down, and I wasn't sure if it was Emma's or mine.

Thump. My head hit the side of the bedframe, and that was it—lights out.

Chapter 7

{Chase}

I strolled into the small square bathroom with only one thought on my mind. Shower. Checking out the bathroom, there were neatly folded towels and travel-sized soaps, shampoos, toothbrush, and toothpaste. A good thing, as I realized my dumbass forgot to bring anything, except the change of clothes I kept in my car for emergencies, and this definitely was what I called an emergency.

The hiss of the shower drenched my face, beating down on my body. I thought about Kira and Angel. My mind spun, trying to come up with ways to get Kira to give me privileged information. I hadn't been bluffing when I said I wasn't giving up. Of course, time wasn't on my side. Not only because Angel was falling deeper and deeper into the darkness, but one of the demons who'd been at the bar probably was already squealing like a bitch. I figured I had less than twenty-four hours before Alastair and his goons showed up to take me out.

Let them come.

My heart did a funny thing in my chest. Speeding up just as

the demon inside came clawing to the surface. I dipped my head back under the stream, hands placed on the tiled wall. Something was building in my chest, a rising darkness I managed to keep at bay, but there was no denying *him* now.

Panic squeezed me, my hands curling into fists.

Shit.

My demon pretty much took advantage of my tiredness and all the crap being drudged up. There was nothing I could do to stop it. Had I known my defenses would weaken coming here? Yes. Was it probably one of the craziest things I'd ever done? No doubt. Was I going to give up? Hell no.

I could only hope *he* didn't shred the room to pieces.

Fifteen minutes had gone by since I'd been in the shower. I turned the faucets, shutting off the water, thinking losing my cool naked in the shower was not a good idea. My hands trembled a little, but I managed to make it out of the shower and tug on a pair of sweats without tearing the sink off the wall.

Who was I kidding?

This place was going to look like a cyclone came through if I wasn't able to get a grip. Just as I entered the bedroom to grab a bottle of water, there was a knock on the door.

Son of a bitch.

Now was not the time for room service.

I put a fist to the wall and yelled, "Go away."

Another knock sounded, louder and harder. The door shook under impact. Whoever was on the other side had a death wish. I growled, eyes going all glow-in-the-dark, and threw open the door. "Did you not hear what—?"

"Oh, I heard you. The whole motel heard you, but I figured you'd want to see me." She pushed the door wide open and strutted her high-heeled mighty self into the center of my room.

I had to say as meatsuits went, this one was top of the line. "I thought you weren't going to help me?" I snapped.

Her brows knitted. "Ah, that. Didn't anyone tell you demons are liars?"

I frowned. "I also thought demons didn't have hearts. What's your deal? Why are you here?" I was hanging on by a thread. Her timing couldn't have been any worse, but I needed to find a way to rein *him* in. This was the whole reason I'd come here—to find a demon with intel.

Making herself right at home, she sat on the edge of the neatly made bed. "Because just as you're not like most halflings, I'm not like most demons."

Swinging the door shut, I turned with a frown. "Meaning what?"

She crossed her long legs, the denim shirt she wore hiking up her thighs. "Are you to going to at least offer me a refreshment?"

"Sorry. The minibar's been ransacked."

"Pity. You look like you could use something to calm the beast. Are you feeling okay, or is the Nevada heat getting to you?"

My scowl only darkened. "How about we cut the crap and you tell me what I want to know and save us both the trouble of dealing with my not-so-friendly side?"

Her lips thinned. "Well, for starters, I've been banished to this realm for over a century."

My mouth dropped. "You're stuck here? I thought demons weren't capable of living on Earth for that amount of time. Maybe a year at most, if they were lucky enough to inhabit a host and find an ample supply of life to steal."

"All true. I told you I was different."

I leaned my back against the wall. "What else?" I didn't like surprises, and Kira was becoming a mystery to me.

She gave me a meaningful look. "If I told you all my secrets, I'd have to kill you."

I opened the door. "Then we're done here." I was seventy percent positive she wanted something from me as well. We were using each other. So I hoped, otherwise I was making a huge mistake.

"I've already said more than I should," she huffed.

I thought back to last night, recalling our conversation. It was hard to draw up the memories when my demon was knocking at the door, but there was one question that stuck with me. "What did you mean when you implied we have something in common?"

She sighed, tapping her foot in the air. "Our bloodlines have crossed."

Swinging the door shut for a second time, I crossed my arms as the wheels in my head started turning, and the conclusion I came to dropped my heart. "You're talking about Travis and Lexi, aren't you?"

She got a far-off look in her red-rimmed eyes, and her lips turned down in what I didn't think demons could show. Emotion. Sadness if I was correct. "How is Devin?"

Holy shit.

This was…the demon who had seduced Dev not once but twice. She was Travis and Lexi's…I refused to say mother, because she had never come to being anything close to resembling a mom. Egg donor?

What did I say to the demon who birthed my two cousins? Nice to meet you, Auntie?

I didn't think so.

My first instinct was to go for the throat.

I choked on my own breath. "What do you want?"

"A chance," she responded.

I shook my head. "No. Hell no. I'm not letting you anywhere near them." My fingers dug into my palms.

A smug smile curved on her bold cherry lips. "I think we both know you'll give me what I want. What other choice do you have?"

I dropped my shoulder, slumping against the wall. Dread blossomed. This was not what I pictured when I made the decision to dance with demons. I hated being cornered, but like she'd said, what choice did I have? I knew I would have to make tough decisions in order to save Angel; I just hadn't realized how much it would reflect back onto my family.

My vision started to turn red, a humming ricocheting between my ears.

"Chase, focus. This is what you want." Her voice had a hypnotic texture, smooth and bewitching. It was a technique I knew well. Compulsion.

"I *am* focused… On ripping your head off." Full possession was right around the corner. Everything was seen through an enflamed haze, and it clicked. Kira was causing this little unbridled outburst inside of me. She was doing something to pull my demon forth, and I had walked right into it like a good, obedient puppy.

"Well, I can see this is going nowhere." She stood up and flashed in front of me, nothing more than a quick blink. Her eyes bathed the room in a reddish glow.

A flare of rage rose up and snatched me. "You made an epic mistake," I managed to mumble. Kicking Kira's ass wasn't part of the plan. But plans changed. I was a flexible kind of guy.

"I don't make mistakes. Humans do." Then the bitch hit me. Not a girly kind of hit either. She punched like Muhammad Ali.

My head snapped back; a hammering thundered and rattled my brain. As stars danced behind my eyes all I could think was this was bad, but my brain never really caught up with the precarious situation I was in. At the mercy of a demon was no place I ever thought I would find myself.

Damn. I really hate demons.

It all went black.

{Angel}

The room wafted with Channel perfume and Kors leather. A pair of snakeskin print Jimmy Choo's came into view and stopped just outside my cell. "I wondered when you would show your face, blondie," I said, not bothering to get up.

"Angel?" Lexi hesitated, tiptoeing closer.

I rolled to my side, looking at her for the first time. "What took you so long? I thought we were BFFs and shit." I was getting tired of pretending to be the "good" Angel, and I was seriously sick of these four walls.

"They wouldn't let me see you." So much emotion in that tiny voice.

"What a pathetic excuse. I thought you cared about me."

"I do care. You know I do." Tears clogged her aqua eyes like a turbulent sea. "You're the only real friend I've ever had."

Ah. Break my heart. I thought I was going to barf something rancid. "Then help me. I can't stay here another night. Lexi, look at me. That awesome tan I used to have. Gone. Now my skin looks like Dumbo's."

Her eyes ran over my pathetic appearance. "You really do need a facial and some vitamin B. Don't get me started on your hair. If I knew what wretched conditions they were keeping you in, I would have…"

"What? Brought in a team of stylists?"

The small dingy space did nothing to dull her sparkle. "I can see your love for clothes and beauty hasn't changed. That's encouraging."

Whatever helped her sleep at night. She was clinging onto hope her friend was still in this body. It was false hope, but I didn't want to crush her poor little spirits. "God, you make me sound like a monster."

She wrinkled her button nose. "Well, you kind of went crazy."

"Disappointed? Don't care. If you came to see your BFF, she's gone out for the evening." Sitting up, I swung my legs over the side of the bed, my bare feet hitting the chilly concrete. "But maybe we could be friends."

She shook her pretty blonde hair, so perfect, not a hair out of place. "I didn't want to believe them. Chase is totally stressed out.

I've never seen him like that. He's out there, putting himself in harm to try to find a way to cure the darkness."

The little wheels in my corrupted mind started to turn. What was he up to? "And if there is no cure?"

She angled her neck to the side, analyzing my face. "I don't think I will ever get used to your eyes."

I blinked.

A glare of sadness crossed her face. "You of all people should know Chase isn't about to take no for an answer."

I would have to have the world's most determined boyfriend on the planet. "Right," I said, tapping a finger on my dry bottom lip.

"Here…" Lexi dug into the pocket of her skinny jeans, pulling out something small. "You look like you could use this." She rolled a tube of lip gloss under the bars.

Stepping on it with my foot, I bent down and picked it up, rolling it between my fingers. A quick flash of another life flickered through my memory. There one second and gone the next. "Thanks, but I don't think having moist lips is going to help me."

"Well, maybe this will." She turned and grabbed something off the floor. "I brought you coffee, too. It's from Starbucks."

Suddenly, my taste buds perked up. Boycotting food sucked. "Peppermint mocha?" I asked, eyeing the cup in her hand.

"Of course. It's still warm." She slipped the green and white cup through the bars, careful not to let them touch her elegant skin.

I whizzed off the bed, taking a long, deep swig. Demon or human, the appreciation for sugar infused coffee was real. "Hmm. Better than I remember," I said, licking my lips, eyes fluttering open.

"Travis said you're refusing to eat. They wouldn't let me see you," she said.

"Travis has never brought me Starbucks. How did you find me if they won't allow you to see me?"

"My brother isn't as smooth as he thinks he is or as cautious as Chase." She shrugged. "I followed them. He's always underestimating me."

Hmm. And maybe I had as well. My hand shot through the cage, capturing her wrist. "Please help me. Please, Lexi. I can't stay inside here another second. I'll lose my mind." I forced my eyes to well, though it was getting harder and harder to draw out tears. Dehydrated, I was sure.

"I want to help you. It kills me to see you like this. But Chase—"

"Doesn't have to know," I interjected. "I just want five minutes to feel the sun on my face. I promise. No funny business. I would never do that to you. You're the only one who hasn't treated me like a monster."

"Five minutes?" she repeated.

I nodded.

Her hand went to one of the many locks, and I held my breath.

Chapter 8

{Chase}

I awoke with a start, and a razor edge of pain sliced through my head. Wincing, I lifted a hand to my forehead, expecting there to be a big, nasty cut. It felt okay, just achy and sore, but otherwise okay, which was not something I could say about my current predicament.

I was sitting in the passenger seat of my car, completely wrong in itself. No one drove my car, and certainly not Kira.

Shitbucket.

The cunning demon had even strapped me in. How considerate. Yet, I was feeling anything but.

A mess of emotions ranging from anger to confusion collided in my stomach as I recalled how she had knocked me out. That was a first. A demon getting the jump on me, and she was female. Not my brightest moment. If Travis had seen it… I never would have been able to live it down.

I took stock. The demon inside me wasn't beating to break free, and the pressure that had been clamping down on my chest was slowly lifting, degree by slow degree. And that meant only one thing—we were headed back to Illinois.

The dream!

Lexi.

It might have only been just that—a dream—but I was done leaving things to chance. When it came to Angel and me, our connection hardly ever made sense. I wouldn't disregard the idea that it had morphed into our subconscious. Who knew the counter effects we were dealing with when it came to the kind of darkness breathing inside her?

I could only hope I wasn't too late and my cousin wasn't having a blonde moment. She wouldn't really let Angel out—so I kept telling myself—but the truth was Lexi had a heart softer than mine. If it was difficult for me, it was going to be harder for Lexi.

"It's about time, Sleeping Beauty," Kira said, interrupting my thoughts. One hand on the wheel, she drove the car expertly with her other hand hanging out the window, platinum hair blowing carelessly in the wind.

"Stop the car," I demanded in a gravelly tone. Being confined in a car on a road trip with the very thing I loathed was certainly not something I ever thought to experience.

No surprise she ignored me. "We're not there yet, and you've already wasted too much time snoring."

"Yeah well, whose fault is that?" I grumbled, shifting forward in my seat.

A hint of a smirk appeared on her lips. "I had no choice. You were about to lose it. I did you a favor, getting you out of town."

I scoffed. "Demons never do favors."

"True. You have something I want, and...I might know a way to save your kynt."

"Kynt? Is that some kind of demon gibberish?" I wasn't about to promise a demon squat.

"It is a very old word for the bond that exists between you and Angel. The three points of Triplici." The way the words rolled off her tongue made me wonder how old Kira was. There was an ancient quality in her voice she tried to hide, but it was ever present when she spoke words no longer used.

"You mean the Triforce?" I questioned with twisted lips.

"Is that what you are calling it? Cute."

I rolled my eyes. "What is it you want from me? I'm not in the mood to spend the next hours swapping life stories." If anything, I wanted to get as far away from her as possible. Being near Kira was making my skin itch.

We approached a bend in the road. As she took a turn twenty miles too fast, I reached up, steadying myself on the fabric ceiling. It was then I caught a glimpse of a mark on the inside of her wrist. *Her* demon mark. I felt as if I was free-flying from the sky, my stomach in my throat, and when I hit the ground, the force took my breath away, leaving me rattled.

The mark was one I knew well. My gaze tapered, and the conversation we'd had in my room about Lexi and Travis rushed back. "How is it you've sired children?" I asked, my heart thundering in my ears.

Her eyes took on a volcanic ember. "I told you I'm different. Whereas most female demons cannot carry a child to full term, I have not once, but twice."

A strand of cuss words left my lips. I thought I was going to be sick. It suddenly became very clear just what she wanted from me.

Kira was their mother.

That bitch.

Outrage. It wasn't an emotion I felt often, but to know this—there wasn't a name foul enough to describe what I was feeling. My hands gripped the sides of the leather seat, followed by the shredding of material echoing in the car. My gut reaction was to burn Kira until she was nothing but ash blowing in the wind.

Teeth barred, my chin jutted out, eyes glowing like burning coals. "If you think I would let you harm my cousins, then you are sadly mistaken."

Her eyes countered mine. "It is you who is mistaken, Chase Winters. I mean them no harm."

I laughed sharply. "Excuse me if I don't believe you."

"I would be concerned if you weren't suspicious."

The new car scent air freshener dangling from the rearview mirror perfumed the interior, making my already upset stomach roll. "You've given me nothing. No answers. And no reason to trust you." Not that I ever would.

"It's a good thing we have a long trip ahead of us. Plenty of time to talk."

The thing was I hadn't planned on spending the entire ride back with this demon in the driver seat. While she was blabbing and taunting me, I was thinking of ways to rid myself of her, but not before I got what I wanted. I had to find a way without giving up anything about Lexi and Travis.

"So talk," I said, folding my arms and staring out the window, barely seeing the dry land covered in sand and red rock formations whip by.

She clucked her tongue. "Not so quick. If I give you the information you seek, I am going to need my own assurances."

"What is it you want from me?"

"Just a favor when I need it," she said.

An open favor to a demon, to be called in whenever her little heart desired. Every fiber in my body was screaming no. But what choice was there? Only one.

Her head angled as she eyed me. "Deal or no deal?"

What was she, a gameshow junkie? I gave a reluctant nod.

"You don't honestly think I would just take your word. Surely, you know that is not how demon deals work."

Oh, I knew well enough about making a deal with Hell. I just had never been dumb enough to strike one.

I held out my wrist. "Get it over with."

She kept her foot steady on the gas, never letting the car slow or waver. With her left hand on the wheel, she used her right index finger to slice across my wrist. I watched as blood pooled, streaming down my arm. Then she took that razor sharp nail and opened a small gash on her own wrist, but the color of her blood was black. She smashed our two wounds together, mixing her gunkiness with mine. Her lips formed a chant I couldn't pretend to understand.

A blood oath.

The area around the cut seared. I yanked my hand back from under her grasp and glanced down. As usual, the wound began to slowly heal. It wasn't a deep cut and should have been gone from sight, unscarred within minutes, except it did leave a scar, a bright red one in the shape of her mark.

The deal was done. I was bound to my word, to come when she summoned and give her what she sought. God only knew when or what she would ask of me, but it seemed like a small price for what I was getting in return.

My brow lifted and my body tensed. "Happy now?"

A sadistic grin curled her lips. "For the first time in over a decade." Gliding down the highway, a light mist of rain fell from the cloudy sky. She told me what I sought, every gritty, knee-buckling detail. The drizzle was background noise as she spoke, listening as she revealed a method to ridding Angel of the darkness that claimed her soul.

I gasped at one point, uncertainty weaving through me like tangled vines, intertwining around my organs and squeezing. "I don't believe you," I spat, disgust spewing in the air.

"What? Did you think breaking a bond from Hell would be a piece of cake?"

No. I hadn't been that daft, but…

I'd rally a whole slew of Divisa if necessary. Whatever it would take to protect those I loved. What she was telling me had to be done made the demon inside me shiver and not in a good way.

Intrigue shone beyond her red-rimmed eyes. "I have to say, your reaction is fascinating. Or rather, the reaction I can feel from your demon is what I find interesting."

I rubbed my damp palms on the thighs of my jeans. My body had broken out in a cold sweat. "He tends to get upset when her safety is threatened."

"As do you, I see. If you do nothing, her life is damned. Your dearly devoted wears the mark of servitude to Hell. The only way to save her is to step into the darkness with her. What do you have to lose?"

She was right. What did I have to lose?

And with that being said, it was time Kira and I went our separate ways. Our journey together ended here. There was no way on this green earth I was going to let her anywhere near my family. She might have bested me in the motel, but it was time to reciprocate. I might not be able to kill the she-devil, and it was impossible for Lexi and Travis to hide from her. They both bore her mark, which meant if Kira really wanted to find them, there was nothing I could do about it. I got the feeling what Kira wanted was for me to assure my cousins she didn't mean to hurt them.

No go.

I had already sealed my fate, soul be damned, and someday I would pay the price for the deal I struck. Someday was not going to be today.

No doubt Kira expected me to do something foolish, and she was absolutely right. I just don't think she expected I would also put myself in danger. Cruising down the highway at speeds over seventy, I shifted my eyes up, peering at the side mirror to check the road was clear. Things were about to get bumpy.

Kira glanced over at me with wariness. I grinned and gave no other warning. She blinked, and during that nanosecond, I extended my arms in nothing but a blur, grasping the wheel. Then

I yanked with all my might.

Bon voyage, mother trucker.

Motionless, her eyes went wide. The sound of rubber shrieking was followed immediately by the ear-piercing crunch of metal, like a sonic blast that shook me to my very core. Glass fragmented, showering the inside of the car and nicking my flesh as I was thrown from every which angle in my seat, but I didn't feel it.

While the car tumbled and rolled again and again across the pavement, I went for the blade sheathed in my sock. The bone-shattering impact of each complete spin made the simple process of reaching down difficult, but I battled against gravity until my fingers wrapped around the handle.

The demon herself couldn't be sent back to Hell, but I could force her out of her host. It would buy me the time I needed to get to Angel.

I was quite acquainted with the feeling of spinning wildly out of control. Kira? Not so much. She let out a war cry of frustration, snapping her seatbelt. *Bad move, bitch.* Her head whacked the roof of the car, neck angling in a way a human's was not meant to bend.

Shit had definitely gone downhill.

When she came back down, she dove straight at me, nails extended like claws and flaxen hair floating around her face. It made my job of running the blade into her heart as simple as pie.

She basically landed on it. I gave my wrist a twist, driving the dagger home. "Apstergo," I said.

As soon as I finished the chant to expel the demon from her body, the car finally stopped rolling. It teetered on two wheels before falling back down to the ground in a tremor that rumbled as if it reached the earth's crust. Kira's weightless body slumped on top of mine, and I waited for that pivotal moment when she disintegrated to ash.

Damn demons.

Of course she wouldn't follow protocol. Pushing aside the body of some nameless woman who'd been unfortunately possessed by Kira, I dragged in a long deep breath, and as soon as I was sure my lungs were working, I padded my hands over my body. Hella-freakin'-lujah. I was still in one piece. Mostly. No missing limbs—maybe a broken rib or two—and the cuts would heal in a few hours. In a situation like this, it was good to be supernatural.

Removing my seatbelt, I leaned to my left and kicked the door with my foot. Blood seeped down the side of my face and dripped down the back of my throat. The door clattered to the ground, and I stepped out of the car, taking in my surroundings. There was a line of trees in the distance. The car had tumbled off the shoulder into the grass.

I climbed up the embankment and looked down at my

handiwork. Good grief. My car insurance was going to cost me a fortune. Two totaled cars in a year. I sighed at seeing another one of my vehicles charred.

The roar of flames licked the car and caught, burning metal and melting plastic. A steam of heat rose up in the vicinity, creating a mirage. Smoke billowed in the air, escalating and disappearing into the clouds. It carried the smell of roasting oil and grease, hardly pleasant.

Dusting the glass and dirt off my rather ratty clothes, I ran a hand through my hair, shaking loose any debris. I needed new transportation and quick. I could travel the entire way running, and heck, it probably would have been faster, but I'd only wear myself out. Saving Angel was going to be exhausting in itself.

So I was going to "borrow" the first car I came upon, and hopefully the burning pile of metal beside me would only aid my plight. As luck would have it, I didn't have to wait long.

A silver sedan flew by, breaking when the driver caught a glimpse of the crash and me beaten up on the side of the road. I walked up to the driver's side window.

"Hey, do you need me to call for help?" a man with slightly receding hair and crow's feet around his brown eyes asked.

Granted, this wasn't my first rodeo. Travis and I had been known to hotwire and hijack cars for shits and giggles, mostly Dev's until he bought us cars of our own. I doubted Devin was going to get a kick out of me doing so now, but desperate measures and all.

Holding the man's gaze captive with mine, I said, "I need to borrow your car, mate. But don't worry it will be returned. There is no need to alert the authorities. I'm just a friend using your car for a few days. Do you understand?"

He nodded.

"Good." It was far easier than hotwiring, but not nearly as fun. "You have quite a walk home. Better be on your way." That should buy me a few days. Just long enough to do what I had to do. No harm done.

At least that was the idea.

And my plans had a way of backfiring in epic proportions.

Without a second thought, I slid into the driver's seat, wrapped my fingers around the key, and turned the engine over. I put my foot on the gas and steered the vehicle back onto the highway with one sole purpose.

Two state lines later, I came to a fork in the road, and its symbolism to my current situation hit me. Do I go left or right? Could I really do what Kira had suggested? Even now, thinking about it, my demon balked and the man rebuffed. It went against my very nature to protect her at all costs. And that was where the conflict came.

When it came down to it, would I actually be able to follow

through? I was scared I wouldn't, but even more scared I would.

Chapter 9

{Chase}

I made the long trip back to Illinois in record, law breaking speeds, only stopping to pee and grab a bite to eat. My eyes darted to the rearview mirror for the hundredth time, making sure a demon wasn't stupid enough to trail me. I thought for sure I'd be pulling over to exercise my ninja skills, but maybe Kira had something to do with my uneventful trip back.

It was hard to admit that maybe, just maybe not all demons were self-serving assholes.

I went straight to Angel, not bothering to stop home or let anyone know I was back. The need to see her with my own eyes overwhelmed any other function—including food.

I did not pass go or collect my two hundred dollars.

This was it. Do or die.

Walking down the stairs, I detached myself as much as I could, knowing I was about to partake in something that would darken my soul, whatever was left of it.

My stomach lurched.

Angel was lying on the mattress, curled on her side with her back to the door. I expected her to jolt out of bed and start cussing at me, demanding I let her out. So the fact she didn't even acknowledge I was here was unnerving, especially since my body was having a sensory seizure. Tingles of every emotion, and some I didn't even know I was capable of, rocketed around my organs.

My heart rate picked up as I reached into my pocket, pulling out a set of keys. Maybe she was sleeping, probably a darn good thing. "Angel?"

Not a muscle twitched.

With an objective eye, I looked at her. Too skinny. Too pale. Too still.

Something was wrong.

My hand shook as I turned the key, the lock clicking open, followed by the second and then the third. Slipping inside, I quickly closed and locked the door behind me. I called her name again, returning the keys to my pocket. The jingling sound vibrated through the soundless room.

There was no answer, and by now, the Angel I'd come to expect would've been jumping down my throat.

Please God, tell me I'm not too late.

I refused to believe it.

Zapping to her side, I sat on the edge of the mattress. Her face was partially hidden by a curtain of dark hair. I brushed back the strands, my pulse throbbing at being this close to her. The days I'd been gone had done a number on me physically and mentally. I could only imagine what it had been like for her. Guilt started to weasel into my belly. "Angel, I'm—"

The air whooshed out of my lungs on a grunt as her feet slammed into the center of my gut. It knocked me off the bed, but I caught myself and crouched on the tip of my toes, hand touching the ground for support. *Dirty little sneak.* I knew better to let my guard down.

She took her split-second of surprise and jumped to her feet. With a feral cry, she lunged off the bed, coming down on me. I could have darted to the side, but I was afraid she would hurt herself, which was not what I wanted. Landing on my back, her legs locked around my waist, squeezing like a pair vice grips.

"What do you think you're doing?" I hissed, reaching up as her arms wrapped around my neck.

"Shut up." She pulled back, putting her full weight into the movement, and down we went, tumbling to the floor.

I rolled, making sure I took the brunt of the impact and groaned as her body hit mine. The damn wiggle worm twisted, throwing her legs over mine and weaving them between my legs. "If you wanted to snuggle, all you had to do was ask. No need to get aggressive, unless of course you like it."

Her answer was to press her lips to my ear lobe and take a

nip. It wasn't hard, but a warning. She wasn't playing around.

"I always thought you had a kinky side," I said.

Anger made her cheeks flush. Straddling me, her hand snaked down over my hips, going for my pocket. "Of course you would turn this into something perverted." Her mouth grazed the side of my jaw.

I snatched her wrist. "If you bite me again, so help me, Angel…"

She smiled tightly as she tried to yank her arm free. "You'll what?"

If she only knew what I was planning to do to her… But I said nothing. I let her go and she scrambled to her feet, hands curled at her side. "That's what I thought. You don't have the balls to hurt me. Now let me out of here."

Standing, I met her gaze. "You know I can't do that."

"Give me the key," she demanded, shooting forward.

I took a step back, out of her reach. I didn't care if the devil himself was knocking on the door. Hell wouldn't be cackling much longer. "I have something else in mind."

Her chest rose quickly, and I could sense her panic. "You don't understand. They're waiting for me."

"I don't care."

I recognized the wild look that sprang into her eyes, like a crazed hyena. She was about to lose control. *Dammit.* This was not how I'd envisioned things going. Granted, I didn't think she would cooperate, but actually fighting her had not crossed my mind. We would have to do this the hard way.

She exercised a whirlwind kick, knee bent at a ninety-degree angle. The power pack whooshed into my gut and momentarily stunned me. Hot pain jarred me to the bones. "Where the hell did you learn to do that?"

Her chest rose quickly from exertion. "I learned from the best. You. And there is a whole lot more where that came from."

My brows shot up.

She rolled her eyes. "I've watched you fight countless times."

"Watching is a whole lot different than being able to execute moves like that, sweetheart."

She shrugged. "I'm a natural."

"And I have more experience," I countered, keeping a steady eye on her.

Angel was fast—I'd give her that—but I was faster. And a good thing. Spinning around, she jabbed her elbow into my side and used the heel of her palm to hit me in the chest. I darted behind her before she could sweep a kick to my legs. She pivoted around, swinging her arm in an arch that just barely missed my chin. Ducking, air rushed over my jaw and I wrapped my arms around her waist, drawing her back against my chest. I pinned her arms with mine.

She went wild underneath me, wiggling like crazy. "Let me go!" she screeched, as if I was hurting her, another one of her manipulation tactics.

"Are you going to be reasonable?" I asked, although the probability of reasoning with her was up there with lunacy. "It's your choice. We can do this the easy way or the hard way. If you fight me, I promise you're not going to like what happens."

Rocking forward and then backward, she used the momentum to her advantage, slamming my back into the wall. "I think you got it backward, douchebag."

I held her easily, but hearing her call me douche brought back so many fond memories, I couldn't help the tiny grin tugging at my lips.

Her elbow thrust into my stomach and she sprang free. "Because I'm seriously going to kick your ass."

When had she become so slippery...and scrappy?

I sprang forward to grab her just as her knee flew straight up. Thanking my quick reflexes and knowing this was one of her all-time favorite moves, I managed to avoid getting my manhood literally crushed. "Will you just stop and listen to me for one second before you hurt yourself?"

"Hurt myself?" she echoed in a way that said I was going to regret it. Laughing, her voice became high-pitched. "The ones who are going to get hurt are you, Lexi, Travis, Devin, Emma... Do you need me to go on?"

I'd had enough of the games and the fighting. This time when her hands flew at my face, I snatched her wrists, backing her against the wall. I used my body to trap her and restrain her hands above her head. "Now you're going to listen to me whether you want to or not." Leaning down, I brought our faces so they were only a few inches apart.

She closed her eyes, squeezing them shut.

"You don't have to look at me, but you are going to hear me out." I pressed my forehead to hers, letting the warmth of her skin calm me. She was still alive, and somewhere behind the magenta eyes and the bad attitude was the girl I loved with all my soul. Taking a deep breath, I had to try one last time to get through to her. Just in case… "This isn't you, Angel Eyes. You might lash out at me now and again, but you would never hurt me. Hurt anyone."

Her body arched, agony stinging her voice. "I said, get your grubs off me."

My eyes traced the contours of her face. "You're letting Hell control you, and the Angel I know doesn't bow to anyone, especially not to a demon. She wouldn't dream of it."

Beads of sweat dotted her brow. Tendrils of dark hair clung to her neck.

"I swore to protect to you and somehow I've failed, but I'll be damn if I'm going to give up on you. Never," I vowed with more passion than I'd ever felt.

Besides the ragged rise and fall of her breathing, she didn't move a muscle.

"I know how strong you are. You proved that tonight, but I'm not just talking physically. Only *you* can control your destiny. Hell doesn't get to decide for you." I wanted to shake the shit out of her, rattle her brain cells until she started thinking clearly again. "Show me you're not weak."

Her eyes flew open, the circle of red luminous and powerful. "There is nothing weak about me." There was a gravelly texture to her voice. It was sort of robotic.

As beautiful as her unearthly eyes were, I despised them. Hated what they stood for. Detested what they meant. The only light I saw in what Hell had done to her was they hadn't been able to sever our connection. And that made us fiercer. Chase and Angel. We were epic, and our story wasn't going to end here—end like this. "Prove it. Prove me wrong." I knew it was a long shot, goading her, but I was betting on her taking the bait.

Her lips thinned and a shudder rolled through her, racking against my body.

My chest tightened. "Please come back to me, Angel. Please. You have to. I can't live in this world without you. I love you too much. I won't let them take you from me, but you have to fight. I need you to fight to live." I framed her face with my fingers as words I never thought possible spilled out of my mouth.

A heartbeat passed. Her lashes fluttered down. Then they opened. Blue eyes churned, clear and brilliant, shimmering like starlight. A tear trickled down her pale cheek, lips quaking. "I-I'm so sorry, Chase." Her brows knitted, eyes I thought I might never see again swam with a thousand unsaid emotions. "I can't stop it. I don't know what to do."

Before she could utter another word, I pulled her against me, burying my face into her hair. "Don't think about that now." An erratic blend of feelings channeled between us, making it hard to do what came next.

I admired her, loved her, needed her. And if we ever made it through this, I would tell her every day of our lives.

"Angel…"

"There is a war coming, Chase," she whispered.

I weaved my fingers through her hair. "Let them bring it. I will destroy them."

She slumped in my arms, hope sucking right out of her. "We can't win." Her lip trembled. "You're issuing our death."

"We will win. And if I die, you're coming with me," I breathed into her ear and closed my eyes. My hand slipped behind me, twisting around and gripping the cool handle tucked under my shirt. I pressed a soft kiss to her temple, lingering. "I love you."

The blade felt like barbwire in my grasp, and the demon

inside me screamed in protest, thrashing and kicking, attempting to surface and overthrow what I was going to do, I wanted to rage. With my heart in my throat, I positioned myself. There was a very good chance I was going to vomit.

Her body stiffened, sensing the sudden and abrupt change. She pulled back and I let her, eyes searching my face. "Chase?"

"It's I who am. Sorry. This is entirely my fault. If I had just stayed away from you…" I let my voice trail off, unable to stop staring at her. Then I plunged the knife into her side, right into the heart of our identical demon mark, the one that started it all when I saved her life for a servitude to Hell.

Energy hummed through me, shocking me every couple seconds. I hadn't been prepared for the sharp pain that hissed at my hip, but it was nothing compared to what Angel was feeling.

Please God don't take her from me. Not my Angel.

Chapter 10

{Angel}

Golden eyes stared back into mine, tortured with agony. Hope crashed into razor sharp disappointment and disbelief. He stabbed me. I gasped, unable to believe Chase had stabbed me. He would never hurt me. Ever.

But I had bigger problems. Much bigger. Pain. It sizzled through my veins, starting at the entry point where the blade had pierced my skin and spreading like wildfire. Burning. It was a pain I remembered well and never thought I'd feel again. The night Chase brought me back from the dead.

A scream tore from my throat, cold sweat gathering above my lip. My body bucked from the trembles of misery draining me of energy. I shook my head back and forth, hair whipping me in the face. "I-I can't… It's everywhere. It…hurts. So much, Chase. Please…you have…to make it stop."

Sweeping me off my feet, Chase laid me down on the mattress as I whimpered and thrashed. "It's going to be okay. Try to relax. It will be over in seconds."

How could he possibly think it was going to be okay? I was going to bleed out if he didn't get me to a doctor. Glancing down at my hands gripping the wound, I expected to see gobs and gobs of sticky blood covering my fingers. So imagine my shock when there was none. Not a damn drop.

WTH.

What was going on?

"No! No!" I repeated over and over, punctuating each *no* with increased panic. I tried to sit up, but it only made things ten times worse, so I slumped back down onto the mattress. Grabbing his hand, I squeezed. "Chase, it's killing me."

His luminous amber eyes lit the entire room, brighter than I ever remembered seeing them, and I understood that whatever I was going through, it was affecting him too. Nowhere near the same level, but our unique link made the impossible possible. "Don't fight it," he whispered.

Wetness gathered on my cheeks, and I clenched my jaw, tasting the tartness of blood. It felt like the fire would never end. Licking and lapping at my skin, burning away my organs. "What have…you done?" I asked, curling up and clutching my side.

With a pained expression, Chase crouched in front of me, eyes pleading with mine to understand. "It was the only way to get you back."

He hadn't answered my question. Typical Chase fashion.

Evasive.

I pushed up my shirt, needing to be free of the scratchy material against the extremely sensitive spot. Gazing down, I saw the marks. *Well, that's not normal either. Good flippin-grief. What now?*

The intricate designs still bled into my skin, but it was the ink that morphed. Swirling from just under my armpit down to my hip, the marks were awash in a stunning, bold sapphire. "Chase?" My voice shook as his name choked at the back of my throat.

Stilled, his eyes were fastened to the undeniable "Breathe," he said.

Easier said than done. My head fell back and I forced my muscles to relax, no longer fighting against the pain that rocked my body. I took a long deep breath that sounded close to a sigh. Within moments, the blaze slowly began to subside and I couldn't have been more relieved. For a time there, I had been positive I was going to kick the bucket. I should have known Chase would never let that happen. I should have trusted him.

Like the floodgates had been opened, an overwhelming current of memories flashed back. All the horrible things I'd said. Every threat I'd made. It was like watching myself in a movie—a horror flick.

For a shattering moment, I wasn't sure who I was. It wasn't a pleasant feeling, not knowing if I was really me or that other ugly part.

WEIL

You're Angel Morgan. You grew up in Arizona. Your mom is your best friend. And this mind-bending gorgeous male hovering over you is your boyfriend.

I blinked, anticipating the darkness rising up and taking over. "Well, that just happened."

A corner of his mouth lifted as Chase leaned down, placing a kiss on my damp forehead. The utter relief ricocheting off him was a viable thing in the small space. I, on the other hand, wasn't sure what I was feeling other than intense exhaustion. My limbs were so weak, as if I'd been stranded on an island without food or drink. I was dehydrated, and I ached in places you wouldn't imagine. It sucked. The inside of my thighs. The back of my neck. I swore even the tip of my nose throbbed.

My lashes fluttered up, locking eyes with the guy who never gave up on me. I lifted my hand, wanting to feel the side of his cheek, but it never made it. Chase sucked in a sharp breath, and I was almost afraid to ask. "What is it?" *Please tell me it was only an enormous pimple.* In a knee-jerk reaction, I quickly cast my eyes downward.

Chase wasn't having it. He placed his thumb and index finger on my chin, tipping my face upward. His gaze captured mine. "Your eyes. They're purple."

Say what? I had mentally psyched myself up to hear him tell me my eyes were demon red, but purple…that was new.

Unfortunately, I was going to have to dwell on my newfound eye color later, because I was having trouble keeping them open. "Chase, something's wrong."

"I'm sure it's just temporary," he said, downplaying his concern.

I shook my head, my vision starting to blur. "That's not what I mean."

"Angel...Angel," he called, his voice going distant as the room spun. It was hard to hear over the buzzing that vibrated between my ears.

I felt myself falling, a black hole sucking me into oblivion, and I swayed. Chase caught me, soothing me with the sound of my name on his lips.

"I've got you, and I'm never letting go." At least that was what I thought he said.

{Chase}

Clamping down the emotions jackhammering in my chest, I kicked the door open, never happier to leave behind this burrow and to see sunlight. Wood splintered under impact. The hunters were going to need a new front door, but I didn't care about the mosquitos getting in or the hunter's secrecy.

What I hadn't expected to see was Lexi climbing out of an SUV and Emma pointing one of her arrows at my head.

Shit.

"Doesn't anyone follow orders?" I grumbled.

Lexi came flying around the car as soon as she saw who I had in my arms and stopped abruptly, eyes bouncing from Angel to me and back to Angel. "Chase?" She hesitated, confusion circling in her eyes.

I drew in a shallow breath. "It's okay. She's okay." Or so I kept telling myself, but I wasn't sure anything would ever be the same again. And I wasn't *okay* with that. Someone was going to pay for the hell she'd gone through. There would come a time when my desire for revenge wouldn't be silenced.

Angel's body shuddered against mine as it had in intervals for the last forty-five minutes. I just wanted to get her somewhere safe. Realistically, the connection between her and Alastair might have been severed, but I wasn't stupid enough to believe they would stop looking for her.

Lexi's aqua eyes glistened with tears. "How did you—?"

"It's not important now. What *is* imperative is that she sleeps *and* we let no one know where she is."

She nodded, unable to take her eyes off the frail-looking Angel clinging to me. "We'll protect her," she promised fiercely.

I could always count on family. Rotating toward my car, I met my first roadblock. Barely over five feet, hair the color of autumn and cynical emerald eyes, Emma Deen was a constant thorn in my side. "You can stop pointing that thing in my face."

She tipped her chin, nodding over my shoulder toward a door half swinging off its hinges. "Do you destroy everything in your path?"

Ugh. Her voice grated on my ears. I winced. This was one of those times having roommates sucked. "Not now. You and I will talk later." About why my cousin was with her, among other things. "I kind of have my arms full."

"Don't you always?" she mumbled, lowering her weapon and walking straight up to me. She kept her expression blank. "What color are her eyes?" Her hand reached out to pull back the dark hair curtaining Angel's face, beaded with a cold sweat.

I growled deep in my chest. "Touch her and die." Angel nuzzled her face into the alcove between my neck and shoulder. I could have easily brushed past her, but I just didn't have the fight inside me.

"Christ. What did you do?" she demanded.

"What I had to. Brought her back from the depths of Hell's claws." A part of me had hardened, turning cold forever.

"This conversation isn't over. I want to hear everything."

Of course the hunters would have an interest in how I'd broken the link between Angel and Hell, but I would be damned before I let them use her for a science experiment. "We'll see."

"Winters!" she called as I swept past her. "You owe me."

I knew I did. It was because of Emma I'd been able to keep

Angel hidden and from becoming Hell's anchor on Earth. If we hadn't teamed up, the outcome might have been very grim for humankind and for Angel.

Frozen for a single heartbeat, I nodded and then I was gone.

There would be a time and a place to pay that debt. I ran to my "borrowed" car, concealed under overgrown brush and the weeping branches of a willow. After carefully tucking Angel into the back seat, I hustled behind the wheel, taking one last glance over my shoulder at Angel to ensure she hadn't pulled a disappearing act. Her eyes drifted closed, knees pressed against her chest in a fetal position.

Satisfied that she wasn't going anywhere, I hit the gas, preparing for another short road trip. The idea of getting behind the wheel wasn't thrilling, but as I drove, I let my mind wander. A dangerous thing.

Angel had fallen into a fitful, but deep sleep. She tossed in the back seat, occasionally letting out little moans of distress. Her body needed rest probably more than it needed anything else. Freeing her from the demon-darkness had taken its toll. I refused to let my mind drift toward how close I'd come to losing her. If I'd been a few hours later, it might have been too late. The blackness had nearly taken over her humanity. Her road to recovery wouldn't be without challenges.

I let out a long, ragged breath, finally letting go of all the pressure building inside me the last few days. As I listened to the sweet evenness of her breathing, I knew that when she woke up, she should be around familiar surroundings, in a place that made her feel safe and secure. Somewhere that oozed tons of love and fond memories. College had been nothing but a curse, bringing angst and misery. It wasn't home.

Pulling into the driveway of the only home I'd ever known, pressure clamped down my chest. I stopped the car beside Devin's, staring at the two-story farmhouse. The porch light was still on as it was every evening. It brought an affectionate smile to my lips.

I sat in the car, in the balmy twilight, gazing at the vast woods beyond. They seemed to stretch endlessly in either direction, but I knew better, knowing every off beaten path. Evergreens, maples, and even poison ivy thrived in those woods along with other things.

My eyes wandered to the dark and still house next door. No life moved inside. Chloe must be at work, which I'd been counting on. The last thing I wanted to do was explain to her mom why her daughter looked like she was in a coma. I still had to deal with Dev, just not tonight.

Gathering Angel, I shot across the yard to her empty house and managed to unlock the front door one-handed. *Still got it.* I climbed the stairs in the dark and crossed to her bedroom, depositing a worn-out Angel on the bed.

    I could only sit and stare at her. She needed rest, I told myself. We both did, but my mind was churning. Not worrying about Angel went against my nature. I didn't know how to turn it off. Peeling back the blanket, I crawled in alongside her, lying on my side. I interlaced our fingers, needing to touch her. Her chest rose and fell in a sigh, quieting my anxious heart. Together, the outside world didn't seem to matter. All that did was we were here.

    I closed my eyes and finally allowed myself to sleep.

Chapter 11

{Chase}

Groggy, I opened my eyes and blinked multiple times. I waited for the immediate sense of panic that followed each time I woke. Today, it never came. I was filled with these dazzling tingles and a sense of tranquility I wasn't sure I would ever feel again. It was in that moment I remembered where I was and what I'd done.

I turned toward the girl still sleeping peacefully beside me. Her head was curved on the pillow, dark hair fanning out against the silver sheets. It had only been a few weeks since she'd become demon bipolar, but it felt like a year. More than anything, I wanted to pull her into my arms. Instead, I ran my fingers over my jaw before I carefully swung my legs over the side of the bed.

My stomach let out a demon-sized growl. Besides being hungry, I was feeling optimistic. There was something about being home, with Angel tucked safely in her bed, that calmed both sides of me.

I moseyed into the kitchen with nothing but food on the brain. Unfortunately, I wasn't the only one with that idea. Dev was sitting at the table, a mug of coffee and a bowl of cereal sitting in front of him. Glancing around for a few seconds, I made sure I was in the right house. Angel and I both lived in old, huge farmhouses, but that was were the similarities ended. Chloe had a much different design style. There was no way Dev would have a leopard print rug and matching dish towels hanging off the stove.

"What are you doing here?" I asked.

"Hmm. I was going to ask you the same thing." I took the seat across from him at the table, and Dev slid his uneaten bowl of Captain Crunch toward me. "Here, you look like you could use this."

I never turned down a bowl of cereal. "Thanks. I can't remember the last time I ate." Shoveling a spoonful into my mouth, I mumbled, "What time is it?"

He took a sip of his coffee. "A little after four."

"In the morning?" Maybe I should have asked what day it was. "Wow. I can't believe I slept that long." Or that Angel was still snoring logs. Over twelve hours.

"You look like crap."

I snickered. "Thanks old man. What are you doing up, anyway? Got the munchies?"

Behind his salt and pepper beard, his lips tipped. "I forgot how funny you are. When I realized you were here, I couldn't sleep."

I rubbed the back of my neck, hating that I caused him stress. "I'm sorry. I didn't mean to worry you. I figured you'd be at *home*."

"Yeah, well…"

"I got it." He didn't need to spell it out. Chloe and Dev had sleepovers. He probably had a key. Moving on.

He leaned forward, elbows on the table. "Are you going to tell me what's going on? Not that I'm not happy to see you, but I know you. Is everyone okay?"

I poured myself another bowl of the Captain. "Lexi and Travis are fine. I imagine they'll be on their way home soon."

He uttered a sigh of relief. "And Angel?"

Fumbling with the spoon, I stared into the bowl. "She's been better."

"Tell me what happened. The last I heard was her father was back. Are you guys in trouble?" he asked, genuine concern in his voice.

"More than usual?" I added, cynically.

He gave me one of his stern, yet dependable looks.

"He's not going to be a problem."

"Chase, did you…?"

Devin knew what I was capable of. That was no secret, so it didn't bother me in the slightest that he immediately jumped to the conclusion I'd killed Chris. "No, but I wish I had. It was Angel," I added.

He gasped.

Twirling the spoon with the milk, I mumbled, "And that was the start of a demon domino effect."

"I think you better start from the beginning," Dev said.

And I did, unloading all the sordid details about her father, the transformation in Angel, having to keep her hidden, and the lengths I went to get her back, all of the nitty-gritty—except for Kira. I left out her name, and luckily, he didn't ask. The last thing I wanted to do was add an extra layer of stress and anxiety. When I finished purging myself of all the crap I'd been through, I actually felt better.

Devin tipped his head back, suddenly looking much older than I remembered. "I never should have let you guys go. Maybe then this wouldn't have happened."

I slammed my fist down on the table, harder than I'd meant to. The bowl clattered on the wood top. "This isn't your fault, Uncle Dev."

He arched his brows. "But you blame yourself. Chase, at some point you have to stop always taking the fault. This wasn't the life you asked for. If anyone is to be blamed, it's Hell."

Logically, I knew he was right, but I wasn't a logical person. "We're going to need some more Captain Crunch," I said, staring into the empty box.

His coffee mug was pressed to his slightly curved lips.

"What's new? I'll go to the store and get some groceries before you clear out Chloe's pantry."

"What are you going to tell her?"

"I don't want to worry her yet. You're sure she is going to wake up?" he asked, eyes glancing toward the stairs.

I wasn't sure of anything, but I sincerely believed Angel was a fighter. "She has to."

He leaned forward. "You Chase, are fierce, a protector. I know that you love just as fiercely. It's who you are. Let's face it. I tried to do my best to keep Lexi, and Travis safe, but without you, it would have been a thousand times harder. I don't know how I would have done any of this without you."

Emotion clogged the back of my throat. I hadn't expected the well of feelings to rise up and grip me. Since the moment I closed the doors on Angel's prison, with her red eyes staring back at me, I'd been in a constant state of suppressing any type of feeling. If I hadn't, there was no way I would have been able to withstand seeing her suffer, hearing her pleas, feeling her pain, or imagining a life without her.

Now, it was coming to the surface.

Devin stood up and laid a hand on my shoulder, giving it a quick squeeze before going to set his mug in the sink. "Oh…" He paused and turned back around. "Whose car is parked in the driveway?"

I cleared my throat. "It's probably better you don't know."

"That's what I was afraid of."

~*~*~*~

Her lashes lifted. Wispy sunlight caught those strange eyes meeting mine for a brief second, and I wasn't sure I would ever get used to the color. Violet eyes, a perfect blend of her blue human eyes and her red demon eyes. Angel had slept for nearly twenty-eight hours, waking up for only a few minutes when I laid her in the back seat of my car.

I bit the inside of my cheek as her lashes swept down. Angel was beautiful to me—flawless. An exuberant amount of relief pinged through me. She was home, no longer connected to Hell and not trying to kill me.

Her long lashes lifted again and our eyes locked, a sweet flush creeping across her cheeks. My eyes dipped and her lips parted, causing a hunger to stir inside me.

{Angel}

Chase's handsome face came into focus. The sun was highlighting the sharp angles of his jaw through a window I knew well. It faced his bedroom.

I was home.

It was surreal. I kept blinking just to make sure this wasn't a dream. When his fingers lightly ran under my chin, I thought I might cry. They felt very real.

There were a million things I wanted to say, but I had no idea where to start. I was lucid for the first time in…I wasn't sure how long. I felt like myself, but I didn't—something was different. As I gazed into his eyes, I realized one thing hadn't altered—my feelings for Chase. They were tremendous. They were strengthening. They were overwhelming.

I might be a complete basket case, but I was certain of one thing. I'd been saved by his infinite love.

Without a word spoken between us, I leaned forward to kiss his jaw, the stubble he was sporting tickling my lips. I nipped playfully at his chin and then pressed my lips softly to his. "Thank you," I whispered, resting my head back down on the pillow beside him so we were face-to-face.

His eyes morphed into incandescent gold slits, and a shiver skated over my skin. He let out a shuddering breath. "I was terrified the entire time you were lost. I've never been so scared out of my mind that I would never be able to hold you again."

My arms tightened around him.

"And when I did see *you*, I was afraid it might be the last time I'd ever hear your laugh or see your smile."

My heart tripped, dancing. "Chase…"

"Don't you dare," he said, putting a finger to my lips. "I know what you're going to say and you don't owe me an apology. None of this would have ever happened if I had just stayed away from you." His chest heaved. "I'm scared shitless that we'll never be the same again. That you won't love me the way you did."

"Stop," I said, blinking back tears. "How can you say that?"

"Angel, I've taken so much from you, from your life. My world has almost killed you, taken you from me, and destroyed you. How can't I feel responsible for altering your life so much?" His jaw locked.

"None of that matters. You saved me. You always save me."

He cast his eyes downward. "I promised you that you would be safe. I lied. You'll never be safe with me."

"That's such bullshit. I owe you my life. *You* brought me home. *You* always know what I need even when I don't. *You* love me no matter what stupid thing I've said or done. And…I love you. That's never going to change." I softly rubbed the pad of my thumb over his lower lip.

He closed his eyes. "Say it again."

I leaned forward, pressing my lips smoothly against his and whispered, "I love you more than I ever thought possible. Nothing you can say, nothing you do will ever change that. You'll always be a part of me."

His lips parted on a sharp inhale. "I only want you to be happy." He slid his hands over my hips as he pulled me into his lap, eyes searching mine.

"*You* make me happy," I said, tracing my fingers over the nape of his neck.

He lowered his forehead, pressing it against mine. "What I did—"

I pressed a finger to his lips, silencing him and shaking my head. "I don't want to talk about it. Not yet." There was a goose-sized lump in my throat, and I forced the tears that threatened to take over back down. "I don't want you to regret the choice you made bargaining for my soul."

His bright golden eyes twinkled as he looked down at me. "I would make the same choice a thousand times over. You're worth every fight, every bloodshed, and I'll never stop fighting for you." He placed his mouth to my ear, his breath tickling the sensitive area. "I love you, Angel Eyes."

I was breathless, and he hadn't even kissed me yet.

It was so easy to slip into his arms, slip back into this radiant feeling he enticed inside me with just one steaming look. We might have only been apart for a few weeks, but gazing into his dreamy eyes, it felt like a lifetime. I wanted him to make me forget everything else but him. I wanted him to hold me and never let go.

Chase seemed to be able to know what I wanted without my having to tell him. I could thank our bond for that and his deep feelings for me.

One of his hands moved to my thigh, slipping his fingers

under the cotton material of my long shirt. As his hand inched up, his lips made a hot line of kisses down my throat, causing warmth to flood over my body. This was real. He was real.

And I didn't want to think or feel anything but this moment, if only for a little bit. "Will you love me?" I whispered. The embarrassment I was feeling leaked through my voice, staining my cheeks.

"Now?" he growled, his lips reaching my jawline.

I nodded, unable to speak as I watched his irises meld from silver to gold.

"Are you sure? You're not too tired?" There was heat in his tone.

I rolled my eyes. "I think I've slept long enough. Make me feel again," I murmured.

I never saw him move, but suddenly his lips were on mine, and it was as magical as I remembered. My hand moved into the silky strands of his hair, our breath mingling as I deepened the kiss. I wanted, *needed* more of him. It felt like forever since he'd kissed me, and I let my eyes drift closed, my insides lighting up from the power of his kiss.

His arms dropped to my waist, and then I was lying on my back, staring up into his face. "Are you feeling anything yet?"

I wrapped my legs around his as we lay hip to hip, his weight sinking into me in the most delicious way. I traced my finger over the curve of his cheek. "Exceedingly happy," I said, along with more emotion than I could name. Chase evoked all of it and so much more.

Chapter 12

{Chase}

Every limb in my body was buzzing with the aftereffects of being with Angel. I didn't know what I'd been expecting when she woke up—who she'd be or what she would remember. She had definitely caught me by surprise.

Slipping on my rumbled shirt, I sat on the edge of the bed as Angel clutched the sheets to her chin. There was this shy quality in her expression and a sense of what-in-God's-name-do-I-do-now?

Angling my knee on the bed, I peered down at her and my heart skipped a beat. "How about a shower?" I suggested. "Then you should eat."

"Okay." She glanced up at me, soft eyes drifting over the planes of my face in a dreamlike trance.

Hesitating a moment longer, I eventually forced myself to stand up. She was only going to be in the next room. At least that was what I kept telling myself. It did nothing to stop the panic fluttering in my chest or the fact I just wanted her close to me.

Who was I kidding?

REDEEMING ANGEL

I was afraid if I blinked she would be gone. We might have some serious separation anxiety for a while. Or a decade.

Placing a fresh towel on the bathroom vanity, she followed me into the confined space. Her eyes took in everything, familiarizing herself with her things as if she was seeing them for the first time. Then her gaze landed on her reflection, and she let out a loud gasp. Leaning forward, her hand flew to her face as she tilted her head from side-to-side. "What am I going to tell my mom?"

Wide eyes the color of polished amethysts stared back. I said the first thing that popped into my mind. "We'll tell her you got contacts." Anything, as long as the defeated look was erased from her face. I knew how much it would bother Angel to lie to her mom, but I also knew she wasn't ready to talk about what had gone down.

Her bottom lip quivered, and I thought she might cry, finally break down, and I knew it would send me over the edge. But just as her eyes started to glisten, her chin lifted and she pulled it together.

Angel never ceased to amaze.

"Okay. I can do that," she said, meeting my eyes in the mirror.

I nodded.

What a pair we were. No one could ever say our relationship

was dull. Unhealthy? Hell yes, but never boring.

The hiss of the shower sounded almost immediately after the door closed behind me. I leaned against the wall and closed my eyes. How the hell was I going to leave her alone?

{Angel}

I'd taken countless showers. It was a mundane task, but this shower was like none of the others. There was an immense appreciation for something as simple as having hot water spray over my face in a waterfall effect. The water didn't sputter or turn brown. There weren't spiders dangling from the ceiling or some ugly as sin creature scampering underfoot.

Everything was exactly where I'd left it. I ran my fingers over the variety of bottles and jars, wanting to touch it all. Opening my shampoo bottle, I dragged in a deep breath of honeysuckle and ripe strawberries. I wanted to drench my body in the scent; it was that good. Oh. My. God. A razor. I could kiss the little beauty tool. Once glance at my pale skin confirmed my legs had definitely seen better days.

A few times I pressed my shaky hands to my face, but the steady stream of water washed away the grime and sweat stuck to my body. The shower worked with the sugar and caffeine Chase had left for me, clearing a few of the cobwebs so I could put my mind to other things.

Like seeing my mom.

Overall, it felt good, like cleansing the soul in a way.

I opened the door, a fog of steam following me into the bedroom and floating along the floor. Clutching the towel to my chest, I went into the room, my eyes immediately drawn to Chase pacing the floor.

He exhaled, leaning against the window. "I was two seconds from breaking the door down. I thought you passed out in there."

My lips curved up. "Sorry," I said, padding across the carpet to my dresser. I opened the top drawer. My gamer shirts and comfy clothes lay in disorder in the drawer. If I'd been alone, I would have taken out each piece just to look at them.

I pulled out an outfit. With an armful of clothes and my other hand still clamping the towel, I stood up and turned around, smacking into Chase. I let out a little shriek. "You're never going to stop doing that, are you? Sneaking up on me?"

One side of his lips tilted up. He twined a piece of my damp hair around his finger, inhaling the fresh and sweet scent of my shampoo. "Feel better?"

My heart fluttered at his nearness. "Much." I glanced at the clock on my nightstand. It was eleven in the morning. "Is my mom home?" I realized I didn't even know what day it was.

The strand of hair slipped through his fingertips, and he brushed it behind my ear. "She is, but she doesn't know we're here. I talked to Devin this morning."

Part of me wanted to run into Mom's room and climb into her bed. I bit my lip. "How long have I been sleeping?"

"It doesn't matter. You needed it."

He was being evasive. What else was new?

"You hungry?" he quickly asked.

Now that I had a moment to think about food, I was craving grease and cheese. "Actually, I think I could eat an entire pizza."

He pressed a kiss to my forehead. "I'll call for delivery and wait for you downstairs."

As soon as the door closed, I stared at my room. The silver bedding always reminded me of Chase's eyes. There were video games stacked in one corner. Some girls collected makeup, but I hoarded games. Silence stretched over the room, and it was killing me. With silence came thoughts, voices, and memories. I didn't want to think, but my mind jumped and danced from thought to thought, bouncing back and forth between who I'd been and who I was. I wanted to shut it all off.

My stomach dipped.

I was growing to hate the sound of nothing.

Shaking my head, I blinked back tears and refocused on the rumpled bed where not long ago Chase and I had been, wrapped up in nothing but each other. God, I didn't know where I'd be without him. He never gave up on me even when I was horrible and a bitch. Suddenly, standing in the middle of a room surrounded by all my things, I felt so lost. I knew the person I'd once been, but I didn't know who I was now. The only thing I did know was I could never go back to being that girl. She was gone, taken from me long before the darkness took me.

And I was okay with it. I accepted that my life would always be different, but I'd been naive to think loving Chase would be enough. Maybe it had been…once. I still wasn't sure how he'd been able to bring me back. I could only recall snippets of that night, falling in and out of consciousness. The memories of when the darkness seized my mind and body were murky, like swimming through a swamp of muddy and slimy waters.

Tugging on my clothes, I sat on the bed, needing a moment to gather myself before I went downstairs, not that it mattered. My emotions weren't something I could hide from Chase. I sat with my hands folded in my lap, staring at the fibers of carpet on the floor, doing my best not to lose my shit. The tears were right there, waiting for me to let them loose, but I was afraid once I started I wouldn't be able to stop.

Shaking out my damp hair, I stood and crossed the room, knowing I couldn't be alone in this room another second. I needed to see him. The sight of him gave me strength. I'm sure there was a more technical name for what our bond did to me. All I knew was when I was with him, he took away a majority of my fear, uncertainty, and sadness.

Pizza. The smell hit me as I rounded the corner of the stairs, and a smile began to spread on my lips. Chase was behind the counter with a half-eaten slice dangling from his mouth and a plate in one hand. There were three boxes on the counter, one of them already missing three slices.

"Did you save me any?" I asked, scooting up on one of the barstools.

He slid me a can of pop and handed me a plate. "You said you could eat a whole pizza, so this one's yours."

"And the other two?" I teased.

He took a bite. "All mine."

I opened the box in front of me, and my belly made a series of noises that sounded like my stomach was munching on my innards. When it came to pizza, I always ordered the same weird combination, and Chase knew exactly how I liked it. Cheese and black olives. His consideration of the small things made him deserve the best boyfriend award.

With the first bite, my taste buds exploded in a foodgasm. "God, I missed this," I mumbled, my mouth full.

Guilt shadowed behind his eyes, and I could sense it through our bond. How long would it be before he stopped blaming himself? I wasn't the only one who was going need time to mend the scars left behind.

"Don't do that," I whispered, placing my hand over his on the counter. "I can't have you look at me like that every time one of us makes an offhanded comment. We both need to move past this…somehow."

He turned his hand over so ours were pressed palm to palm, linking our fingers. "I know. It's just harder to control my emotions when I'm around you. The time apart has messed with my abilities. Being in the same room with you makes my emotions go haywire."

"Me too," I admitted, stroking the side of his thumb. "What are we going to do?"

"We'll figure it out. Later."

In the meantime, I was deathly afraid the darkness was not really gone, but still residing inside me, growing little by little until it was able to take me.

There it was—the dark cloud hanging over my head.

Chase and I had very different coping methods. He went looking for trouble, the kind that meant whacking off demon heads. And I wanted to pretend it never happened. Neither was healthy, but in a situation like ours, I didn't think there was a wrong or right way to deal with the kind of trauma we'd endured.

I would love Dr. Phil to try to analyze us.

The thought made me smile to myself.

"What's so funny?" he asked, plucking another piece from the box.

"I was just thinking that we would make a great reality show."

He cocked his head, pondering. "Yeah, I can definitely see myself on TV."

Of course he could. Plucking a black olive from my pizza, I threw it at his head. My aim was dead on, but Chase had the reflexes of a mongoose. He promptly caught it in midair with his mouth.

"Nice toss," he said, grinning.

I internally sighed, glad to have things back on a less serious path, and took another T. rex-sized bite out of my pizza. Chase lifted his gaze over my head and smirked. It was the twinkle of mischief in his silvery eyes that gave me pause.

"I thought I smelled pizza," said someone behind me.

I dropped my food on the plate and spun around, faster than normal. The sound of her voice made my heart kick. "Mom!" I leapt from my seat and threw my arms around her. She smelled and looked like home—the lingering scent of the perfume she wore religiously, the old worn Minnie Mouse pajamas and house slippers.

She engulfed me in a hug. "I'm the one who should be surprised. Why didn't you tell me you were coming? I would have, I don't know, gone shopping or something." After another squeeze, she pulled back, eyes roaming over my face. Concern replaced her surprise. "Honey, are you crying?" Her gentle hands framed my face.

I swiped at my eyes, not realizing tears were spilling down my cheeks, and stared at the floor. "It's nothing. I'm just being a sappy girl. Bad time of the month."

"Awkward. And that is my cue to leave," Chase announced, his chair scooting across the floor.

I knew he wanted to give me time with Mom, but I was afraid. It wasn't necessarily him leaving that freaked me out, but being alone with Mom. What if something happened? What if I hurt her? What if she asked questions I couldn't answer? "Chase?"

He stopped in the doorway and arched a brow. I couldn't believe how much I missed seeing the silver stud above his eye. "I'm just going next door to clean up," he said, but his eyes said so much more. They assured me everything was going to be fine, and if I did need him, he would know.

I nodded, and then he disappeared.

Her hand flew to her heart. "I don't know how you ever get used to that."

"I don't."

She had watched our exchange, sensing something was up, and placed a hand on each of my shoulders, studying my face. "What is going on? You've lost weight. And what did you do to your eyes? Does it have anything to do with demons?" Her ramble of questions was typical Mom.

"*Mom*, there is no need for a full-blown freak out." Sarcasm. It was my companion. Anything else would have only triggered her warning bells.

"That's not an answer."

"What was the question?" I asked, playing ignorant.

"Angel, I can't believe I've actually missed your sarcasm, but God help me, I have."

"That makes two of us," I muttered.

"So, are you going to explain the eyes, or am I going to have to interrogate Chase?" she pushed.

I swallowed. God no. He would crack under the *mom* pressure, especially if she offered to make him dinner. I shrugged, about ready to spew a bunch of lies, but I couldn't. She trusted me, and had always been truthful. I owed her the same.

Could I really tell her I'd killed my father? Her ex-husband? Not that he'd actually been the same man we'd once known.

Could I actually say I'd been possessed by Hell?

There was no way I could tell her I'd been held captive because I had wanted to unleash demons on Earth. She would be appalled. I was appalled.

"This is going to call for more pizza," I said soberly. I had no clue what I was going to say or how detailed I'd be.

She raised a honey-colored brow. "And wine," she added.

"Mom, it's not even one o'clock, and if you say it is somewhere, I'm going to my room."

"Glad to see college hasn't changed you too much. Except for the eyes," she said, stretching to reach the top shelf on the cabinet. After retrieving a stemmed glass and a half-empty bottle of Muscato, she took a seat on the stool beside me.

I plucked a black olive. "It wasn't school that altered my appearance."

She pulled a swig from her glass. "I kind of figured that out on my own. Demons?"

"When isn't it?"

Worry jumped into her eyes. "You're okay though?"

"Yeah. Of course. The eyes are just a byproduct of a hiccup in my bond with Chase. It's nothing, really." Downplaying was apparently the route I was going to take. Not quite a lie, yet not the whole truth. Worked for me.

"Is it permanent?"

I lifted the still slightly damp hair off my neck, keeping my eyes averted. "I don't know, but I think so."

She was slow to respond. "Angel, don't be afraid to look at me. I'm not going to condemn you. Whatever did happen, you're still my daughter. Nothing is ever going to change that, certainly not the color of your eyes. Anyway, they're beautiful, just like you."

I wrinkled my nose. "That's just the wine talking."

She laughed. "Even so, doesn't make it any less true. I'm so glad you're here. I want to hear about all the other stuff. School. Living on campus. *Chase*..." She said his name in a gooey kind of tone. "But first, I have something important to tell. I was actually going to call you, but this is much better."

I groaned, but was secretly glad she didn't press for more details. When Mom said *important*, I immediately thought of her relationship with Devin. There was no denying things between them were moving in a certain direction. "Okay, now you're freaking *me* out," I said, glancing at her hands to see if there was a shiny new diamond.

"It's nothing bad. I've just made some big changes."

I picked at the crust on my plate, my appetite vanishing. "To your life or the house?"

Nervous energy rolled off her. "Sort of both."

"Just spit it out."

Both of her hands spread out on top of the counter. "I put the house on the market," she blurted.

Confusion and trepidation weaved through my belly. Believe it or not, I'd actually really grown to love my little hick town. The idea of moving again filled me with dread. She knew how much the people here meant to me, what Chase meant to me, and I legitimately thought she was happy with Devin. What had changed? To make me have to choose between her and Chase was cruel, especially after everything I'd gone through. "You're selling our house? Why?"

An emotion crossed her face. A wistful gleam. "Well honey, Devin and I have decided to move in together."

"What? Are you insane?"

Chapter 13

{Angel}

Where love was concerned, Mom didn't have the best track record. I mean, her last husband had turned into a drunk, landed in jail, and ultimately was used by Hell. He had a black soul, the kind Hell gravitated to.

I thought for sure Chase would come barreling through the front door at the speed of light due to the rise in my blood pressure. He was definitely listening, but I was past the point of caring. "Don't you think you're moving a little fast?" I asked, pizza getting cold.

She twirled the stem of her glass on the counter. "It might seem that way, but with you gone at college, Dev and I have gotten more serious. And it seems like such a waste having this big old house empty most of the time."

I made an ugly face. Gross. She'd just implied she spent most of her night's next door. I could have done without that image. "Can we not mention you and Dev...*together*?"

Mom smiled warmly. "He's an amazing man and an even

better kisser."

OMG. I buried my face in my hands, groaning. *Make her stop.* I swear she made a game out of embarrassing the crap out of me. The more uncomfortable I got, the louder she generally laughed, but her tactics never failed to make my cheeks burn. The second she started telling me how famous Devin's butt was, I was walking out. But then I realized something. Whether she did so intentionally or not, her awkward teasing made me feel more normal than I had in weeks.

Still didn't change the fact I didn't want my mom to move in with Devin. *I* didn't want to move in with Devin. I started to visualize what my life would be like if Mom and Devin got married. It got me thinking. Lexi would constantly be in my stuff, always trying to dress me up. Travis and I would be duking it out for Internet connection. And Chase…

My head lifted. Oh God. Chase and me. Under the same roof. Twenty-four hours a day. I needed oxygen. Suddenly, living together wasn't such a bad idea after all.

Mom thrust her fingers through her tousled hair. "I know that look. What are you thinking?"

"Chase and I are going to live together," I whispered.

"I wondered when you were going to make that connection. Actually, I'm surprised it wasn't your first thought. You sure you don't have a fever?" She lifted her hand as if to place it against my forehead.

I rolled my eyes. "Funny. I leave for a few months and suddenly you think you're a comedian."

"Comedian or not, I'm still your mom, and there are going to be rules. Very strict rules."

It was my turn to laugh. Mom didn't know the meaning of strict, and really what was the point? There was pretty much nothing left for Chase and I to possibly do.

"I know how much you care for each other," she stated.

Did she really though? I wasn't sure Mom grasped the depth of our feelings. She knew we were serious and I loved him. She knew we shared an unexplainable bond, which summarized our relationship—unexplainable. Not rhyme or reason.

"But," she continued, "that doesn't mean I'm okay with you shacking up."

Shacking? Who still uses the word shacking? "I get your drift. Oh, and I'm not calling him dad."

She laughed. "I think you're getting ahead of yourself. I never said anything about marrying him."

True, but I knew Mom, and she would never make such a huge step unless she loved Devin and was hoping it would lead to the sound of wedding bells. The woman was a hopeless romantic if there ever was one.

Maybe this meant she would be giving up her daisy dukes, but something told me that wasn't happening anytime soon.

"You're sure you're okay with this? Nothing is set in stone. I don't have to sell the house. I can—"

"Mom, stop. It's fine. I swear." I could see how important this was to her, and by God, if Devin made her happy, who was I to stand in the way? It was like she said; we were all away at college, and I would feel better knowing Devin would be around to look after her.

Argh. College.

I'd already missed so much of my classes there was no way I would be able to catch up. Knowing Chase, he had probably used his wily methods to ensure I was getting straight As. However considerate his efforts were, I didn't want to bs my way through school. As it was, I would probably have to retake the semester, and so would Chase. I just had to convince him. He had his methods, and I had mine.

"Okay then," she said, taking a bite of cold pizza and making a funny face. "How about I make us all a family dinner tomorrow? You look like you could use a home-cooked meal."

"I'd like that."

Change. Change. It was all around me. Everywhere—inside me. Reminders that nothing would be the same. I felt it then, a thread of darkness, residing in me, curving and weaving around my soul.

I don't know what happened. I sort of just checked out, withdrew inside myself. The next thing I knew, Mom was calling my name and I was blinking rapidly, trying to focus on where I was.

"Angel, are you okay?" Her smile slowly fell.

No. I was far from okay, Mom. I'd just spent almost a month locked in a dungeon possessed by a darker side of me. And I don't think it's fully gone.

Instead I said, "Yeah. I'm fine. I'm just happy to be home."

Expression filled with tenderness, she reached up and brushed one side of my face.

The darker side had once been strong enough to manifest and take over.

Never again, I vowed.

~*~*~*~

Questions. I only had about a gazillion of them. Chase and I hadn't had the *talk* about what happened, neither of us anxious to relive those moments. I remember the pain clearly. It was the before and after that were fuzzy, and he was the only person with answers.

"Really? You bought a new car?" was the first thing that popped out of my mouth.

A shit-eating grin unfolded on his lips. "I *borrowed* it."

My eyes went wide with understanding. Borrowed my butt. "Chase!"

He bumped my shoulder with his. "Don't worry. It will be safely returned to the owner. No harm done."

"Uh-huh." We were sitting on the stoop of my front porch, watching the wheat field across the street grow. What else did you do in Spring Valley?

The sharp autumn sunlight bounced off his silver eyes. It was the middle of October, and in Illinois that meant the weather changed from day to day and temps ranged from eighty to twenty. The leaves had started to turn and flutter to the ground, like little drops of fire in the trees. It would only take one good storm to strip the trees of their covering.

"Everything is so quiet here. It makes me nervous," I said.

"The calm before the storm." He fidgeted, and I couldn't help but notice how often his eyes darted over the yard.

"Are you going to tell me what's got your boxers wadded up?"

His lips twitched. "You just can't stop thinking about me half-naked, can you?"

That was his sad attempt at trying to avoid the question. I wasn't letting it go. I pinched him on the side at the sensitive area above his hip. "Tell me or I'll be forced to hurt you."

He placed a hand over my knee. "I planned on telling you, but I wanted more time with you before dealing with the past and what's to come. I'm selfish like that."

I placed my hand over his, lacing our fingers together. There was this urge inside me to touch him as much as possible. "Well, thanks to you, we have time to be selfish with each other."

His chest heaved. "You're right. I guess I should tell you what happened in Vegas."

"You went to Vegas. Without me?"

"Yeah well, you were kind of indisposed. But trust me, Angel Eyes; it wasn't a vacation. I went in search of a demon who might have answers to stop the darkness from spreading, from overpowering you."

"A demon?" Outrage city came pouring out. "You trusted a demon?"

"No. Nobody said anything about trust. I'm not completely witless. Anyway, I knew what I was getting into. This wasn't the first time I'd gone in search of demons."

"You're just a world of wonder. Why did you never tell me?"

He folded his hands, propping his elbows on his thighs. "There are some things from the past, things I've done I don't want shadowing the way I feel about you. I've never felt like this about anyone, and I'm bound to make mistakes."

"I know who you are, and I know you're not perfect."

He snorted.

"We've both done things that have damaged us, but I don't need all the details of your sordid past. I love who you are," I said to make sure we were clear.

After a moment of silence, he said, "The only way I knew how to save you was to step into the darkness with you."

"I could sense you. Even when there was nothing but blackness, I felt you. It was the only thing that kept me going."

"Our bond is stronger. I was counting on it." His skin was still a golden summer tan. I was jealous, looking down at my own pasty arms. "When I was searching for a way to bring you back, I had to make a deal."

My lips turned down. "What kind of deal?" I asked, scooting to the edge of the step.

His eyes said it all.

"Chase! You didn't."

"What did you expect me to do? There was no other way. I wasn't about to leave you there another minute."

I knew that while I'd gone cuckoo, Chase had suffered. There had been moments of clarity where I felt his pain, but hearing the anguish in his voice, struck a chord. "And you're worried about the deal you made?" I never knew Chase to let a demon get the better of him. It was disconcerting.

His gaze got lost in the distance. "It's not the deal I'm concerned about."

I raised a brow. "What then?"

He deadpanned. "It's the demon. She's different than any I've encountered. And..."

She? It was stupid, but I was suddenly filled with jealousy. Me? Jealous of a demon? Redonkulous. But there was something in the way he spoke about her that caused my internal girlfriend radar to go berserk-o.

"Before you jump to all the wrong conclusions," he said, sensing the fibers of my jealousy through our link. "She's Lexi and Travis's mom."

My mouth hit the ground, immediately dousing my irrational possessiveness. "Uh, say what?"

Fingers dove into his ragged hair. "I know. That was exactly how I felt."

"Oh my God." I got a sick feeling in my gut. "What does she want?"

"She says she wants to reconnect with Travis and Lexi."

"And you don't believe that's all?"

"No."

The first lesson Chase taught me was to never trust a demon, no matter what they promised. "What are we going to do?"

"I honestly have no idea, and that's what's bothering me. If Kira really wants to find Travis and Lexi, there's not much I can do about it. I've been trying to decide if I should tell them or not."

"Do you think they have any interest in seeing her?" Demon or not, she was their mom, and I knew how much my best friend longed for a "real" family. Yet there was nothing *real* about a demon.

"We've spent our lives running from and fighting demons. It's hard for me to imagine they would want anything to do with her."

Chase's feelings for his father were very black and white, and I could hardly blame him. I hated Alastair, but Chase's hate went deeper—a lifetime deep.

Some people come into your life as blessings; others come into your life as lessons. Kira was definitely a lesson—and we were still waiting to see what lesson we'd learn. One thing I did know—it wasn't going to be good. When she called in her deal with Chase, he'd have no choice but to answer.

Damn her.

I wanted five minutes alone with the demon. She'd messed with the wrong guy—my guy. A burn started in the pit of my chest, rising. "She wants to use you."

"I know." Helpless anger etched into his face, matching mine.

That was the thing with our bond. We frequently altered each other's moods without being aware.

Just awesome. As if we didn't have enough on our plates, we also had to worry about mama drama.

Chapter 14

{Chase}

It felt as if a tremendous weight had been lifted off my chest. Telling Angel about Kira lessened my stress levels. Now if only Angel would do the same. She was hiding something. I was sure of it.

And it wasn't just the zonking out into space that had me concerned. She was putting an exuberant amount of effort in keeping her emotions from me—no easy feat considering. I know she'd been through an ordeal, but what I didn't understand was, if something was wrong, why wasn't she talking to me? How was I supposed to fix it if I didn't know what was wrong?

I wanted to call her out on it, but I also didn't want to push her. She had made it clear she wasn't ready to talk, and granted I wasn't all too thrilled to relive those moments either.

It hurt a little not having her let me in. Maybe more than I wanted to admit.

Still, I was going to give her the time and space she needed to recover. It would be sort of presumptuous to think nothing had changed. That *she* hadn't changed. In reality, the moment I'd set my eyes on her, I'd known her world would never be the same. Darkness and doom followed me like a rain cloud.

Seeing her struggle only emphasized my desire to kill Alastair. Not just send him back to his domain, but wipe him from all realms. "I'm going to destroy his black soul," I promised to no one in particular. It was one I made to myself frequently and one I meant to keep, damn anyone who stood in my way.

Angel had her way of dealing with what happened. This was mine.

"What are you thinking about?" she asked, sneaking up behind me and wrapping her arms around my waist.

My heart thudded in my chest. "Nothing. Everything."

She rested her cheek on my back. "Do you want to talk it out?"

Smirking, I turned around, linking my hands at the small of her back. "I hate psychobabble."

"What a coincidence. Me too."

"Come on. I told Dev we'd take care of our car situation. Want to ride along?"

"To return our "borrowed" car?"

My brow arched.

She rubbed the tip of her nose against mine. "Sure. I'd love to be your partner in crime."

I twined my arm around her waist. "Good. Saves me from having to convince you. Let me grab the keys, sidekick, and then we can see how many laws we can break on the way."

"As long as we get home without flipping any cars."

I coughed as we walked across the yard toward my house, an arm still looped around her. If she only knew what happened to my last car. "Now what fun would that be?"

"Can't wait," she mumbled as we climbed the porch steps.

I opened the front door with a smile on my face and was greeted by chaos. There were bodies everywhere, all talking over each other. I almost shut the door and turned back around, but Lexi let out one of her high-pitched squeals, making me cringe. In a blink, she was hugging the life out of my girlfriend. They lost their balance and went down in a tangle of curls and girly shrieks. Tears were flowing down Lexi's cheeks, brightening her aqua eyes. For someone who had a ballet dancer's body, she was strong and spirited.

"You're really okay," Lexi gushed.

"I'm still bonded to your hotheaded cousin, so I'm not sure that justifies me being okay," Angel replied, her voice muffled by Lexi's natural sun-drenched blonde hair.

Lexi giggled. A second later her hand flew to her mouth. "Oh my God. Your eyes."

Angel looked like she wanted to curl up in a hole and die. I could have throttled Lexi.

"How come all the cool stuff happens to you?" Lexi asked.

Angel rolled her eyes.

"Well, this didn't take long," I muttered. The whole gang was here. Travis, Lexi, Emma, Hayden, and Craig were all spread out in my family room. Silence followed Lex's squeals of happiness, and all eyes were on Angel.

Cheeks flushed, I gave her and Lexi a hand, pulling them to their feet. I kept Angel's hand linked with mine as we stepped into the room.

I tensed, waiting to see what was going to happen next.

Travis swooped across the room, engulfing Angel in another hug and lifting her off her feet. "Thank God you're back. Chase was driving us all insane."

She laughed lightly. "I don't doubt it. I'm just glad he never gave up."

"Chase? Give up? As if he would. I don't think quitting is in his vocabulary." He set her down, and I snuffed the immediate desire to wind our fingers together. The yearning to constantly touch her was always present in the back of my mind.

She took a step backward so our arms brushed. "There are a lot of words *not* in his vocab."

Travis got one of his silly grins. "That's for sure."

Enough was enough. A guy could only stand aside while

being talked about as if he wasn't there for long. Sixty seconds was about all I could take. "I'm standing right here," I grumbled, taking a seat on the arm of the recliner. Angel sat in the chair, legs tucked underneath her. She nibbled on her lower lip, looking like she was ready to run for the door if necessary. "So what's this all about?" I asked, eyes scanning the room.

And then like a dam being broken, the room erupted into questions galore. They were flung at Angel and me, one right after the other.

What dumb thing did you do this time?

How did you bring her back?

Why didn't you call?

Are we going to order food?

I took a deep breath. "Everyone chill out."

"How can you be so calm?" Craig scowled, his broad shoulders stiffening. "There is an influx of demon activity and we're on the cusp of war. Why the shit aren't you freaking out? How can we trust her?"

"Be careful what you say next, Craig." My voice was low, but it carried across the room.

{Angel}

I flinched.

Something told me things might get ugly fast, as they usually did in a room filled with demon DNA. Chase's eyes went from silver to gold in a wink.

"You don't have to trust me," I interjected before things got heated. "But whether you do or not doesn't change the fact we are all going to be under fire sooner rather than later. Just because Hell can't use me anymore, doesn't mean they won't find a way."

"Angel's right," Travis said. "Losing their key is going to royally piss them off."

"What are we supposed to do about it?" Lexi asked.

"There is only one thing to do. We take out the big players. The higher demons. And I'm not just sending them back to Hell. I'm going to destroy *his* soul." It wasn't lost on anyone that Chase had suddenly switched to referring to a certain demon.

"Alastair?" Travis interjected.

"No way, dude," Hayden added, propping his elbows on his knees beside Lexi on the sofa. "How do you plan on doing that?"

"Can it even be done?" Craig asked, intrigue in his beefy expression.

Chase shrugged. "I guess I'll find out. I'm done playing the cat and mouse game."

"Oh great. That's our grand plan?" Lexi threw her arms in the air.

"You got a better one, little cuz?" His smoky eyes challenged.

She slumped back into the couch. "Don't you ever wish our

lives weren't so complicated?"

"Some people should thank their lucky stars that everything I wish for does not come true," he replied coolly.

I rolled my eyes. *Good grief.*

"Okay, so how do we go about destroying the soul of a higher demon?" Hayden asked, always so loyal and trustworthy. He would walk blindly into a battle because Chase asked.

Chase shook his head. "If you guys had half a brain, you would all walk away now."

"You always were a showoff," Travis sneered. Emma and he were smooshed onto the loveseat. She'd been quiet, which worried me. The hunter was indubitably plotting away.

"You'll be putting yourself and those around you at risk. I can't be responsible for anyone else getting hurt. Or worse…"

Travis's gaze narrowed. "Can it be done?"

"Is the sky purple?" he retorted.

"Meaning you have no idea if it's possible," Emma finally chimed in. This was right up her alley.

"I have a source," Chase informed. His body language said, don't ask questions.

I groaned. Fan-freaking-tastic. More dealings with Kira. If he struck any more contracts with this particular demon, he was going to end up being indebted to her in this life and beyond.

I wasn't the only one suspicious. Lexi was onto him, and she was not in the least put off by his stubborn tone. "What kind of source?"

"Let me worry about the details," he said irritated. "And in the meantime, we send as many of those assholes as we can back down to roast in Hell."

Emma cleared her throat. "Speak for yourself, half-breed," she hissed. "I've had enough of demons."

I think everyone in the room got whiplash, heads turned so fast in her direction. "Giving up the family biz?" Chase scratched his head, looking doubtful.

Emma glanced to Travis briefly. "Let's worry about keeping Earth from burning and extinguish these bastards. I can't retire if we're all dead."

She had a point. "I don't expect any of you to stand by my side. I can't promise that you'll come out of this unscarred…or at all."

The room lapsed in silence, the severity of our situation settling over us. This wasn't about us anymore; it could very well affect the world. No pressure.

Chase played with my hair, twirling the strands around his fingers as they worked out patrol details around town. The demons *I* had let loose before being caged were our immediate problem. Hell was coming with backup.

I cast my attention to the wheat fields outside, the room of people fading into the background. My nerves felt shot, and there was a buzz humming between my ears. What I wouldn't give for five minutes of blissful silence.

"You ready to go?" Chased asked in what felt like only minutes later.

I blinked. *Oh crap.* I'd forgotten all about returning our "borrowed" car.

The room had pretty much cleared out; only Lexi lingered behind. I smiled. It was all I could do, because inside I was a mess, and I didn't want Chase to know. Keeping those feelings from him required effort, and I wasn't sure how long I would be able to hold out.

I was stronger than I used to be; yet I still didn't know exactly what I was doing. There was untapped potential and power inside me. I felt it simmering and swirling under the surface, ready to break free, but had no idea how. And that scared me almost as much as losing myself again to the darkness.

Chase was already burdened with worry and had done so much for me. This was something I would find a way to handle on my own. Looking up, I met his eyes. "Let's ride."

Leaning down, he whispered a ludicrous response in my ear.

I whacked him on the arm, smiling faintly. "You're still a dickwad."

Unfolding his legs, he stood. "And that makes you happy?"

I hopped to my feet, eager to get some fresh country air. "Yeah, it does."

He gave me a wicked grin. "It's nice to know I still have no clue how your mind works."

The feeling was mutual. You'd think being able to sense each other's emotions would have made it easier. Not the case. Sometimes I wondered if it made it more complicated. "Ditto."

Part 2

Being deeply loved by someone gives you strength, while loving someone deeply gives you courage.

—Lao Tzu

Chapter 15

{Angel}

The sun had gone down and with it a cold slapped over the air, punching from the northeast. A storm was coming, the kind that made you want to stay inside, curl up, and sip a hot drink. Sitting by the window in my room, I wrapped my hands around a mug of tea. *Patter. Ping. Pang.* The rain pelted against the glass. I watched it curtain the view and waited for the next round of lightning to ignite the gloomy sky.

Two days had gone by.

And this was the first time I was alone for more than five minutes. I needed it.

Often I found myself staring into space for no good reason, and I wasn't the only one who noticed. They all worried, waiting to see if the darkness might rear its ugly head. And who could blame them?

I clasped my arms around myself as if I could protect myself from such a terrible invasion. The darker Angel had been strong enough to manifest outside of me. What Chase had done wasn't a permanent solution. At least that was my assumption. I finally admitted to myself what I hadn't wanted to believe. My soul wasn't wiped clean. There were still tendrils of blackness entwining around my soul. I could feel them—faint, but they were there all the same.

It was the moments I caught myself lost to time and space that I realized I needed to find a way to overpower the darkness. Never again would I let it control me. Chase, Lexi, and Travis all found ways to control their demons. I would too.

Flattening my hand against the window, I felt the rain pepper the glass. My eyes peered next door at the Winters' house. I didn't have the heart to tell Chase and burden him with another problem. Between Alastair and Kira, he had more than his fair share of stress.

But Lexi…

She was strong—her control profound. If anyone could teach me, it was Lexi. Secrets weren't secrets for long if Lexi knew, but this time, she was going to have to keep her trap sealed or I would compel her. I hated sneaking around and lying, mostly because I plain sucked ass at it, but also because it wasn't something I wanted to come between my relationships with the people I cared about. Lies turned into more lies, until you found yourself trapped in a web created by your own deception. Lies hurt. They destroyed.

REDEEMING ANGEL

But a voice in my head told me this one little white lie was to ultimately protect those I loved. And it wasn't as if I would never tell him. I would—after the demon storm passed and I was able to handle the darkness.

I laid my cheek against the cool glass and closed my eyes. The world faded—

—Chase was in my room, standing in front of me with eyes smoldering gold. A familiar tingle of panic twisted in my gut. Demons. They weren't just nearby; they were here. In my room.

"How did they get here?" I gasped.

"Demons aren't bound by physical laws, but unworldly," Chase said, keeping his gaze glued on the three demons that moseyed out from the shadows. "They come and go in our realm as they please. Our marks allow us to do the same. Their biggest problem is staying here, which is why they seek us out first. Our life source allows them to stay here longer than a human's would."

I understood what he was trying to tell me. I could move like them, fight like them, because physical laws no longer bound me. Change. My limbs trembled lightly at first, then more noticeably.

Four more demons hissed from behind the others, fourteen scarlet eyes radiating through the room spotlighted on Chase and me. *Holy freaking Christmas cake.*

Confusion gave way to terrifying panic. I hadn't expected my first face time with demons since my separation from Hell to be in my bedroom. It felt like an invasion of my privacy, and I didn't like it.

However much it irked me, it was becoming clear I needed to zip up my big girl pants and fight. Chase couldn't save us alone, but how much help could I be if I could barely stay upright? I don't know what it was, but the sight of demons in all their hideous glory, drooling on my carpet and filling the room with their rancid stench, made me woozy.

I checked myself, chin jutting in the air.

Sparing me a quick glance from the corner of his eyes, he asked, "You good?"

I nodded, at a loss for words. Control. I needed to be in control right now, and caving to the fear and self-doubt wasn't going to help me.

Chase rushed headlong into battle like a bowling ball striking the pins. Demons hit the ground. He twisted around but wasn't quite quick enough—out of character for Chase. And my nightmare began. The demon brought his arm around Chase's neck, placing him in a brutal chokehold.

Hisss time hasss come to an end, a ragged voice whispered. I couldn't tell which one spoke, as none of their mouths moved.

Steeling myself, I whipped at him, snarling. "Let him go, you asshole."

Chase bent down, using the momentum to send the demon behind him sailing through the air. *Crash.* The mirror above my dresser shattered to a gazillion pieces, glass spraying over the room. His gaze narrowed as he straightened, deflecting another bone-jarring punch, but it didn't matter how many blows he dodged. They were swarming around him like stink on shit.

I ground my teeth and forced myself into action. "I can do this. I can do this." I spun, whirling a kick in the air straight at what I thought was a stomach. *Smack!*

God that felt amazing. I wanted to do it again. And again.

"Angel, watch out—"

I didn't even register the impact until I was on my back and my pain scale went from zero to ten in seconds. The demon who had slammed his foot into my chest hovered over me, grinning like a sadistic prick. To think, I had once upon a time been able to command these creatures. It would have been a pretty darn handy skill to have right about now.

Pushing up on my arms, I scooted my butt across the floor until I bumped into my bed.

Must kill. Must have. Must die.

Power. Taste good.

Mine, all mine.

I feared the voices were in my head. They stacked one on top of the other, loud and persistent. This couldn't possibly be the end. Chase and I had fought too hard, been through too much to die like this, but the demons stalked, closing in around me with their thoughts echoing in my head.

I wanted to crawl under the bed and cover my ears.

Breaking free, Chase managed to circle around and help me to my feet. If there had been time, I would have given him props for such quick maneuvering. We stood shoulder to shoulder as our uninvited guests closed in, nothing but my full-sized bed between us.

"Got any brilliant ideas?" he asked.

"I thought that was your job."

"Yeah well, you won't like what I have in mind." His eyes shifted to the window on our left.

"Probably not," I stated flatly. Knowing the way his mind worked, we were about thirty seconds away from crashing through that window and dropping two stories to the ground. I wasn't too keen about having my brains splattered over my yard.

I blinked. If I didn't do something quick, I was going to be picking glass out of my hair for weeks. Squaring my shoulders, there was this sudden crackling under my skin, traveling down my forearm. Shock held me immobile as I stared down at my arms. Chase's fingers spread over my hip, and as soon as he touched me, a bolt of static radiated between us.

He snatched his hand back, scowling. "What the hell?"

REDEEMING ANGEL

A white-hot blast of light shot from my hands, the force shoving me backward. An explosion rippled through the air, shaking the floorboards under my feet. Shit, it shook the whole house. I hit the ground, my ears ringing and fingertips burning. Plaster fell from the ceiling, chunks showering the room. I thought the ceiling was going to come crashing down. Demon arms flew one way and legs the other until they burst into ash, raining over me.

Pain ruptured and rushed down my arms, confusion swirling as I clutched my arms over my face to shield myself from not only the blinding light, but also the debris.

When the light finally fizzled out and the dust settled, I started to crawl on my hands, calling out Chase's name. He never answered. And he never would.

Shaking my head incisively, I couldn't believe what I was seeing. His body lay at an awkward angle at the foot of the bed. Blood pooled around his face, flowing freely from his mouth. His eyes were open, a soft gray, but they lacked the life I loved. The life I couldn't live without. Chase was my rock. Without him, I was lost in the world. I screamed. Again. And Again. His name tearing from the depths of my soul—

Gasping, I jolted upright. Panic cloaked me as my wild eyes scanned the surroundings, Chase's name lodged in my throat. I didn't remember how I'd gotten here. Or where *here* was…

I was in my bedroom, tucked into a ball still sitting in front of the window. The sun was in the process of rising, peeking through the ends of the blinds. My eyes darted from corner to corner, covering every nook, my heart pounding ferociously. There were no red eyes in the shadows. No lifeless Chase sprawled on my floor. No blood. But my fingers were tingling and the ends of my nightshirt were singed. "What the hell?" I muttered.

Cold tremors rocked through me as I lifted my cheek off the damp window. How had I gotten here? The last thing I remembered was fighting, the voices, and Chase… Oh God. He had been… I couldn't even form the thought.

My heartbeat sped, my lungs constricting. He was nowhere in sight, and I didn't know if I should be relieved or losing my mind. Scrambling off the window seat, I went to grab my phone. Two frantic steps and familiar sensations pricked at me. Something soft tickled my hair.

"Chase," I whispered, gazing into his silver eyes.

They twinkled like starlight. "Angel."

Even though I was trying to push down the emotions, some of them eked through. *In.* I inhaled. *Out.* I exhaled. *In. Out.* I repeated over and over until I was sure I was breathing again. "You're alive."

"What did I miss?"

Nothing. Everything. A sudden burst of happiness gathered inside me. I threw my arms around his neck, burying my face into the front of his shirt. "I'm so glad you're here."

His hands combed gently down the length of my hair. "Where else would I be?"

"Dead," I mumbled, shuddering.

"I thought we had this discussion. I'm not easy to kill."

Very true, but he also hadn't had a nightmare so real it was hard to believe it hadn't happened. The demons. The explosion. And Chase. *Christ, Mary Mother, and Joseph.*

It was my fault. The blast of light had been what caused him to stop breathing. I had killed Chase. *Me.*

He placed two fingers under my chin and tilted my face back. "What's going on, Angel Eyes? You woke up screaming my name."

"Is that such a bad thing?" I asked, using a pathetic attempt at humor to diffuse the very real fear still throbbing inside me.

"It wouldn't be if you didn't sound like you were being murdered."

"Thanks for putting that vivid image in my head. It was just a dream." *Just a dream*, I echoed in my head. *Not real.* Then I scoffed. "Scratch that. It was a nightmare." Dreams made me think about sugarplums and dancing fairies. What I experienced was nothing short of horrifying.

"Want to talk about it?" he asked, his breath warm against my temple.

I picked at the sheets, avoiding his eyes. "I don't want to talk at all." Even as the words left my mouth, I knew he wasn't going to like it. It was a total cop-out. I knew it. He knew it. But if I started to talk about the dream, I dreaded it would all unravel. All of it. The darkness. The captivity. The helplessness. The urges. And then there was the depth of my love for him. It scared me sometimes to love someone as deeply as I loved Chase.

"You've been saying that a lot lately. Eventually, that excuse won't be enough. You're going to have to tell me what's going on."

"Eventually," I murmured, staring at his lips. Without thinking, I leaned over and pressed my mouth tightly against his. There was only one thing that would surely make me forget the nightmare, my fears, everything. And it started with Chase's lips.

He was surprised, but quickly gave in. Wrapping me in his arms, he smelled insanely good, and his lips burned hot against mine, working ferociously.

"You're overdressed," I said as my fingers pushed at the ends of his shirt, impatient with the need to feel him. Seeing him dead, even in a dream, made me want to feel him alive. And Chase never felt more alive than when he was kissing me.

Warmth leapt into his face, softening the lines around his

amber eyes. "The wanting you. Does it ever stop?"

Heat spiked, radiating in my eyes. "I hope not." There was a cord between our hearts, binding us together, and I wouldn't want it any other way.

Dappled morning sunlight brightened the room as Chase ran his hands up and down my arms in a way that managed to arouse and soothe at the same time. He leaned down and kissed the curve of my mouth. His arms came around me and wrapped me in a long, deep kiss. "Satisfied?" he whispered.

"Hardly." I drew him down again, lingering over the sinful taste of him and leaned into his sumptuous kiss. I needed much, much more. "This might take a while."

"We've got forever."

I hoped so.

{Chase}

With one lingering glance over my shoulder, I slipped out of her room, carefully closing the door behind me. Angel had finally fallen back to sleep. I couldn't help but worry. I'd give her another day or two tops. My patience was running thin. She was struggling, and it was my natural instinct to want to help, ease the conflict she was feeling. I didn't need a shrink to tell me Angel had problems.

Who didn't?

Hers just happened to be exceptional. She was different now, but still the same. Profound, I know. I couldn't pinpoint precisely what was different. Physically she looked the same, except of course the eyes. Anything was better than the demon eyes. Honestly, they were quite beautiful on her, illuminating like a tropical sunset.

Inside, she was broken. I felt glimpses of the turmoil spinning inside her.

Tiptoeing down the hall, I passed Chloe's room, and once I hit the top of the stairs, I broke into turbo. I moved quieter when I was traveling at mach ten.

My mind was thinking ahead to a few things I needed to take care of as I rushed into my house, skidding to a halt. Lexi was in the kitchen being a busybody, pretending to cook. I adored my cousin, but she only experimented with food when something was bothering her.

"What's wrong?" I asked, leaning my forearms on the counter.

There was a smidge of flour on her cheek and a whole lot more on the counter. "Are you still recovering from that injury?"

"What injury?" I replied, eyes tapering.

She jabbed a wooden spoon into a bowl and began stirring with fervor. "Whatever head injury turned you into an abrupt goon."

I gave her a puzzled look. "Okay. I'm missing something.

REDEEMING ANGEL

What did I do?"

She spun, whipping the spoon from the bowl into the air, flinging cookie dough on the floor. "How could you do that?"

I suppressed a laugh. "Again. No clue what we're talking about."

"You took off like that, not letting us know what you planned on doing. The next thing I know you've swooped Angel away. You didn't bother to call or let me know she was okay."

"I'm guessing sorry isn't going to cut it."

She swung the spoon at my head. Thankfully, my ninja reflexes kept my noggin from suffering an egg-sized lump. "You jerk. I was worried sick. The least you could have done was send me a text."

"I'm sorry, Lex. Truly. It all happened so fast and I wasn't thinking straight. I just wanted to get her out of there and somewhere safe."

Buzz. Buzz. Buzz. The kitchen timer sounded. She popped across the room and back in a heartbeat. "And I'm so grateful you did, but jeesh, Chase. I was really worried. I didn't even know if you made it out of there alive."

"You can see I'm fine."

"But are you really?"

Me? There wasn't time to think about how I was feeling. I ran a hand through my hair and wondered when the last time I'd showered was. The last few days had been insane. "It doesn't matter. All that matters right now is she's home."

Lexi sighed and leaned a hip against the lower cabinets, most of the irritation dispelling from her face. "I figured you'd need me, even if you didn't."

"I'm glad you're here, Lex. She could really use a friend." Angel wasn't the only one who was struggling. There was something different about my youngest cousin. She looked a little pale and her eyes were slightly puffy as if she'd been crying. "Are you sure there's nothing wrong?"

"Nothing I can't handle."

She was right as usual. Leaving her to trash the kitchen, I pulled out my phone and climbed the stairs to my room. I sent a quick text. **We need to talk.**

Chapter 16

{Angel}

I knocked on Lexi's bedroom door and fussed with my hair as I waited for her to answer. Nibbling on my lip, I wondered if this wasn't one of my more harebrained ideas. Would getting Lexi involved with my problems only make things more complicated? Or worse, get her hurt? That was the very last thing I wanted to do.

But I didn't know what other choice I had.

"Come in," she yelled from the other side.

What was that I heard in her voice? Hurt? Tears?

I knew in my gut something had been up with her these last few days, but I hadn't been able to pinpoint just what. Not to mention my focus had been elsewhere, and now I was feeling like a pretty craptastic friend.

I turned the handle, stepping into Lexi's very romantic and lovely room. All of her furniture was a soft white, and there were assorted shades of pink butterflies dancing on the walls. Tucked in the corner was a vanity covered in makeup and perfume bottles. It was the perfect sanctuary for someone as tenderhearted as Lexi.

She gave me a tentative smile, turning in the chair, her eyes too bright. Yep. Tears had definitely been shed.

"Hey," I said.

Hastily she brushed at her cheeks. "Hey, bestie. Chase let you off the leash?"

"Hilarious. Did you get a sense of humor while I was gone?" Truth be told, Chase was just in the next room, probably hanging on our every word.

"Each time I think about you in that place I want to hurl."

I belly flopped onto her bed, resting my chin in my hands. "Hmm. Me too. But, I don't want to talk about it. Let's talk about you and why you're crying."

She slumped into the back of the plush chair, the façade she'd been trying to keep hold of faded. "Colin and I had our first fight."

"Oh." Chase and I disagreed all the time. We had as many tiffs as we did laughs, but our bond made things different for us. I knew how he was feeling and vice versa. We knew there was no one else. No matter how much of a dickwad he could be, he would never break my heart.

I swung my body over the edge of the mattress. "You want to talk about it?"

She shrugged. "I thought he was different. I was wrong. He

said it was all too much for him to handle. Demons. Hunters. End of the world. And the sucky part is I can't blame him."

"I'm sorry, Lexi. But if he couldn't deal with our world, then he wasn't worth your time." Holy buckets. This was my world now, too. I wasn't an outsider who knew their secret. I was part of the secret.

Her lip quivered and I thought, *here comes the waterworks*, but I watched, impressed, as she reigned in those tough, painful emotions. "I refuse to shed another tear for that jackass."

That's my girl. "Do you want me to have Chase—?"

"No! Absolutely not. I don't want him dead."

"Right. Too messy."

Her pouty lips gave a slight twitch. "God, I really missed the crud out of you."

And I knew just what she needed to take her mind off what's-his-name. "Think you can find the energy for some sh-shopping?" I tripped over the words. "I really need some new clothes." Inside I was cringing, but this was the only way I could think to get away from prying ears and her mind off Colin.

She slipped on her sunglasses. "You had me at shopping."

Lexi's idea of boyfriend therapy was going on a spending splurge. We each had our own agendas, but I really wished my friend had another hobby.

The mall.

It was the antichrist.

During our car ride, we spent the whole time guy bashing. She needed it, and I didn't mind. Mentally bashing Chase had been a hobby of mine when I first moved to Spring Valley. I'd grown quite good at it.

She'd quickly moved from self-pity to hating Colin's guts.

One thing remained constant, no matter how Lexi was feeling, her ability to dress to impress was on point. It was sickening really. Lexi didn't have a bad day. For me, every day was a bad hair day or an I-have-nothing-to-wear day. The fact that Lexi wore stilettos shopping made me question whether she was human at all, even half, and she looked amazing doing it. She could probably run a double marathon in those things without breaking a sweat.

Definitely not an ounce of human.

As we rode up the escalator, Lexi reapplied her lip gloss. "How did you not see that guy totally checking out your ass?"

"What?" I said, looking over my shoulder. A group of three guys snickered on the opposite side of the escalator.

"How can you be so oblivious?" she asked, shoving her tube of gloss back into her handbag.

My fingers trailed along the railing. "It's a gift. Guess my charm of irresistibility hasn't worn off."

"Seriously, why do you get all the cool abilities?"

I wouldn't call being the key that almost destroyed Earth cool. But hey, what did I know? "If we could trade, I'd give you all my guy magnet mojo."

Her phone jingled. When she looked at the screen with a frown and ignored the call, I realized who it was.

"Is that the douchebag?" I asked, as we stepped off the escalator and straight into the nearest store.

"Yep."

"Aren't you going to answer?" I prodded when her phone continued to vibrate and light up.

"Nope. I'm so over him." I didn't know who she was trying to convince more, me or herself.

"Uh-huh." No way in hell I believed that. "Maybe you should tell him that," I muttered when her phone started buzzing again.

Her heels clacked on the floor as she made a beeline to inspect a pair of red wedges. "Oh, he'll figure it out. Anyway, I'm done ranting about my absent love life. What is it you want to tell me that you don't want Chase to know about?"

I tripped. "Umm," I fumbled, uncertain how to approach the subject. I gingerly began to rummage through a bin filled with brightly-colored tube socks I had no intention of buying.

"You don't honestly believe I bought the whole 'I need new clothes' excuse. Spit it out, girl. You can tell me anything."

That's what I was counting on. "I need your help."

"Okay." She looked at me from head to toe. "Yellow is not your color, especially now with your kickass eyes. It washes out your skin tone." Her eyes squinted at my feet. "First, let's find you a pair of really great shoes, something to emphasize those legs—"

"Lexi, I don't want a makeover. And BTW, I love these shoes." A semi-attractive guy walked by us, smiling appreciatively as he eyed me up. I groaned inwardly.

"And it shows," she mumbled under her breath.

I peered down at my Converses. They were comfy. That was all I cared about. "I heard that. You forget I've have sensitive hearing now."

Sitting on a nearby bench, her fingers twiddled with the straps on her shoes. "So does this have anything to do with what happened to you?" She slipped off her heel, replacing it with the red wedge.

I let out an automatic sigh and pretended to be really interested in a pair of pumps with four-inch heels. I don't know why I was so nervous to tell her. "I guess in a way it does. I need you to teach me to control the darkness."

She gulped, glancing up. "I thought…"

"It was gone?" I finished, sitting down beside her. "Most of it is. At least for now, but I still feel it every now and then. It sneaks up on me when I'm the most vulnerable."

Her voice tightened. "And you don't want Chase to know?"

I shook my head. "Not yet. He is so consumed with revenge and ending Alastair. I don't want to burden him. He would only worry more, and when it comes to dealing with demons, distractions can be deadly."

Pulling the shoe out of the box, she slipped it on her right foot. "Why are you so sure the darkness is still inside you?"

My shoulder lifted in a one-sided shrug. "There's this feeling in me..." Along with the voice, but I omitted that part. "It's familiar and foreign at the same time. Okay, I know that sounds like crazy talk, but I don't know how to explain it."

"You nailed it. That's pretty much how I feel twenty-four seven. It's like all the things that make you human feel as if they're fading away."

"Oh my God. Yes."

"I don't know how it's possible, but I can't make sense of anything Hell does."

I couldn't imagine what passersby thought catching pieces of our conversation, but somewhere along the way I'd become immune to the world around me. "What Chase did to save me was only a temporary solution. If I don't find a way to control it, Hell will have the advantage once again."

"Shit," she swore.

"I never want to feel like that. Lost. Not in control. Will you help me?"

"I might not agree with your reasons for keeping this from Chase," she said, "but of course I will. I can't have my BFF fly off the rails again."

My attention was drawn to the smoothie stand across the mall. I was dying for a peach-strawberry, the greatest smoothie known to man. "When do we start?"

"Now," she stated.

"Now?" I echoed. What could I possibly learn in the mall?

She held up only her index finger. "Lesson number one. No smoothie."

I frowned. "Are you screwing with me?"

She drew an air circle around her face. "Does this look like I'm screwing with you?"

Ugh. "How is this going to help? I'm dying of thirst."

She folded her arms, pouty pink lips pursed. "Only because you think you are. Your mind is telling you that you *need* to have a drink. Conquer the urge."

I was seriously thinking about knocking her flat on her ass and making a mad dash across the mall. Good God. I was a crazy person. "Fine." I shook out my hair, exhaling. "You're right."

She looped her arm through mine, and we stood. "See that wasn't so bad."

"So you're not getting those shoes?"

REDEEMING ANGEL

She plucked the red wedges from the shelf. "Did you hit your head? These shoes were made for my feet. This is your test, not mine. I already know my limitations. Shopping is not one of them. It's my anchor. It helps me keep the beastly part of me from making poor decisions."

I rolled my eyes and pouted as she dragged me into yet another store. Although my mind was still on the peach-strawberry smoothie, I started to question asking Lexi for help. Her methods made absolutely no sense to me right, but I was desperate, and she did have way more experience when it came to demon matters than I did.

By the time we left the mall, I expected to feel relieved. Instead, there was this pressure of unease clamping down on my heart, and it wasn't from all the body lotion samples. I'd tried so many I smelled like I worked at Bath and Body Works, minus the cheery attitude. It would take more than bubbles to turn this frown upside down.

At least Lexi agreed to help me—however bizarre her methods were. That made my hours of suffering worth it.

I guess.

Chapter 17

{Angel}

"Fight me," I said.

Chase and I just finished a perimeter walk. I couldn't sit inside, twiddling my thumbs and doing nothing. My tortured mind ended up getting the best of me.

Lexi had been helping me with the mental stuff, control and whatnot. We'd only been at it for a week, and already I felt reinvigorated, but I didn't just want to be mentally stronger than the darkness; I also wanted to be physically strong. I wanted to test myself, see what I could do with these abilities I was given. Sitting in my room, playing video games for hours, wasn't going to save the world.

Not that I thought little old me was going to become Earth's champion alone, but I never wanted to be at the mercy of a demon again. I was tired of being scared and weak.

Chase gave a stunted laugh. "I'm not going to fight you, Angel Eyes."

I tilted my head as we walked down my driveway toward the

house. "Chase, this isn't a joke."

The half-grin faded from his lips, and he rubbed the back of his neck, eyeing me. "I can see that," he said, but it wasn't what he meant. He wasn't taking me seriously.

I was going to have to find a way to change that. Whether Chase liked it or not, Hell was furious, and we were the prime targets. It suddenly became important I learn how to defend myself, instead of always looking for him to save me. "I'm stronger. If we're going to beat Alastair, then I need to fight."

His eyes darkened, flashing with a glint of gold. I could only guess that the idea of me fighting against his father didn't make him happy. "I'd agree with you, but then we'd both be wrong."

"Chase," I whined. "Be serious."

"No."

I hated that single, short word. "No?" I echoed.

"No!" His voice got heated. "Any hero ideas you've conjured in that pretty head of yours, forget them. You're not going anywhere near the bastard. Understood?"

I stepped forward, my eyes on his, completely undeterred. "You are being so unreasonable. I can do this, Chase. I'm not the same girl."

We were toe-to-toe and his gaze softened. "I know, but I've come too close to losing you. I'm trying to keep you safe."

It was going take a whole lot more than one of his dreamy

looks to persuade me this wasn't a good idea. My mind was set. I sighed. "You leave me no choice." Sometimes the big dope needed to be forced, so I struck out, hitting him with a closed fist on the chest. It was a sad, feeble attempt, but hey, a girl had to start somewhere. And the idea was to provoke him, which normally wasn't hard. Add my mouth to the equation and it was a done deal.

His lips thinned. "Angel," he growled.

"What? Are you afraid I'll kick your ass?" We both knew that wasn't even a possibility, but…

"No. I'm afraid I'll hurt you."

"You already said that," I pointed out.

"Then let me tell you again." And he did. Three more times he said no.

When he finished, I said, "I heal, remember. Thanks to you."

"How can I forget?" he mumbled, tangling a hand through his dark hair.

"I want to learn, Chase. I want you to teach me. You're the best."

A brisk fall breeze picked up the slight waves at the ends of his hair. "Flattery isn't going to get me to teach you to fight."

"How about this?" Unbidden, I took a step closer to him, pressing my lips softly to his. "Does that change your mind?"

His eyes were closed for a beat. Hard bands wrapped around

my upper arms. "This is absurd."

I angled my face to the side just so I could feel his breath on my cheek. Then I threw my elbow into his gut, not holding back. *Touchdown.* "Still think it's absurd?"

He grimaced. "You're serious about this?"

I twisted in his arms until he loosened his hold. "I am. Do you need another demonstration of my seriousness?"

"In an hour, you might be wishing you'd never thrown that hit."

"Maybe. But it's my choice. I'll deal with the consequences."

He gently flicked the end of my nose, and I could see the surrender in his eyes. "Speed, stamina, and quick wits will save your life. You still have the knife I gave you?"

Swallowing, I nodded.

"Good."

"So, I'll be learning how to use it?"

"Yes, against my better judgment, and because we're working with daggers, you'll have to get up close and personal to render a demon extinct. You have to be prepared for anything, always. Demons are not only fast, but devious. You ready?"

"Yes," I replied.

Putting a few feet of space between us, he eyed me up and down, making me feel like a bug under a microscope. "Okay. Come at me."

It took me a moment to register what he'd said. This was what I wanted, but now I was feeling self-conscious and silly. "How do—?"

"You've done it before," he said, grinning.

Yes, but never with the intent to actually hurt him. My expression was pinched with concentration as I figured out what to do next. The idea of fighting was much easier in my head. Did I lead with my right foot or left? Did I tuck my thumb under or cross it over the others? I was totally overthinking each action.

"Don't think. Just act. Pretend I'm the jerk you wanted to punch when we first met."

"That won't be hard to do," I mumbled.

His silver-studded brow went up.

But it did help to think about the strife he frequently stirred inside me. We did the whole song and dance, me on the offence and Chase on the defense. He was patient, encouraging, and didn't make me feel like a ninny.

"There you go." Chase nodded as he deflected one of my blows. "Use your speed, and move with purpose. You want to use your small frame to your advantage."

I knew he wasn't trying to insult me, but I hated being called small. Wiping the sweat off my brow with the back of my hand, I motioned for him to come at me again.

He didn't hesitate.

REDEEMING ANGEL

Chase launched himself at me, and this time I blocked his jab, but just barely. He didn't even give me a second to gloat over my small triumph. God, he could move that body like a ninja. Even with my enhanced skills, I still wasn't as fast or precise in my movements. With more practice, I might be able to defend myself, but actually besting Chase? I wasn't sure I would ever acquire that ability.

"You're holding back," I hurled. "Don't."

"Angel, I—"

"Don't," I emphasized. "A demon wouldn't think twice about ending me. Don't go easy on me. How else am I going to stay alive?"

He straightened. "That's why you have me. There is no need to push so hard, not yet."

My response was to throw a right hook straight for his pretty-boy face. I got nothing but air, but he could see my determination, and that was when my training really started, when it no longer became a game for him.

I couldn't even block most of Chase's attacks. He went through several more techniques, but I was starting to realize how much I had to learn. It would be a miracle if I managed to kill two demons, let alone one.

"Watch me." He swung out, the heel of his hand slipped past my arms and into the side of my gut. The impact sent me sprawling on my butt with a sharp spike of pain followed by throbbing. I was momentarily robbed of air, and when I finally inhaled, I slowly breathed through the agony.

Chase was crouched in front of me. "You okay?" he asked, concern flickering over his face.

I clenched my teeth, looking up at the sky. "Yeah." All I wanted to do was not move from this spot. My body ached; even my armpits ached.

He looked down at me, doubtful. "We're done for the day. I won't mar your skin. It will break me to see the bruises I caused, even if only for a short time. I won't hurt you, Angel."

I sat up, grabbing his forearm. "I'm fine. It just startled me." Then because I'd seen the conflict in his eyes and I could feel the inner turmoil causing a ruckus inside of him, I used both hands and tugged.

He came toppling down on top of me.

{Chase}

I could have caught myself, but where would the fun be in that? And after the last hour of sweating and grueling paces, we needed a little entertainment. Cheeks red with exertion, she let out a squeal of laughter. Real laughter. Her resilience and persistence impressed me. It was impossible to deny that Angel Eyes had the heart of a fighter.

Grabbing ahold of her wrist, I trapped her with my body, pinning her to the ground. Her laughter proved to be infectious, and I reveled in the sound. I reached over, prying her fingers loose and brought her injured knuckles to my lips. I kissed each one. "I should have taught you how to survive in my world a long time ago." My arm tightened around her.

Her smile spread, lighting up her eyes as her gaze settled on me. "Are you admitting I was right?"

I pushed the hair out of her face. Large eyes, framed by dark lashes were beaming, and her cheeks were pinked by the sun, the wind, and the fight. "I have no idea what you're talking about." I stared at her for a long while. "Have I ever told you that I think you're the bravest person I've ever met?"

She angled her head. "I don't think so, but you can try."

"You're the bravest person I've ever met," I said.

She grinned, amused. "Not true, but I like the sound of it."

"We're going to get through this." I brushed pieces of her dark hair off her forehead. "That's what people do. They mend."

"I guess," she agreed, sounding anything but convinced. A shadow cast in her violet eyes.

"And sometimes you end up stronger at the broken places."

"Do you know what I want?"

"I could guess." I pressed my lips to hers.

She placed her hands on my chest. "So much for reading my

mind. I might not be Wonder Woman, but I can do things that make you wonder."

Unable to deny myself the pleasure, I meshed my lips against hers, my tongue slipping between her teeth. The kiss was slow at first, but like everything with us, it sped into something wild.

Somehow, my worries vanished and her hand inched up my shirt, her nails embedding in my skin. I couldn't get close enough to her. Couldn't get enough of her. Would it always be like this? I could go on just kissing her for an eternity, but of course something always intervened.

This time it was a someone.

"Is that all you guys do? You're worse than bunnies," interrupted a voice.

I closed my eyes and groaned. "Please tell me I'm hearing things."

Angel buried her face in my shoulder and giggled. Her heart thumped crazily, a mimic of mine.

I popped my jaw. "What are you doing here, Emma? Don't you have a home?"

She shot me a dirty look. "Lexi was worried, so Travis and I got conned into a search party. Looks like my tracking skills are better."

Rolling over, the softness of the grass absorbed my weight. "Your timing sucks."

Emma grinned. "I know."

Sitting up, Angel inhaled, a blank expression crossing her face.

My heart sunk. Terror burned in my chest like a fistful of acid. "Angel?" I called.

She didn't respond, her skin paling.

No. No. No.

Emma's body stiffened, her shoulders squaring. "I thought you said she was better," she murmured.

"She is." So I kept telling myself.

"Really? Then what's wrong with her?" Emma asked with a tremor.

"Nothing," I demanded. "She needs time to heal. You better than anyone should know what it's like being held against your will." The fear radiating inside me made me snappy, but Emma's feelings weren't my first priority.

Emma took a step backward. "I get it. She's fragile."

Angel got to her feet, that glassy, faraway look still in her eyes. "I'm not fragile!" she shouted.

Just as I leapt up, her arm swung out, fingers extended. I thought she was going to bitch slap Emma across the mouth, but to my great surprise, a ball of fire shot from her fingertips.

What the…?

For a moment, I was mesmerized as I watched the flickering flame move through the air. Suspended in time, I waited for someone to yell code red, because this couldn't possibly be real.

Emma ducked, and she barely missed being incinerated. Unfortunately the tree behind her wasn't so lucky. "Umm, Chase. *That* was not normal."

Okay. Fine. She wasn't a fragile human. Point taken. Angel's spirit had never been weak. She had always been brave, sharp, and reckless. And now her fingers spit embers of havoc. I'd known there would be consequences due to the transformations Angel's body and soul had undergone. I just never imagined this.

Before she could set off another round of fireballs, I flashed in front of her. Sparks of gold twinkled in her violet irises as I stared at her face. "You don't want to do this, Angel Eyes."

The shock of what she had done must have brought her to her senses. Her hands shook as she intently studied her fingers. "What did I just do?" Her voice quivered and the cloudiness cleared from her eyes.

"It's okay," I assured tenderly, reaching for her.

In an instant, horror transpired in her face. Horror and fear. "No," she shouted, backing away from me. "No. It's not." She widened the distance between us. "St-stay away from me. You have to stay away."

I moved toward her, determined. "Angel," I said, latching onto her arm.

With a quick jerk, she wiggled out of my grasp. "Don't touch me!" she hissed. "Just let me go. *Please.*"

My hands fell to my sides.

All I could do was stare as she took off, running toward the tree line at the back of the house. *Let her go? No…Yes…No!* It took a great amount of willpower to not go after her. Every cell in my body woke up when I lost sight of her, stretching to reach out to her, desperate to make things better for her.

Except I didn't know how. Nothing I could say or do would make it better. *I* had barely processed what I witnessed.

"What did I miss?" Lexi asked, suddenly appearing at my side. Her aqua eyes narrowed. "Where's Angel going?"

Emma came to stand beside her, the three of us all staring at the spot where Angel had disappeared into the woods. "You missed me nearly pissing my pants," Emma said.

Lexi's gaze slid sideways. "I would have paid to see that."

"I need to find her," I declared. She might not want me to follow her, but it was too risky allowing her to go off on her own, especially in the woods.

Lexi placed a hand on my arm before I had the chance to speed off. "Let me. You look like you could use a few minutes to calm down."

She was right. I tangled my fingers in my hair, pushing out a breath, and nodded. This whole day seemed surreal, from Angel harassing me to teach her to fight to her fingers spitting fire. I let

Lexi go. In the meantime, there was something I needed to take care of as well. And I was dreading it.

Chapter 18

{Chase}

As reluctant as I was to leave, it was more important than ever that I had this little sit-down. Yet, it didn't stop a seed of guilt from sprouting in my gut. Angel wasn't the only one keeping secrets. I wanted to tell her where I was going and why, but divulging any information at this point would only suck her in deeper, the very last thing I wanted to do. The whole point was to get her as far removed from Hell as possible.

And where I was going was as close as walking through the gates of Hell.

The door jingled over my head as I strolled into the Village Diner. A quick scan of the nearly empty restaurant and she was easy to pick out.

She had a type.

Slut.

I slide into the corner booth across from Kira in her new human form. This one was no less beautiful and probably left most men drooling in her wake. I only drooled over one girl.

"Well, isn't this quaint?" she said, her dark crimson eyes roaming over the homey café. "Can a girl at least get a decent martini?"

"Hardly. Try the coffee." Under the table, I carefully extracted my blade, lying it in my lap. "You look like you could use a cup."

She pouted, and it was an expression I'd seen countless times on Lexi. I flexed my fists on top of the table, hating that this demon had any part in my cousins' existence. "That was a dirty trick you pulled on me."

Having Kira so close to home, so close to Lexi and Travis, made my muscles tighten. I stretched out a hand on the table. "Really? I thought it was one of my finer moments."

She twirled her fork between her fingers. "It's reckless to anger a demon, especially one as old as I am." The spears of the fork came down on the table right in between my index and middle fingers. The wood splintered under impact.

I sat back in my seat, my free hand resting over the back of the booth. "I'm not impressed. Seriously? The almost stabbing me with a fork is all you've got? I know all about enraging demons. I've been doing it my whole life."

"But I bet this is the first time you've ever found yourself indebted to one."

I saw fury. "You got me there. Unless you count the time I bargained with death." I scratched at the stubble sprouting on my chin." You know, now that I'm thinking about it, I'm not entirely sure what I traded in that deal. My soul? Pretty damn sure I lost that a long time ago."

"Souls are overrated, unless you're dead." Repositioning herself on the worn-out leather seat, Kira ran a hand down her long champagne colored hair, smoothing it into place. "I assume you took my advice and it was successful?"

I hesitated, not comfortable with divulging information I considered none of her business, but it wasn't like I could hide Angel away. Angel would definitely not go for that. "I did what I needed to."

"So Chase Winters, why did you summon me then? Or did you just want to hang out with your aunt Kira and have a heart-to-heart?"

"You demented witch." Ripping the fork from the table, I sent it flying across the booth. I had damn good aim. If I had wanted to hit her heart, I wouldn't have missed. My intent had not been to wound her, but to send a warning.

She gave a throaty laugh. "Come on now." She yanked, pulling the fork out of the meaty flesh of her shoulder. "You know there is no such thing as witches. I'm a demon, honey. Not a witch. God's honest truth."

Hilarious. I fought not to be amused. "Oh, I can think of many things to call you, and not a single one of them will ever be family."

"Whether you like it or not, I'm not going anywhere."

I pressed my tongue to the roof of my mouth. "Maybe not, but Alastair is."

"A vacation perhaps?"

"I was thinking of something a little bit more permanent."

She arched a brow. "What did you have in mind?"

"That's why I called you," I replied.

There was no denying the intrigue in her gaze. "You already know I don't give away that kind of information for free."

I wasn't sure she had any information to give, and the idea of owing this particular demon another "favor" made me want to lash out. My frown deepened. "Can it be done?"

"There has always been talk. War? Grace? Final death? You name it. There's been some kind of whisper surrounding what demons desire and fear most. Of course most of it is utter crap."

That wasn't deflating. "You aren't making this deal very tempting."

"I didn't say I didn't have information that might be of value. With age comes wisdom, and I am very, very old."

"It shows."

"And you claim I'm the wicked one. Does your precious Angel know where you are?" she sneered.

Anger bubbled up inside me. There was an underlying threat

in her tone, and it made me go King Kong protective. "Don't say her name."

"You're more fun when you're angry." She looked at me through lower lashes as she took a sip of her watered-down drink. "I didn't want her to get bored while we had all the fun, so I sent her a gift. I hope she isn't afraid of dogs."

Vision blurring in a haze of murderous red, I slammed my fist onto the table, knocking a glass on the floor. I wanted to litter the restaurant with her body parts with no concern for who witnessed.

"You should calm down. We wouldn't want to make a scene," she mocked.

Calm? Calm! I. Utterly. Exploded.

Launching myself at the demon, I grabbed ahold of her neck, forcing her to look at me. "If a single hair is harmed on her head, I'll end you," I seethed, venom dripping from my threat. And I meant every word.

I loved to make scenes.

With or without Kira's help, I would find a way to destroy the soul of a demon, and Kira had just been bumped up to number two on my dead list.

{Angel}

I wasn't sure how far I expected to get, but after a minute of running, I realized he wasn't going to come after me, and I wasn't sure if I was feeling relief or trepidation.

Get it together, Morgan.

My limbs trembled as I walked aimlessly, no real destination, as long as no one was near me. I stared at my hands, seeing smudges of black soot on my nails. My eyes felt like they were going to pop out of my head.

Holy flamethrower.

Fire? Fire! It literally erupted from my fingers. There was still a warm prickle vibrating just under the skin.

I felt dizzy thinking about it. What was wrong with me? What had I been thinking, fighting with Chase, getting him to give me a few lessons how not to get killed? Bad idea all around. I'd barely begun to deal with the lingering darkness.

As my mind revolved, circling back to the dream, I tripped over my feet and fell, banging my knees into the cool, hard ground. The air, which had been slightly warm earlier, was now chilled, and the scent of smoke clung to my nose, mixing with wildflowers and grass.

What if I accidently hurt him? What if I had attacked him instead of Emma? Why had I attacked at all?

If I hurt my friends… If I hurt Chase…

It would break me, shatter my heart into a thousand little pieces. As much as Chase might get under my skin, I would never put him in harm's way. If I had known…

The nightmare.

It came back to me in an arctic gust. Chase splattered in his own blood. The odd angle of his colorless and lifeless body. I closed my eyes, willing the images to stop, fingers digging into the dirt.

As easily as my body had been dragged backward, it now whisked forward. Darkness and body collided together.

I peeled my eyes open. A spooky cluster of clouds moved overhead, creating shadows over the forest floor. I was still sprawled on the ground, pine needles and gravel embedded on my palms.

A pair of really stellar red wedges came into focus. I craned my neck, glancing upward. Lexi anchored her hands on her hips, hovering over me. "What are you doing on the ground?"

I thought I was going to cry. "I screwed up on a global scale."

"Not from where I stand. You didn't kill anyone."

"But I could have," I said, pushing to my feet. I winced as the scrape on my knee stung from the stretching movement.

"I got the cliff notes of what happened. We all have a choice, to be good or to let the darkness rule. Human or not, the choice is still there."

I only wish it were that easy. "I've done enough damage, but what I'm most concerned about is how much more I will cause."

"Did you really throw a ball of fire at Emma?" There was a

hint of hilarity on Lexi's pixie face.

I pushed to my feet, brushing my hands on my pants, and shrugged, but before I could confirm or deny, Lexi gasped.

"Oh God." She paled.

And all I could think was now what did I do?

"Do you know what caused those tracks?" she asked.

I rooted my feet in the ground, afraid I knew exactly what had made those marks in the dirt. "Hell's timing really sucks," I muttered.

A howl raptured the night, stealing my breath. Not a wolf's howl, but that of a hellhound— many of them from the numerous howls that followed.

"Do you smell that? The scent of rot is in the air." Lexi's eyes morphed into slices of amber.

I inhaled deeply, but I only smelled pine from the trees. And…Chase? I smelled Chase, and it was better than the earthy forest. It was delicious. Mouthwatering. Made me wish we hadn't been interrupted before. I could still taste him.

"You able to fight?" she asked.

I wasn't sure, but there was only one way to find out. "Don't have much of a choice."

A hound stepped out from under a bush, dirty and dark hair matted. Three others moseyed out from different corners of the woods, eyes glowing like rubies in the shade.

"Whatever you do, don't die. Chase will never forgive me." She took a step back so her body was shielding me. "And this might be a really great time to practice your new pyro skills."

If it were only that simple. I wasn't sure I ever wanted to do it again, and I didn't have the foggiest idea how I'd managed to produce the little spits of fire. I was out of time.

A twig snapped.

My head whizzed to the left, and I saw beady, red eyes peeking through the wall of green foliage.

The hellhounds weren't just nearby; they were here.

At my side, a snarl punctured the air, stretching out. I bent, reaching for the blade tucked into my sock. On instinct, I turned, realizing two of the hounds had launched a sneak attack. I stood and swiped out my blade, the tip slashing the creature's neck, but it was only a nick. I was so not ready for this, and my faith in my skills was lacking.

I palmed my blade.

Scrambling over weeds and twigs, I latched onto the handle, waiting. Instantly the air became hotter, filling with the putrid pants of mutt. What I assumed was the leader of this gruesome pack gave a short growl. Then they attacked.

I arched left and stepped right, narrowly avoiding pointed nails and razor teeth. My blade blindly swung in the air, and a few times I got lucky, slicing through decaying flesh. Black goo dripped down the end of my blade, touching my skin. I wanted to shiver, to squeal, and run around in circles with my arms flailing.

The hound jumped, pushing me to the ground. I landed with a hard thud, my side throbbing. A second later, I was pinned and teeth snapping in vicious chomps went for my neck. I wiggled and only ended up gnawing my back on the brittle floor.

As the hound hunched over me, I jerked my knee up, barreling into its gut. The beast was so much stronger than I anticipated and barely budged. Jaws nipping, saliva dribbled from his muzzle, leaking onto my hair and the side of my face.

Disgusting. Fowl.

This is it. They're going to munch my face off.

I tried to summon my fire the same way I had not long ago, believing I could gain the upper hand, but I was so new to this and didn't know what I was actually supposed to do. As expected, I couldn't generate even a spark. *So much for my flaming fingers.*

As I was about to close my eyes and say a prayer, Lexi appeared behind the hound, golden eyes glowing. Her hands moved in a blur on either side of the creature's large head, and then she gave one quick twist, snapping its neck.

I wasted no time getting back on my feet. They were everywhere. Hellhounds. Hellhounds. Hellhounds. They swarmed around us like flies, growling instead of buzzing. I trembled, the blade seeming to gain ten pounds in my grasp. I'd been without real physical activity for too long, and after the beating I put my body through today training with Chase, this was too much, too soon. I wasn't sure how much longer I could keep up and still remain on my feet.

Another hound sprang at me, black-stained teeth bared. I spun back and kicked my heel out, slamming into its muzzle. The mutt whimpered as he rolled away. There was no time to breathe a sigh of relief as yet another hellhound lunged for me.

I reacted with the first thing that came to mind. I popped it in the snout. The hound went to the ground but quickly twisted and nipped at my ankles.

I don't think so.

Hopping up, I stomped down on the hound's head, and with a twirl of my dagger, I punched the blade into the creature's belly and took a step back.

"Nicely done," Lexi said from behind me, panting with exertion.

I bent down and grabbed my knife, wiping the dust against the material of my thigh. Tingles radiated in my stomach as something solid pressed against my back. Fear and adrenaline drove my actions as I threw my elbow behind me and raised my blade.

Chase ducked just as I sliced downward in an arc. If I had been faster or he had been slower…

"Idiot!" I screamed. "I almost stabbed you." He knew better than to creep up on me when I was armed. Or at least you would think he would.

Ruthlessness radiated in his eyes. "I guess those lessons paid off."

Chase! He was here.

Yes, my body sighed in relief.

He reached the creatures, using two of them as punching bags. So much rage. It was a viable force, surrounding him inside and out. Eyes blazing amber, he gave a wide slash with my dagger, clipping the hound's spine and nearly removing its head.

The woods went eerily quiet, and I knew Chase and Lexi had finished off the pack. I shook my head to clear the surge of dizziness.

Chase's gentle hands framed either side of my face, steadying my rapid breathing and heartbeat. His eyes morphed into a soft heather gray. "You okay?" he asked, his gaze running over every cell of my body.

I drank in the horror scene around me, the mossy ground scattered with the putrid ash of Hell. Nothing about my life or me was okay. "Define okay?"

Chapter 19

{Angel}

I'd spent the first seventeen years of my life sheltered and protected by a woman who only wanted me to be happy. She moved us to the quiet, small town of Spring Valley and into a house she made a home in the hope of a better life—a fresh start.

Now, I knew more about the concealed world around me, more than I ever wanted to know. I'd experienced firsthand the inner workings of Hell. I knew demons inhabited human bodies, drawn to the thirst for souls. It gave them power and life, allowing them to survive longer on Earth.

Fear added spice to the delectable soul.

As miserable as my life had been when my parents were together, nothing compared to the misery I'd felt locked inside the underground bunker. It wasn't even that I'd been held against my will that tormented me. It had been and always would be the losing myself to the demon Angel.

Remembering caused pain to scrape across my heart, over and over again, leaving me raw and vulnerable. I hurt.

Tiny flickers of red burned in my eyes, and black smudges of mascara ran down the corners. Through the reflection I watched as demon Angel smiled and waved mockingly at me.

Power.

Kill.

Thirst.

Hot.

The words played through my mind like a terrible song. I wanted to shatter the mirror, to run away, but my vision was going dark.

My brows furrowed as I tried to stay focused on my image. The encounter with the hellhounds combined with the unleashing of power I didn't know I possessed must have provoked the darkness to rise. The worst was happening.

"No!" I commanded my reflection. "I'm not letting you in."

I blinked.

And then…

Nothing. I must have blacked out or something. Those blank spots in my memory were piling up, but for now I was just glad it was over.

The red flecks in my eyes were gone.

I quickly tossed my hair into a messy bun and slapped ice-cold water on my face. It came down to a battle of wills and war of power. The past ceased to matter.

Temples throbbing, I stalked out of my room and hunted for Chase, although it wasn't much of a hunt. He was easy to find thanks to my built-in GPS. I needed a distraction.

What better way than a little physical one-on-one combat? Chase's favorite.

My evenings were all about training.

And I wouldn't have it any other way. Social life? I wasn't good company nowadays. Education? There would be time for that later. After the hellhound attack, Chase—to my surprise—was more determined about the idea of me learning to defend myself.

Halle-freaking-lujah.

Mom was at work, so she was none the wiser.

Throwing open the front door, I smacked into a wall, or what felt like a wall. My nose pressed to Chase's chest. He was so much taller than me, dwarfing me in every way possible.

"Did you see that?" he asked, angling his head toward the sign stuck in the middle of my yard.

My eyes shifted around him. "Looks like we're going to be one big happy Brady Bunch." A realtor had come out the day before and put up the for sale sign.

"*If* someone buys it," he added.

"They would be out of their mind if they did. Maybe I should talk to my mom about having a disclosure added to the listing. *Neighbors are part demon. Often have unexpected hostile visitors.*"

He snickered.

I rested my head on his shoulder, taking a moment to just enjoy his presence. Our lives had been so turbulent lately and he was still tiptoeing around me, not that I could blame him, we hadn't taken more than five minutes for *us* time.

A date?

Sadly, I couldn't remember our last date. It wasn't fair to either of us. Chase, even with all his flaws, was an outstanding guy. He was my rock. There was no way I would have been able to get through the last months without him. He inspired me to want to overcome the trials of being scarred by the Underworld.

"I know those cute little wrinkle lines on your forehead. What are you thinking about?"

"Just how lucky I am to have you," I replied.

He wrapped his arms around me, tugging me into his embrace. I looped my hands at his neck and buried my face in him. The dark scent that was uniquely Chase caused a string of fireflies to flutter through my belly. "You don't have to do this, you know," he said, his cheek brushing against mine.

He hadn't shaved and the little stumble grated on my skin, but not in a painful way. It was quite a tickle. Regardless, I found it comforting. "I know, but it is something I *need* to do."

He nodded, understanding pooling in his silver eyes. "Okay then."

"Can you hold me for a few more minutes first?"

"We can always go upstairs—"

I elbowed him in the side. "After we finish this…and you've showered…if you're lucky."

A few minutes later, Lexi bounced outside. Her long caramel locks were swept up into a high ponytail, swishing from side to side with the sway of her hips. Skin naturally sun-kissed, excitement and anticipation were brimming in her almond-shaped eyes. "What did I miss?"

"Nothing," I answered, a smile still pulling at my lips.

"Goodie. Chase promised I could help. I really need the diversion."

Chase and I shared a look. We had briefly discussed Lexi and Colin's breakup. Of course, I had to talk Chase out of ripping Colin limb for limb, his jerk reaction to anyone who hurt the people he cared about. I'd been genuinely close to compelling him to chill out.

"Let's see if we can get you to light up today," she said with far more glee and confidence than I was feeling.

I nodded, flexing my fingers. "I hope you know what you're getting into," I mumbled.

Fifteen minutes into it and already my patience was in tatters. No matter how hard I tried, I hadn't been able to summon fire again. I was starting to think the whole thing had been a figment of my imagination, a one-time deal, which might not be a bad thing.

I wasn't any closer to producing a spark than I was at finishing my freshman year of college. Zilch. And my frustration was through the roof. Mastering this ability felt important. I could finally do something other than be bait. That was if I figured out how my trigger finger worked.

"You're overthinking it, and it's making you tense," Chase said.

"Thank you, Captain Obvious." My shoe scuffed the ground. "I need coffee." Fuel. Something to help me focus.

"More energy is the last thing you need. I can feel the power vibrating off you, and it's making my demon itchy."

We started bantering back and forth like usual, neither of us noticing that Lexi's attention was focused on something behind us. Not until she said, "Guys…guys…guys!"

On the third time, Chase whipped his head toward Lexi and yelled, "What now?"

Her aqua eyes were pinned over my shoulder, touched with a fraction of gold. "I think we have trouble."

Chase's hair was disheveled from the cool winds, and as he turned, his features closed off. My marks were tingling at my hip in overdrive, and I knew the moment I turned around, I would be face-to-face with a demon. I didn't move with haste. Actually, I would have liked to close my eyes and walk away. But, it was too late for that.

Up close, Kira was more beautiful. The kind of beautiful that made me want to hit the gym and watch a gazillion makeup tutorials on YouTube. If I knew nothing of demons, I would have thought of Kira as a modern day goddess. She had a quality about her.

I didn't need Chase to tell me who she was. I knew the second I laid eyes on her, and I didn't understand how Lexi didn't immediately recognize her own mother. It wasn't that she looked like Lexi, but it more her mannerisms. A lump gathered in my esophagus as uncertainty clouded the air. No one knew what to do next. There were a few prolonged moments of awkward silence before Lexi could no longer stand it.

"Who the hell are you?" she snapped.

"I'm a personal friend of Chase's," Kira said in a way that implied they were close. I wanted to rip the honey-blonde locks from her head.

Lexi took it in a different direction, her eyes leaping between Chase and Kira. The spark of demon in her eyes spread. "If you're cheating on my best friend..." she growled.

His face puckered. "Ew. Gross, Lex!" he cut in before she could defame his character.

I loved my best friend for caring enough about me to call out her own family, even though it couldn't be farther from the truth. In another situation, I might have found it funny, but the tension that settled between us made my blood fizzle with energy.

"You wouldn't be the first to be seduced by a demon," Lexi justified.

Dark fire snapped in his eyes.

Oh boy.

{Chase}

Ragged breaths scraped through my nose and lungs, and I felt my inner demon working. Seeing Kira at the house I grew up in, feet away from Lexi, magnified my rage. I wanted to cut her in half and send her into a confetti of ash.

But Kira had proven she wasn't like the demons I was accustomed to. The same rules didn't apply, and I didn't think she abided by their rules either. In a way, it kind of made sense we were related. Rules weren't our thing.

"Chase?" Angel lowered her voice, wordlessly asking what was going on.

I ignored her, refusing to let Kira out of my sight. "What do you think you're doing here?" I hissed, my body instantly stepping out in front of the girls. Kira had nerve, I'd give her that, but that was all she would get. After everything she'd done, I wanted to rip out her sticky bits.

"So you do know her?" Lexi demanded. Her foot stomped the ground, causing a tremble under my feet.

At this point, her feelings were the least of my concern. If I had to be a jackass to keep her safe, so be it. "It's not your concern, Lex. Go inside. I'll take care of this," I replied flatly, teeth gritted. I expected the next revolution to erupt, but before Lexi could utter a protest, Kira overstepped her boundaries.

"Lexi," Kira said in a slow drawl like she was savoring the sound. "What a beautiful name for such a beautiful, young woman."

Lexi's turquoise eyes narrowed. "Are you hitting on me? Because I don't date demons."

Angel choked behind me.

I just shook my head. *What have I gotten myself into?* No matter how I played this out in my mind, it all ended with my balls cracked.

Kira let out a sultry laugh. "Sorry sweets, your dad is much more to my taste. Is your brother around?" Her eyes moved to the house.

Lexi's started to glow. "Chase, what is going on?"

There were whole parts of my brain that were trying to stop me from lying, but the stupid parts won. "Nothing is going on, except this demon isn't welcome here."

Kira leered. "Now, that isn't any way to treat family.

Especially, after everything I did to help you and...Angel, is it?"

She knew damn well what her name was. There was no need for the coyness. My expression darkened, and I wondered if it had been no accident that I'd stepped foot in that bar.

Lexi's attention zinged between us, and I had been dreading this the second I realized who Kira was to my family. A splay of emotions navigated over Lexi's face.

"Chase and I spent plenty of time catching up on his little trip to Vegas, didn't we luv?"

Lexi twisted up to look at me and flinched. "This is the demon you sought for information? My mother?"

In the distance, I registered the purr of an engine and tires crunching over gravel, but I dismissed it, wincing. "It wasn't like that. I didn't know who she was until later."

Lexi's face pinched. "Just splendid. And that makes it okay? Were you ever going to tell me?"

She had a right to be angry. I was pissed with myself, with the world, with Kira, and with the Pope. "I don't know," I admitted.

No reaction whatsoever.

And that alarmed me.

But Angel had plenty to say as she stepped forward, her chin in the air. "Oh, bless your little heart. I just bet it was difficult for you to come here and throw a big old turd in our faces," she spat.

"You got yourself a girl with spunk."

"So I've been told," I grumbled.

A car pulled into our driveway and out stepped frat boy.

Oh for fuck sake.

Lexi still was unresponsive, eyes glazed. Kira was smirking, clearly amused. Angel's mouth fell open. And Colin's timing was impeccable. "My life is a three-ring circus," I muttered, eyeing Lexi's…whatever he was. It was still unclear to me what their relationship status was.

"What do you get when a human, a demon, and a hothead walk into a bar?" Angel whispered.

Only Angel would pick a time like this to make a joke. "You're killing me here, Angel Eyes."

"Well, it was either make a horrible joke, or let you tear into both of them. I thought dry humor was better than violence in this situation. Things are already pretty heated and tense."

Like a dog with his tail between his legs, Colin strutted over the lawn, completely oblivious to the crockpot of shit he just walked into.

Or maybe he knew and was willing to risk it all in the name of love.

Fool.

"Spring Valley is kind of out of your way, isn't it, Conner?" I asked when it became clear no one was saying anything.

He shoved his hands into his front pockets, rocking back on

his heels. "It's Colin, and I'm here to see Lexi," he said, eyes rotating to my cousin.

Some people just need a high five. With a chair. In the face.

Lexi was still staring at Kira. Kira was staring at her. And I was sure a nuclear bomb wouldn't break the trance. Mother and daughter seeing each other for the first time, I guess I should be glad no one had lost a limb. Travis seeing Kira might be another story.

Nobody knew what to do or say next. I rubbed the back of my tense neck. "Lexi, get Colin out of here. Stay in the house and lock the doors," I ordered, taking control of the situation. "Oh, call Emma and Travis. We need to talk."

Her lips thinned. "You bet your ass we do." After one extended glance at Kira, she stomped off, dragging a dazed and confused Colin behind her.

As Kira started to step forward, Lexi's name on the edge of her lips, Angel moved in, nothing but a streak of auburn hair as she blocked her path, too fast for a human. "Don't think about it," she warned.

Fear. Real fear, for the first time, popped in Kira's scarlet eyes. Her body went stiff. I mean, I knew Angel could be scary, but this was unexpected, and then Kira said, "I wondered if this would be your fate."

Huh?

REDEEMING ANGEL

I trailed Angel's movements, sidetracked by how quickly she had moved from one spot to another. She was glaring wide-eyed at her open palm, a bolt of shock thundering through her body. I averted my eyes downward, and sucked in a sharp breath. All five of her fingers were flickering with fire. Seeing it a second time did nothing to lesson my amazement.

Apparently Kira wasn't as floored as the rest of us. "What are you ranting about?" I commanded. It crossed my mind to also add a few threats, like salt in an open wound.

Kira's voice came out unusually dry and quiet. "Not until she douses the flames."

I glared, feeling as if this might be an advantage. As much as I wanted to give her the middle finger and tell her to stick it, I needed Kira.

And it burned my butt.

"Angel, any chance you can extinguish those firecrackers?"

She looked at me then at her hands, confusion wrinkling her forehead. She didn't know how to summon the fire, so it only made sense that she also didn't know how to get rid of it. Her heart rate kicked up, transferring through our bond. I did what came instinctually, calming the panic that just started to eek through her.

Swallowing hard, she shook her hands like you would a match.

Kira released a breath, raising her brows. "You might want to work on your control there, luv."

I blinked, preparing to snatch Kira by her slender neck. The backstabbing demon owed me answers, and I was going to get them by any methods necessary.

But she was gone.

Son. Of. A. Bitch.

Looks like I'm going demon hunting.

Chapter 20

{Angel}

A dark cluster of clouds moved in front of the pale moon, creating a dull, almost tarnish color. The tips of my fingers were warm, degrees hotter than the rest of my body. "Where did she go?" I did a full circle to check my back.

"To Hell would be too much to ask for," Chase muttered.

I snorted. I loved that he could make me forget, even for a second, that moments ago I'd been the girl on fire. "When do you think he'll come?" I felt the time clock ticking. I had to believe good triumphed over evil. It kept me sane.

He came toward me, rubbing his hands up and down my arms. "Soon. Too soon."

I shivered, despite the intense heat radiating from his body. "That's what I'm afraid of."

"How are you feeling?" He lifted my fingers in the air, examining them for marks or scars. There were none. "Does it hurt you?"

I felt his unease. Anything that could possibly cause me pain stirred Chase's alpha tendencies. "I-I don't think so."

He shot me a questioning look.

"My brain sort of shuts off. I don't feel anything at all except…" I lifted my head. "Power."

He dropped his gaze, placing a kiss on the palm of each hand. "I'm glad."

My heart cartwheeled at the intense relief in his words. I pulled back and ran my fingers up his chest. "What are you going to say to Lexi and Travis?" Worry gathered in my stomach. This was not the time to cause strife between us, but maybe that was precisely what Kira wanted.

"What can I say? I should have told them, but I was so consumed with keeping you safe, and part of me hoped I'd never have to see her face again. Stupid, I know."

"It's not stupid. Nothing you ever do is out of malice."

"*She's* different, Angel."

"Yeah, I'm starting to understand that." Lexi and Travis were the only Divisa known to be born from a demon. If there were others, Chase had never met them. That in itself said how different Kira was, but that didn't mean she was trustworthy.

I'd never met a demon that was.

"Does that make her more dangerous? She's never tried to hurt them before," I voiced the questions somersaulting in my head.

His eyes shifted to the house, where Lexi and Colin were having a not-so-calm argument. Emotions were running high. "Not that I know of, but demons don't usually discriminate. We're all one and the same to them."

"I saw her mark. It's so strange seeing it on a demon." I'd only ever seen Travis and Lexi's demon mark on them. Most of the other demons I'd encountered wore Chase's mark and were under Alastair's rule.

"Makes it real." His voice dropped.

I saw the gleam in his eyes. *Trouble.* I looped my hands around his waist. "Oh no you don't. Leave them be."

He scowled, brows pinching together.

"I think Lexi can handle herself," I added, flattening my hands on his chest, not that I would ever in a million years be able to physically stop Chase. If he wanted to get in the house, my little muscles weren't going to hold him.

A low growl started at the back of his throat, and his eyes lit up like a comet.

I rolled mine, and I was about to say something smart, but suddenly I started seeing stars. A wave of intense heat rippled through my body, making my vision go hazy like the Mojave Desert. The darkness came, sweeping over me like a storm, swift and violent. I swore I felt my atoms splitting in half.

"Angel? What's wrong?" His voice echoed inside me, muffled

by the voices in my head.

Kill.

Punish.

It's your gift. Your purpose.

"Everything," I whispered. My head sliced in two, pain blistering from the center out, pulsing and hammering. I winced, fighting to stay on my feet. The noise in my head was almost too much to bear, and I wanted to drop to my knees.

Chase's steadiness and the strength of his biceps kept me upright. My insides twisted with dread as I clung to him. I ransacked my brain, trying to figure out what was happening, why I was suddenly sick and feverish. The first thing that popped into my head was this was the aftereffect from using a power I didn't fully understand. It was staggering, and if I had to go through this each time, I was less inclined to learn to control it. Something in my molecular makeup had adverse reactions to demons and to my magic fire fingers.

Fighting a swell of frustration, I felt the *other* Angel rise up, wanting to come out and play. Wreak some havoc on the world. *She'd* had a taste of power, and a nibble wasn't enough. The last thing I wanted to do was fall apart.

Not in front of Chase.

I bit my tongue until I tasted blood.

"That's it. I've been patient long enough," he rumbled.

"You're going to tell me what is going on." There was no room for negotiations.

And frankly, I was too exhausted to argue. The wall blocking my secret came crumbling down, along with my energy level. I was beat.

He swooped me off my feet, and I squeezed my eyes shut, knowing what was going to come next. Already I was feeling lightheaded, and Chase running only made me close to losing my lunch. I buried my face in his shirt, securing my arms around his neck. The tiniest movement sent a wave of pinpricks.

As gently as possible, he laid me on his bed, and I curled up, waiting for the room to stop spinning. It was the woodsy scent of his sheets and the room in general that calmed the whirlwind. I knew he wanted answers, but he wasn't cramming the questions down my throat.

Sitting on the edge of the bed, he pushed the hair out of my face, his fingers lingering over my cheek, and cursed. "Are you still in pain?"

"I'm okay," I answered. "I swear."

His mouth went slack. "Is this the first time it's happened?"

I swallowed a dry lump and shook my head.

"I swear to God I'll kill them."

"Shh." I scooted up on the bed, leaning my shoulder against his. For no feasible reason I was nervous. "I didn't know how to tell you before…" I started chomping on my nails. "You risked so much for me, never resting until you brought me back. I couldn't stand to disappoint you."

"What do you mean? Why would you think I could ever be disappointed in you?"

He could be sweet without meaning to. It made me love him that much more. I exhaled. "The darkness isn't gone."

His facial expression didn't budge.

"I expected you to be surprised. Why aren't you the teensiest bit surprised?"

He gave a one-shoulder shrug. "I had my suspicions."

"And you didn't say anything?"

His brow shot up, mocking me.

"Okay, touché. I should have told you instead of trying to hide it, but I wanted to find a way to conquer the darkness before it conquered me."

"And did you?"

Now it was my turn to shrug. "Not entirely, but Lexi's been helping me."

"Lexi?" he repeated.

My stomach flopped at seeing the swift flicker of hurt in his eyes, gone as quickly as it had appeared. "Yeah. I didn't want to burden you. You've been so focused on Alastair, and I know how important it is to you, to all of us."

"Nothing is as important as you."

Gulp.

Dammit. I felt guiltier than ever. I cast my eyes downward unable to look at him. "I thought I could handle it. I needed to."

His fingers tipped my chin. "I understand you need to do this yourself, for *you*. But it doesn't change the fact that I want to protect you. I want to slaughter every demon who comes within a hundred mile radius of you. As much as it pains me, this is one battle I can't fight for you."

I forced my eyes to meet his, but I couldn't stop being nervous and had to look away. "The darkness, it's nothing more than a shadow, but what if I can't control it? What if everything you did and went through was all in vain?"

"Don't think for one second that I regret anything I've done. I would do it all over again in a heartbeat. I only wish I could have prevented…" He pulled me closer and I climbed into his lap, burying my face in the crook of his neck. His hand stroked the soft material at my lower back.

We stayed like that for a few minutes, wrapped up in each other.

"What about the nightmares?" he whispered.

"What about them?" I whispered back.

"You don't sleep through the night, not without having at least one."

I frowned, fumbling with the material on the front of his white T-shirt. "Are you spying on me, too?"

"You'd like that," he replied, humor in his tone. "But there's no need. You wake up screaming my name. And Angel, if you're going to scream my name, I'd prefer it wasn't in fear."

My cheeks reddened in half embarrassment and half shame. I rolled off his lap, needing my own air space. "It's just a dream. Who doesn't have them?"

"I might not always be in the room to comfort you, but I'm there. Our bond makes your fear very real for me. Tell me what haunts your sleep."

My gaze was drawn to the network of cracks on the ceiling as I replayed the events of my reoccurring nightmare. "You."

Chase, leaned closer, his eyebrows tightly knit with confusion.

"I've had the same dream night after night. I watch you die." My voice hitched. "And it's because of me. It's my fault."

He swiped his thumb over my cheek, brushing away tears I didn't know were falling. "How is it your fault?" he asked quietly.

"I blast you with these." I held one of my hands in the air, wiggling my fingers. "I've seen your blood soak my bedroom floor countless times. Sometimes I wonder if I'm even dreaming."

His expression was stoic. "It's not real. The darkness is taking advantage of your mind at its weakest state."

"How am I supposed to stop it?" I rushed out the words.

"I know what works for me," he said in a melty voice that did little to calm my pulse.

I cleared my throat, feeling the temperature in the room go up twenty degrees. "Hmm?"

He kissed me like he had all the time in the world, stealing my breath away, and I couldn't remember why I'd ever been nervous to tell him. I let my insecurities get in the way, but one kiss from Chase gave me a boost of assurance.

He would always love me, no matter what.

I placed my hand on his scruffy cheek. "Are you angry with me?"

"Not after that kiss."

I searched his eyes and then gave him a quick peck on the lips.

"Just promise me no more secrets. We're going to face our future together, Angel Eyes. You've given me more than I'd ever thought I'd have. No matter what happens, I need you to know how much I love you. How much I adore you."

Did he expect me to think when he was looking at me with bedroom eyes? I felt his breath on my face. "I swear it."

He kissed me again and I felt him soften.

My eyes closed and I inhaled. I forced myself to pull away so I could whisper, "You smell so good." When I opened them again, a rumble came from the back of his throat and his eyes were burning in the darkening room. "Kiss me again."

His mouth found the curve where my shoulder and neck met. I let myself melt into him, savoring the warmth filling my veins. And the sweet torture began.

I felt his fingers dip into the back of my pants, his warm hands cupping my butt. My heart banged in my chest and skipped as my body reacted to his touch. There were so many things we should be doing, preparing for, but this was the only place I wanted to be.

My fingers buried in his hair. A tickle began at my waist, different than my marks radiating, which they definitely were. It was the feel of his fingers, gathering the ends of my shirt upward. The pads of his fingers occasionally brushed my skin, and I was breathing hard when he finally pulled my shirt over my head. I kicked off my pants, sending them flying off the bed, and then went for his shirt. A wicked grin curled his lips.

My fingers spread over his abs, and a rush of warmth gleamed down my arm. There wasn't a female alive that could argue Chase Winters had a rockin' bod. And he was all mine.

Trailing his fingers down my shoulder, he slipped one under my bra strap. I held my breath as he reached behind me, releasing the clasp. It was utterly ridiculous. This wasn't our first time, but I felt a rush of self-consciousness that made me want to cross my arms in front my chest.

"You're perfect."

"I was thinking the same thing about you," I said shyly.

The corner of his mouth lifted as he moved down to take possession of my lips again. I squirmed, desperate to get closer, and he let out a low moan. I don't know if it was my heightened senses, but every touch, every kiss felt particularly sensitive. When his teeth scraped along my collarbone, I gasped.

Oh wow.

After that, it was all intense feelings of love and passion, brought together by two people who treasured each other reverently. Guys like Chase set the expectations of love at an impossible bar for the rest of the world.

I rolled over so we could spoon, succumbing to the warmth of Chase and the rhythmic beat of his heart. He reached around my waist and pulled me near. My eyes fluttered closed as I relished the feeling of his arms.

Chapter 21

{Chase}

I sat up, the sheets bunching around my waist, and shoved a hand through my rumpled hair. Angel was fast asleep, and she wasn't restless or whimpering my name. Her face looked peaceful, softened and lit by moonlight.

It was hard to leave her after being steeped in the rich glow of loving her. Being close to Angel was magic. She seduced my heart, my soul, and my body, and I wasn't referring to our bonds. The sweet sound of her even breathing enthralled me.

I wanted there to be a day when I didn't have to leave her in the middle of the night. When I could spend night after night with her in my arms, not worrying about what slinked outside my windows. I wasn't sure that day would ever come, but I wasn't giving up without a fight, which was why I was leaving the comforts of my bed and the warmth of Angel's body.

I'd only been back to Spring Valley a few weeks, but I couldn't help but be on edge. *What was taking him so long?* I'd stolen the one thing Hell desired, a way to inhabit Earth, and yet there hadn't been a single demon attack, other than Kira and her pesky dogs. She didn't count. I got the sense she had been banished here. And that brought about more questions.

Who was she really?

Or more importantly, *what* was she?

It worried me.

Kira owed me answers, and by god, she was going to give them to me.

I pressed a light kiss to Angel's temple, careful not to disturb her sleep, and let my eyes roam over her face one last time. Then I slipped out of bed, pulling on a pair of sweats and a wrinkled T-shirt. I moved soundlessly through the room, shoving my phone in my pocket. Downstairs, Colin was crashing on our couch.

I shook my head.

Travis was sitting in the recliner, waiting for me. "You ready?" he asked.

Oh, I was definitely ready, but was he? I had to tell the truth about the demon we were hunting tonight. "Emma coming?"

"Nah. Not tonight. She went home to see her mom and sis."

Good, now I didn't have to worry about being hit in the back with an arrow. "Just like old times, cuz."

"What are we going to do with him?" Travis asked, giving a small nod in Colin's direction.

"I know what I would like to do to him," I mumbled.

"I hear you, but Lex would never forgive us. She still cares about him."

I grunted. "Then we better go before I decide to give him a rug burn with my fist. If he ends up hurting her…"

Travis leaned a shoulder on the doorframe. "I'm right there with you."

We snuck out of our house without waking a soul and headed off into the woods. There was a crisp bit to the autumn night, but I didn't feel. My blood was pumping. I stretched out my senses, listening and looking for the any sign we weren't alone. Dried leaves blanketed the forest floor, crunching under our feet.

After five minutes or so of walking, Travis asked, "Are you going to tell me why we're tracking *this* certain demon?"

My foot snapped a twig. I didn't care if she heard us coming. I wanted her to, and if my demon senses were right, she'd been following us for the last four minutes. "I'm getting around to it." I didn't want to blindside Travis as I had with Lexi. He deserved to know what he was getting into and have the choice to walk away.

"Let me guess, she's hot."

I coughed, suppressing a smirk. "If you're into the whole slutty MILF."

"Okay, you've piqued my interest. Why you haven't put a dagger in her heart yet?"

"Oh, I have. The bitch came back. She's the one who helped

me bring Angel back from the brink of darkness, and she is like no demon I've ever had the displeasure of meeting."

"It sounds like she's gotten her claws in you."

I snorted. He didn't know how close to the truth that rang. Not her claws, but she had managed to what no other demon had. Make me in her debt. A fury balled in the pit of my stomach, my demon growling inside me and causing my eyes to glow. I wanted to bury Kira so far into the Earth's crust she could taste China's soil.

"You think she will tell us how to destroy her own kind?" he asked, skeptic.

I continued to steer us as far from the house as we could get in the woods. "Yeah, I do."

"Why would she do that? I know demons are heartless, backstabbers, but they don't usually turn on each other, unless it's a territorial thing."

"It's not about staking claims."

"Then what is it about?"

I lowered my voice. "For Kira…it's family."

"Kira? What, are you guys on first name basis? And since when do demons care about family? You know firsthand that they don't give two-shits about us."

I know that he was trying to razz me, something we'd always done. A way to keep us grounded while the world around was going up in smoke. "Kinda. She's your mother."

He stumbled, his long legs getting tangled up together. "What. I thought you said—"

My chest heaved. "I did."

Travis froze, clenching and unclenching his fists. If he decided to bloody my face, I wouldn't stop him, but instead he only stood there. "How long have you known?"

"Long enough to piss you off." I kept my eyes on the tall trees in front of me. It was enough to hear the hurt and surprise in his voice. I didn't need to see it in his face as well.

A series of silence followed; the air filling with the chirping of crickets. Indecision and confusion framed his face. "I don't know how I'm supposed to feel. Or what the hell I'm feeling."

I shoved my hands into my pockets. "Look man, you don't have to do this. I can handle it on my own...handle her." I didn't know how to apologize for not telling him sooner. Expressing feelings wasn't my strong suit. With Angel it was so much easier—she already knew how I was feeling without me having to say anything.

He squinted at me, then looked into the dark woods. "How do you plan to track her?"

"I don't." Travis was more than my cousin—he was my best friend, and I should have known he wouldn't abandon me. No way. I knew Travis, and he would see it as missing all the action. It didn't matter who she was. "She's been following us for some time." I could feel her practically breathing down our necks. How could he not?

Abruptly, Travis stopped in his tracks a second time, eyes wildly searching the dark and thick forest as he adjusted his heightened vision. "She's been trailing *us?*"

I nodded. "Since we stepped into the woods."

"Shit," he muttered under his breath. "That explains why my mark's been on fire."

I was going to give him one more shot to bow out before things got real. "You sure about this?"

"Who doesn't have mommy issues? Yeah. Let's do this," he said.

I spun around. "Kira, you can come out now." The cat was out of the bag, no use prolonging the inevitable. Whether I liked it or not, there was nothing I could do to stop Kira from trying to contact Lexi and Travis.

She stepped from the shadows, blonde waves standing out in the twilight. For a change, Kira didn't look like she just came from the clubs. In jeans and a white flowy top the wind blew behind her, she could have easily been mistaken for an angel or a ghost, until they got a glimpse of her eyes…or she opened her mouth.

Her sinister lips curved. "There's no need to yell, luv. You'll wake the dead."

Travis stiffened beside me.

My eyes chilled, sharpening. "Save the endearments for someone who cares."

Travis and Kira locked eyes, and I held my breath. Anger slithered through my veins like poison.

"I've waited for this moment for many years," Kira said in almost a whisper. Her eyes ate Travis up.

He put his hand out, and for a second, I actually thought he was going to hit a chick, not that Kira really counted as a girl. "Don't. I don't want to hear anything you have to say. I'm here for one thing only, and that's Chase. Clear?"

She was less than thrilled, but what had she expected? "So much for the tender family reunion. Fine, have it your way, for now. I know what you're looking for, Chase. I know you want to kill your father, and who could blame you? Demons aren't exactly parents of the year, but...you're going to need my help."

"Why would you *want* to help? What's in it for you?" I demanded, once a cynic always a cynic.

"You would never believe me," she answered.

I folded my arms. "Try me."

"You've done an exceptional job keeping your family safe all this time. Would it kill you to put a tad bit of faith in me?"

Yes, I believed it would kill me, especially when I wanted to put my foot up her ass. "You still haven't told me why I should believe anything that comes out of your mouth. As far as I can tell, you haven't done anything without ensuring you get something in return. Typical demon."

Her eyes kept flicking to Travis who refused to look at her. "Some habits are hard to break."

"So are some human bones, but I'm not above breaking all the ones in your host's body to get what I want."

She laughed, a sound too musical for a demon. "We're more alike than you want to admit, nephew."

"If you won't tell Chase why you're suddenly eager to help us, then tell me. I'm asking you, as your son," Travis said.

An emotion I never expected to see on a demon's face swam in Kira's eyes. I couldn't call it love because demons weren't capable of such a feeling, but an emotion similar. I was taken aback.

She tilted her head to the side. "What I've always wanted. To keep you and your sister safe."

Travis was having none of it. "Yeah well, you haven't exactly done a bang-up job of that, have you?"

"There is so much you don't know, don't understand," Kira said in a rush.

"Enlighten us," I stated.

Her eyes were fixed on me. "The sun will be rising soon and we don't have time to waste. What is important is *you* have the only weapon capable of destroying the flesh and soul of a demon."

Huh? What weapon? "Explain."

"There is only one thing that can end a demon's soul, dissolving them from Hell and Earth, and its fire from the chosen's hands—a demon slayer forged by demons and death."

My mind started to turn, pieces of the puzzle falling into place as I processed what I thought she was saying. A slayer. But it was the "forged by demons and death" that caught my attention. I didn't need Kira to spell it out for me.

Fate had a way of really twisting things up. I slumped against a nearby tree trunk, and the branches overhead shook at the impact. I rubbed my face. "You're not suggesting…"

"I'm doing more than suggesting."

"You better not be wrong." Venom dripped from my words.

Chapter 22

{Angel}

"What color? Naughty 'N Nice or Lacy Not Racy?" Lexi asked, holding two bottles of nail polish in each hand, one a deep red, the other a soft pink.

"You're asking me?" I replied flatly.

"Right." She swirled in her chair toward Emma propped on the floor. "Okay, which one, camo girl? You used to at least have a girly streak."

"Who says I still don't?" Emma grumbled.

"Seriously, this is important stuff."

It was just the three of us, hanging out, having a girls' day like normal college girls. We needed a bit of normalcy before the crap storm on the horizon hit. Lexi had made coffee and cranberry-lemon scones for us.

"Totally. It's not like we have to save the world or anything," I said around a mouthful of my scone, covering my mouth to keep from dropping crumbs all over Lexi's bed.

"Exactly. The way I see it, who says I can't go to war looking my best? At least my nails will be fabulous at my funeral."

"That's not funny," I mumbled.

"Finally, emotion. I wasn't sure if that was my best friend or a zombie on my bed."

I squashed an eye roll. "Sorry. I didn't get much sleep."

Lexi and Emma both grinned. "You never did make it home last night, did you?" Lexi asked.

She knew I didn't, thanks to the morning run-in in the hallway. I crinkled my nose. "Oh, and where is Colin today?"

Lexi pouted. "He slept on the couch while Travis watched him with one eye open."

I giggled. "A-w-k-ward. Does your dad know he spent the night?"

Lexi made a ghastly face. "Are you kidding? No. He would go ape shit. Anyway, he was at your house last night. I guess someone made an offer on your house."

I gagged on air. "What?" Disbelief stared back at me in the mirror behind Lexi.

She angled her head, causing her cherubic curls to fall over one shoulder. "Are you going to miss it?"

If someone would have asked me six months ago, I would have probably said no, but now I couldn't imagine living anywhere else. Even next door. "Yeah, I think I will." Polishing off the last bite of my scone, I rolled on my belly, dangling my feet in the air.

Lexi crossed her legs, taking a sip of her hot tea. She didn't guzzle coffee like it was the fifth food group as Emma and I did. "When do you guys plan on going back to school?"

Emma and I groaned in unison. "I'm thinking of not going back this semester. I've missed too many classes already. I'll probably just start my freshman year over again in the spring." Mom would love that, an entire semester of tuition gone down the crapper.

Emma stretched her legs. "Yeah, I'm kind of thinking college might not be for me."

"Guys! You are not ditching me. I can't go to college on my own."

This time I did roll my eyes. "Yes, you can, Lexi. You were born for college life."

"It just won't be the same without you guys."

And just like that, the three of us started to realize we were growing up and in different directions. Unlikely of friends—a half-demon, a hunter, and a mutated human—but we had been brought together for a reason. I couldn't be more grateful for the bond of friendship we had, and I wanted it to last a lifetime.

Sitting up, I swung my feet over the side of the bed and reached for my cup of coffee. "I don't think our lives are ever going to be the same." My voice had gotten grimmer than I'd intended; I tried to soften the effect with a small smile.

Lexi's brows drew closer together, but she didn't say anything. "Why do you think he hasn't made one threat on our lives? It doesn't make sense."

Emma made a sort of irritated sound in the back of her throat. "Since when does anything a demon does or says make sense?"

"Have you said anything to Travis about, you know?" I asked over my steaming mug.

Lexi shook her head. "Not yet. I still can't wrap my head around it. I mean, I actually saw my mother yesterday, and I didn't even say anything to her."

"Did you want to talk to her?"

She shrugged, swiveling her chair back and forth with the tip of her toes. "No. Yes. Maybe. I shouldn't want to have anything to do with her, but I've always wondered what she looked like. What her name was. Why she chose my dad. Why she left us."

"It's normal to be curious about a parent you've never met," I said.

"I've dreamed about it countless times, good and bad dreams, but not once did I ever dream it would play out like it had. But what I had a hard time understanding is why Chase didn't tell me."

"He didn't do so to hurt you." Of course I came to his defense. It was second nature to me.

"Which is why I'm having a hard time processing. I know

Chase would never intentionally hurt me. From the day I was born, he has only ever protected me, often too much, and it makes me wonder if that's what he's doing. Protecting me still."

"I guess in his way he is."

Lexi's eyes narrowed. "If you know something, you better spill your guts."

I frowned at the floor, struggling with my loyalty to my best friend and my boyfriend. Chase had a reason for everything he did, but he had gone too far this time. "Chase made a deal with Kira to save me."

A unified gasp erupted in the room. "He didn't." Outrage was evident in Lexi's voice. "Idiot," she muttered.

"Moron," Emma added.

"It was the only way she would tell him how to save me," I defended, not because I didn't think he was some days an idiot and a moron, but because he was mine.

Lexi shot to her feet and started to pace in front of the bed, working off the sudden excess energy pumping inside her. "What did she ask for in return? What's his debt?"

I swallowed the coffee, which tasted stale in my mouth. "You…and Travis."

She stopped abruptly, tiny flecks of gold in her sea foam eyes. "*Me?* What does she want?"

My shoulders lifted. "Who knows? She said to talk, but Chase doesn't trust her. He didn't bring her here. Kira came on her own, probably to stir up trouble."

"I'm not so sure," Emma said.

"You can't tell me that you, the hunter, is actually thinking about trusting a demon. What has the world come to?" Lexi plopped down on the bed next to me, her weight sinking the mattress.

"If she meant you harm, why has it taken her almost twenty years to show her face? Have you ever fought a demon with your mark?" Emma asked.

Lexi bit her lip, staring at her pink walls. "We don't always strip-search them before we kill them."

I controlled a smirk tugging on my lips.

"There is something about her… I just can't put my finger on it."

"Chase has the same feeling," I added.

"It's so hard to believe she doesn't have a selfish agenda. Being nice is not in a demon's genetic makeup. They're vindictive, cruel, and a-holes," Lexi said, hitting it on the nose.

Emma's freckle-dusted face contorted into a grin. "Go with the pink. It will compliment your complexion."

Lexi's eyes beamed. Getting a compliment from Emma was uncommon. "Thank you. Was that so hard?"

"Like pulling teeth," Emma mumbled.

REDEEMING ANGEL

It struck me again how different we were, but in this moment, I couldn't be happier to have them by my side.

Chapter 23

{Angel}

I flopped on my bed with a sigh, unable to stop thinking that soon this would no longer be *my* room. Some other girl would be sleeping in the room with walls the color of Chase's eyes, staring at the network of cracks that traveled from the ceiling corner. It was a disconcerting thought, but I couldn't actually expect Mom to live alone in this house forever simply because I'd grown attached to it.

Gah.

I was going to miss this room. A swell of emotion rose in my throat, and I chewed on my lip to keep it from quivering. Again with the changes. Too many of them coming at me all at once, and my future so uncertain. What kind of life would Chase and I have if we couldn't destroy the one demon that had turned my world upside down? Like Chase, Alastair didn't have the type of personality that gave up easily. He wasn't done with me.

The darkness inside me was a constant reminder.

On the flipside, for the first time in weeks, I finally felt as if I was the one in control. Not my fear. Not the seed of darkness inside me. Not my anger. Just me. Learning to defend myself had been a big part of regaining the confidence I'd lost and finding me again.

It was about time.

I was drawing lazy circles over the pattern on my bed, deep in thought when a powerhouse of tingles galloped down my spine. A knock sounded on the door and I blinked. *Chase.*

Turning off the music playing in the background, I yelled for him to come in. Seconds later a gorgeous figure darkened my doorway. It didn't matter if I'd seen him an hour ago or a week; I always had the same overwhelming reaction. And because he was a total hottie and I couldn't help myself, I jumped into his arms, throwing my hands around the nape of his neck.

"Hey," he said, pressing against me and nuzzling his face in my hair.

"Hey yourself."

The tip of his nose butted mine. "Take a walk with me?"

"Perimeter check?"

He shook his head. "Travis and Emma took care of it. Nothing unusual. No sign of trouble. I just thought it was a nice night for a walk."

"You did, did you?" He had something up his sleeve, and whatever it was, it was making him nervous and, in turn, made me suspicious.

A lock of hair fell over his forehead as he shoved his hands into his pockets. "Are you going to be difficult?"

I opened my mouth and then shut it. Chase and I could argue about the color of the sun, but something in his mood led me to believe that today was not the day to be obstinate. "Where are we going?"

"I want to show you something." He held out his hand, waiting for me to take it.

Fine. He wanted to be mysterious, so be it. Some days it was better to indulge Chase. I placed my hand in his, enfolding our fingers together. "Lead the way, Romeo."

Outside, I stretched my face up to the sky, letting the nippy wind wash over my cheeks. Chase scanned the dense, dark surrounding forest before guiding us toward the fields. It was dusk, and I let my eyes adjust, illuminating over the trail.

"Do you remember when you followed me into these fields?"

Wheat tickled my nose. I swatted at the stalks in front of my face. "How can I forget? It was the night I found out you were more than an ass."

He smiled. "That was the most gutsy thing I'd ever done, letting down my guard and taking a chance you'd keep my secret."

"I did keep your secret."

"Yes you did, and I'm glad."

"Well, you sure didn't act like it."

His eyes glowed an uncanny silver in the moonlight. "You didn't exactly make it easy."

The air smelled of autumn spices and Chase. I took it all in, savoring the scent. "Did you bring me out here to take a trip down memory lane?"

"Sort of." Our fingers interlaced as we went deeper into the fields. "Before things can possibly get any crazier, there is something I've been working up the courage to ask you."

"Since when do you lack courage?"

"Just like back then, you're not going to make this easy, are you? That's not our way." We stepped into a circular clearing.

"Make what easy—?" My voice trailed off as I caught sight of light that didn't belong in the middle of a field. Lanterns lit the opening, casting a soft yellow glow over the ground. The wind rustled the stalks of wheat surrounding us and all I could do was stare.

He tipped his head to one side. "I wanted this to be special," he whispered in my ear behind me, his warm breath tickling my neck.

My stomach flipped. I blinked, struck by the romantic gesture. I wasn't sure what this was, but I was beginning to like it. Standing in the center of the circle, I spun around and faced Chase. He sucked in a deep breath, wiping his palms on the back of his jeans before reaching for my hand and threading our fingers.

I squeezed his hand.

Then he dropped to one knee.

My heart did a series of flips. "Oh God."

I think I stopped breathing. I wasn't sure, because I couldn't take my eyes off what he was holding in his other hand. Clenched between his fingers a tiny object glittered under the moon, catching the gentle flicker of lamplight.

My features immediately softened, and I leaned toward him. Emotion pure and undiluted filled me, a bizarre mixture of love and panic and joy and disbelief. "Oh God." I spent most my life imagining this moment, dreaming about it, but nothing came close to seeing Chase on one knee, staring up at me with nerves and love shining in his gray eyes.

There was a very good chance I was going to pass out.

"I know things are crazy right now, but I realized I don't want to live my life with regrets. I want to live every day of my life with you. Every second. There aren't enough ways to tell you how deep my love is for you, but I know you can feel it. I will be in love with you for always, and nothing will ever change that. I want you to be more than my soul mate. I want you to be my wife."

I felt a rush of something utterly foreign fill my lungs. It was air, I realized dumbly. I hadn't even comprehended I'd been holding my breath. "Oh God."

He chuckled deeply. "You said that already."

"I'll probably say it ten more times. Is this real?" I wanted to pinch myself. Hard. Wonderment whirled through me like a windstorm.

"As real as my feelings for you. Angel Chloe Morgan, will you marry me?"

This was Chase Winters on one knee for me. Tears stung my eyes and a lump formed in my throat as I dropped down beside him, framing his face with my shaky hands.

"Say something." He took the pad of his thumb and wiped at the corners of my eyes.

Feeling like an overemotional girl, I said, "I think I'm still in shock." Then I tipped my head forward, pressing my lips to his in a quick kiss that tasted of my salty tears. "I want to sear this moment in my memory forever," I whispered.

"You still haven't said yes."

I smiled. "What else would I say? Yes, I will marry you, Chase—" My brows drew together. "I just realized I don't know what your middle name is."

He laughed and pressed his forehead to mine. "Liam."

"Chase Liam Winters." I meshed our lips together in another quick branding kiss. "I want nothing more in this world than to marry you."

His body shuddered, tension releasing from him all at once.

Wonder clouded his smoky eyes dashed with bits of gold.

Happiness like I'd never known trembled through me like magic. It might have been a simple proposal, but I didn't need flashy or over-the-top. I wasn't that kind of girl, but this had to be the single most swoon-worthy thing he'd ever done or said to me. Then again, he was otherworldly.

We were young, but in so many ways we'd been through a lifetime of ups and downs. It didn't matter if we were nineteen or ninety, there would never be anyone else for me but Chase. Tears clogged my vocal chords. "I'm going to love being your wife."

He laughed, a delicious sound that lightened his gorgeous face into sheer happiness. With a hand not completely steady, he slipped a ring onto to my finger. It fit snuggly. "I didn't want to give you something traditional. I wanted it to be special, like what we have. The stone is a tanzanite. It reminded me of your eyes."

I was going to start crying again. "It's the most beautiful thing I've ever seen." The white gold band wove around the stone much like our matching marks.

"That's how I feel about you."

From the corner of my eye I saw a shooting star gracefully speeding across the dark night. "I love you."

He flashed me a lopsided grin, enveloping me in his arms. "I want to marry you as soon as possible."

"Like now?" My heart sped, and my face lit on fire.

"Not this instant, but soon. Very soon. I want to start our life together without the constant threat of Alastair. When this is all over, I'm going to be rushing you down the aisle."

He wasn't going to hear any arguments from me. I would marry him right here in the middle of a field if he asked. "I'm going to hold you to that, Winters."

One dark brow lifted.

In a blink, he was standing and I was ensnared in his strong embrace. I felt as if I was floating, my body soaring with love. I glimpsed down at the ring on my finger, its weight foreign on my hand. He took a little breath and his arms tightened around me. "Let's go home, fiancée."

I giggled. "I don't think I'm ever going to get used to hearing you say that."

"Maybe we should elope."

I swear my feet didn't touch the ground as we left the grove swallowed by wheat. "Lexi would kill us."

As we leisurely weaved through the fields, we decided not to tell anyone just yet. I felt giddy to have such a huge secret, and honestly, I wasn't sure how long I could keep something like this to myself. My mouth had a tendency to move without communicating with my brain. It was a disease almost.

There were no lights on as we broke through the fields, crossing the road, only the glow of the crescent moon above and a huge sky full of stars. We couldn't stop touching and talking about random things, like where we would go for our honeymoon, whether Chase was going to go bald in his old age, and my personal favorite, how many kids we would have.

"So have you changed your mind about kids?" I asked, tiptoeing to the subject. I enjoyed making him squirm.

"My gut says it's a bad idea. With our genetic makeup, can you imagine what kind of kids we would have?"

I could, and they would be perfect. How could they not? With Chase's incredible looks and my sparkling personality they would be destined for greatness. He must be dense. "And you always trust your gut?" I countered.

"It's kept me alive."

"But has it made you happy? What did your gut say when you met me?" I challenged.

He snorted. "Run. As far and as fast as you can, because this girl is going to get you in trouble."

I smiled. "Wow. That was what my gut told me, too."

"And your gut was right."

I shook my head and looped my arm through his. "Not a chance. Why didn't you listen to your gut?"

He shot me a grin. "You know why. Besides, I tried. I just couldn't stay away from you."

Thinking about the days when we first met and the mix of

feelings I had about my sexy douchebag neighbor brought a smile to my lips and made my insides light up.

    He wrapped his arms around me, pulling our faces close.

    We spent to rest of the night wrapped up in each other, trying to forget about the things we'd soon be facing. It was a night I would always remember. How absolutely loved and cherished he made me feel. I didn't think life could be more blissful than being in love with Chase.

Chapter 24

{Angel}

Moonlight streamed through the sheer curtains, and an eerie feeling I was being watched prickled my skin. Chase was sleeping soundly next to me, a rare sight. I climbed silently from the bed, careful not to wake him, and went to the window. Glancing out into the yard, I could see nothing out of the ordinary.

I shivered.

Whether I could see anything or not, I knew someone was out there.

It wasn't just because it was incredibly dark out, or that the moon was full and the streetlights were out. It was the sudden shift in the air. My heart raced as the demon marks on my side swirled in radiance.

I opened up my night vision, and in the darkness, trailing through the evergreens, was a glowing red light. It didn't take a brainiac to know the light was a demon. I know it was probably a trap, but the fear I'd seen in Kira's eyes combined with my newfound skills gave me a boost of confidence. I wanted to know

REDEEMING ANGEL

who and why a demon was lurking outside my window, although I had a hunch who it was.

After slipping on a pair of worn jeans from the floor, I slid my feet into a pair of sneakers and glanced toward the bed. Chase hadn't moved a wink. He must have been exhausted, and how could I blame him? The real trick was to sneak out of the house without disturbing him *and* make it back. I wasn't holding my breath, but I moved silently down the stairs, avoiding every creak.

I left the front porch and took off toward the woods. My heart was pounding in my ears and my stomach was in knots, but I didn't run back inside like I wanted. As I got closer to the edge of the woods, the hair on the back of my neck stood up, and my demon marks went haywire. I twiddled the ring on my finger.

This was stupid. I knew better than to wander off at night, let alone gone near the woods. No matter how curious and brave I was feeling, nothing was going to lure me into those woods. Not even an entire box of apple cider donuts. As I berated myself, I stopped and stared at the spot where a group of trees were the thickest.

Yikes.

Bewilderment leaped into my violet eyes, and I felt the dizzy sense of vertigo. "You?"

"Who were you expecting, the queen of England?"

"You know who the queen is?" I shook my head. "Never

mind. What are you doing creeping outside my window like a jealous girlfriend?"

Kira stepped out from the shadows. "I wanted to talk."

I took a conscious step backward. "To *me*?"

The ends of her lips tipped up in a not-so-nice smirk. "Well, you're not Queen Elizabeth, although my nephew does treat you like a princess."

I snorted. "So you're not here hoping to catch a glimpse of Travis or Lexi?"

There was something less intimidating about Kira; maybe it was the way she was dressed, in a pair of cute jeans and flat riding boots. "Not tonight, but it would have been an added bonus."

At least she didn't try to deny it. "How many nights have you been out here?"

"Do you want an exact number?" She appeared impatient, eyes lively.

I glared and folded my arms.

She blew out a smoke of hot air. "Every night since they came home, okay? Happy now?"

Far from it. Chase would not like to hear about this. It would definitely set him off into a demon rager, and so would my being alone with Kira. If he were to wake up…

Ugh. Best not to think about those consequences.

The demon and I would be in hot water for sure, and that

thought was enough to make this a short conversation. I glanced at the window just to make sure it was still dark. "I don't have much time, so spit it out already. What did you want to talk to me about?"

Her scarlet eyes lifted behind me. "Honestly, I'm surprised you came alone."

"Who said I'm alone?" Never reveal anything to a demon, lesson number two. Lesson number one: never find yourself alone with a demon. I'd already broken rule number one; it was better to not push my luck.

She wore a dark cloak that covered most of her silvery-blonde hair. "It doesn't really matter whether you believe me or not. I mean you no harm. None of you."

The scary thing was, I believed her. "Okay."

Her shoulders relaxed in a way that her movements were nothing but flickers. "I came to warn you."

Now she had my undivided attention, and the fear I'd been dreading since I returned home became real. I knew what she was going to tell me, what we'd all been waiting for—Alastair to strike back.

"There have been whispers. Alastair is on his way." A breeze suddenly blew through the timbers, kicking up the ends of her cloak and shaking the dried leaves off the branches. They frolicked eerily in the air. "He's gathered his army, and he isn't looking to use you. He wants you very, very dead." She circled me like she was dancing, and I turned to follow, keeping my eyes glued to her.

Funny…that was exactly how I wanted him—dead—body and spirit.

My chin tipped up as the mighty wind teased strands of my hair, thrashing them over my face. "Tell me something I don't already know."

"I plan on it, Lucerna."

I raised my brows. I wasn't fond of being called names I couldn't pronounce. "Just to be clear, I'm not making a deal with you."

And with a snap, the wind died, but the dark clouds above remained. "Consider this a gesture of goodwill."

"I'm listening."

"There is such a power to destroy not just the flesh of a demon, but the soul."

"Chase was right; it's possible," I muttered.

She nodded, but I could tell by the seriousness in her eyes, there was a catch, as there always was with Hell. "It is, but there hasn't been a demon slayer in centuries."

"A demon slayer?" I echoed.

"It takes a unique individual to have the skills necessary to extinguish a demon. Even then, sometimes it's not enough."

I wasn't going to be discouraged, not when the first real seed of hope took root inside me, just waiting to bloom. All it needed was a little rain and sunshine. "Where do we find one?"

"You think you are the first to seek such knowledge? There have been many over the decades who sought out the legends of slayers, but they remained a myth…to most."

And like that my bubble burst. How the hell were we going to find someone who essentially didn't exist? If there hadn't been a slayer in centuries, we were doomed.

Then Kira said, "But you already have a slayer."

Umm. Say what? Elation trekked through my veins. If she was screwing with me, I was going to light her on fire. Somehow. I rummaged my brain. "Do we know them? Who is it?" Immediately, I thought of Emma. I didn't know anyone more badass—Chase excluded of course. "Emma?"

"Not even close."

Okay. Then who?

"It's you, Lucerna," Kira said.

"*Me?*" I shrieked. "Are you insane? I'm not a slayer. I can barely use a knife. I trip over my own feet. And the sight of blood makes me squeamish. There's no way I'm a slayer of anything. You've got your facts screwed up."

"The fire you conjure is not just heat and flames. It's every demon's greatest fear."

I stumbled back a step, pressing a hand to my throat where

my heart had leapt. "I don't believe it. The only reason I can even produce fire is because of Alastair. Why would he give me something that could ultimately destroy him?" It didn't make sense.

"If only the universe was so cut and dry. There are consequences, checks and balances, a way to level the field. When you and Chase defied the laws of death, it forged your first bond and also triggered Alastair's immediate interest in both of you. As you already know, the two of you really fumbled the whole Triplici. For Alastair to get what he wanted, the two of you had to complete the three bonds, each one securing your link directly to Alastair. Only then was he so close to what every demon in Hell wants—freedom—so close he could taste it."

"Oh God," I muttered.

She nodded. "Pretty surreal. There hasn't been a tie between Earth and Hell like yours in centuries, but what Alastair didn't account for was how far Chase was willing to go to save you. Or me," she added, a half grin on her lips. "When Chase broke the connection Hell had over you, severing any chance at invading this realm, Alastair probably realized the fatal flaw in his plan—his own son. I can't help but be amused by the irony of it all. The three bonds that connect you to Chase are complex, as I am sure you've figured out. His natural need to protect you is part of the bond. I'm sure you've sensed it."

Have I ever. There was nothing I wouldn't do to protect him. Our relationship was anything but normal and healthy.

"For Chase to save you," she said, shifting her weight as eagerness filled her gaze, "he had to overcome the ingrain obligation to never hurt you. But the only way to cut the tie was to do just that. In theory, it might sound possible, driving a knife into the person you love to banish the darkness. But, the type of love and affection you share forbids such harm. It is part of the laws of the Triplici. I don't know how he managed to do it." Her voice grew soft at the end and filled with wonder.

My heart skipped. "You don't know Chase. Nothing stands in his way. Not Hell. Not the universe. Nothing."

"I imagine it caused him severe pain," she said.

The thought of him hurting sent a dull ache to my chest. I could recall the torment I'd felt after the blade pierced my skin in sort of a murky perspective. I knew it was my body, but the screams in my head where so much louder than those I actually voiced. My soul had felt as if it was being ripped in half. "He's never said."

"Well for you and the rest of the planet, it was a good thing he did, but having that much blackness extracted from your body all at once leaves scars."

"I've noticed," I murmured.

"You're a smart girl. Those leftover remains of Hell are what give you the ability to destroy demons."

I shoved a hand through my hair. "It doesn't make sense. I'm no one special. I'm not a fighter."

"That's just how the cookie crumbles, Lucerna."

"Why do you keep calling me that?" I barked.

"It means candlelight. It's what demons call someone like you."

Someone like me. A slayer. I couldn't begin to fathom what that meant. "I don't know how to be a slayer," I mumbled more to myself than her.

Kira sent me a dry look. "Well, sweetheart, you better figure it out soon. Alastair is coming. And you're the only chance we have at surviving. The way I see it, your biggest problem isn't learning to control your skills; it's Chase."

My pulse began to level. "What do you mean?"

"That boy will protect you fiercely. He would give up his life before he let you put yourself voluntarily in harm. Some of that is the bond you've created, but I am guessing most of it is his nature. To do what must be done, you will use a great amount of energy. Destroying a demon as old and as powerful of Alastair will be no easy feat. Your body will be depleted—physically and emotionally."

"So you are saying if I do this, I could possibly die?"

A little light went out of her scarlet eyes. "There is always that

REDEEMING ANGEL

chance. It could also separate the ties between Chase and you. Nothing is guaranteed, and the power you have is unpredictable."

"I don't understand. Why tell me all of this? Aren't you afraid I will turn you to ash now that I know what I can do?"

There wasn't any fear or concern in her expression, just an abundance of cockiness. "Is that your plan? To set me aflame?"

I didn't say anything. I let the idea dangle in the air, neither confirming nor denying.

Her lips twitched. "I think you and I both know it would be foolish to kill the only demon on your side. I've proven that I'm invaluable in keeping you alive." She crossed her arms. "Actually, I'm still waiting for a thank-you."

Don't hold your breath. "Release Chase from his deal and I won't incinerate you," I countered, working an angle to my advantage.

Energy crackled through the air surrounding us. I'm guessing she didn't like my proposal. She was a schemer at heart. "I could call your bluff."

God, please let this work—just this one time. Pretty please, with a cherry on top.

I closed my eyes, focusing all my attention on the fragment of darkness that dwelled inside me, summoning it, yet still staying in control. I was beginning to recognize the signature feeling right before my hands became a torch. As I opened my eyes, I let out a small laugh. Orangey-red flames tipped with a touch of blue flared at my fingertips. "Try me." I was loaded and I had the ammunition to do it.

For the first time in my life, I didn't feel powerless—just the opposite. I could take on the world…or Hell.

"Have it your way, *slayer*."

I let out a whoosh of air, the flames burning out.

"But…" Kira said.

Oh, of course there was a but. There was always a but.

"The only way to undo a deal is with anther deal. A trade," she said.

"You want me to make a deal with you?"

"It's the only way. The authority that binds a deal is above my rank. I can make them and enforce them, but I can't break them."

"What kind of crap is that?"

"The laws of the underworld. Never said they were fair. So what is your answer? We're running out of time." Her eyes moved behind me. "Your other half stirs."

I didn't even question how she knew. The thought of Chase waking up and finding me gone sent me into a tizzy. "Give me the deets. What kind of deal are we talking?"

"I'll make it simple. The deal is, if I ever need you to zap a demon, you do it. No questions asked."

Great. She wanted me to be her demon hitman. I thought about what she was asking for two whole seconds before I said,

"You got yourself a deal." The way I saw it, it was a win-win. I didn't really have a problem taking out a demon and making the world a little safer.

Before I realized what her intent was, Kira grabbed my wrist and made an incision with one of her razor-tipped nails.

"Hey!" I protested, attempting to pull my hand away.

Her grasp only tightened. "We're not done yet." She squeezed a few drops of her blood on the wound before it healed. There was this intense heat that burned and sizzled. I snapped back and rubbed at my wrist in an attempt to lessen the sting. "Was that necessary?"

"Unfortunately, it is. Demon rules. Anyway, we're practically family."

I never thought I would have to put my trust in a demon. She better be right, or we were all screwed. "It's done? Chase owes you nothing?" I asked to make things crystal clear.

She smeared the pad of her thumb over her bottom lip and then licked the drops of blood. "The deal's been sealed."

Good, because I really needed to get back inside before Chase awoke and became ballistic. I nodded, my eyes lifting to my second-story window. The light was still out, but a sense of urgency tore through me.

I had only taken a few steps toward the house when Kira called, "I'm hoping my wedding invite won't get lost in the mail—

that is, if we survive."

I had been unconsciously twirling the ring as I walked back. My movements paused for a split second, until I continued on, shaking my head and hurrying my stride.

Damn demons.

Chapter 25

{Chase}

I woke up with the acidic taste of panic in my mouth. Beads of sweat gathered at the back of my neck, and I knew without turning my head Angel was no longer lying in the bed beside me. My stomach plummeted as I jolted upright. "Angel," I called into the darkness.

I didn't really expect an answer, but I couldn't prevent her name from tumbling from my lips.

Tossing the covers aside, my feet hit the ground as the tingles amplified. I lifted my eyes, and her shadow darkened the doorway.

"You're up," she said, sounding a little breathy.

I flashed across the room, grasping her face in both hands and backed her into a wall. "Are you trying to scare me to death?"

"No," she stated.

"Where did you go?"

"To get a drink," she said, but the inflection in her voice posed it more as a question.

My brow shot up.

Eventually she sighed, realizing I wasn't going to be brushed off. "I saw Kira. Happy now?"

Happy? Not in the least. "Do you have a death wish?" I rasped. "Why would you sneak off and see her alone?"

"It wasn't something I planned. It just happened," she answered softly.

"How did it happen?"

Her head bent back, resting on the wall. "I woke up with this feeling something was outside, watching, and I got up to look out the window. Even as I was leaving the house, I knew it was a demon prowling in the woods. And you don't need to tell me it was reckless and stupid to go out there alone."

My chest rose. I didn't know who I wanted to strangle more. Angel or Kira. Why were all the women in my life so utterly troublesome? Maybe it was just women in general. It didn't matter, because I could feel the brim of a fight in our imminent future.

She leaned into me, pressing her hands on my shirt. "Before you start puffing your chest, I'm fine. We just talked. Nothing happened."

I ground my teeth, a hard gleam in my eyes. "I'm trying not to lose my cool. I'm trying to keep you safe, but you keep putting yourself in danger. Angel, I can't—"

"I'm sorry," she interrupted, raising her voice. "I know I'm making things harder. Christ, since the day we met, I've done nothing but make your life more difficult."

I started to tell her she was wrong, couldn't be more wrong, but she wasn't ready to listen.

She shook her head, a soft glint of amber in her irises. "Don't deny it. We both know it's true. If you had stayed away from me, if I hadn't been so curious and nosy, none of this would matter. You would be far safer if we'd never met."

My heart pounded, beating rapidly in time with hers. I framed her face, forcing her to look at me. Her eyes were bright with anger and emotion. "You. Saved. Me."

She snorted. "You have a funny definition of being saved."

"Maybe," I agreed. "But I would rather have known what it feels like to love than be *safe*. We both know I've never been safe a day in my life. What you gave me was so much more."

She pressed her forehead against my chest. "I'm sorry. I don't know what's wrong with me. It's possible the threat of the end of the world is getting to me, or maybe it's the stress of knowing it's up to me to save the world." Her shoulders slumped, and the weight of her body rested on mine.

I linked my hands around her waist. "Kira told you, didn't she?" I asked softly, my cheek brushing her hair. In my mind, it was just another reason to despise my so-called aunt. She hadn't given me a chance to tell Angel myself. Enraged at Kira, my fists clenched at Angel's lower back. "I wanted to be the one who told you."

Her head lifted, bringing the tip of our noses together. "You know?"

I softened the lines on my face. "Kira told me a few nights ago."

Her brows drew together, and I could see the inner workings of her mind as she tried to put together when I'd found out. "When did you see her?"

"Travis and I went looking for her the night she showed up at the house."

"Why didn't you tell me?"

I moved hand from her waist and lifted her wrist. I twirled the ring I'd put on her finger, a symbol of my love. "Because I had other plans, and I didn't want to darken them with thoughts of demons."

She glanced down at the stormy purplish-blue stone. "Do you believe her?"

I lifted her hand to my lips. "There is only one way to find out. We test her theory."

"You want me to kill a demon?"

"Everyone's got to start somewhere," I replied.

The expression on her face was a cross of being on the verge of panic and the need to prove herself. "And after that? What are we going to do?"

She didn't talk about what happened to her often—the darkness and being possessed by it— but I knew it preyed on her. And now this…

"We're going to roll with it," I said.

There was doubt written all over her face. She might not believe in herself, but I sure as hell did. A red mark on her wrist caught my gaze. I twisted her hand around so I could get a better look, and I felt as if I'd been sucker punched. "You made a deal with Kira?" I hissed.

She snatched her wrist out of my grasp. "I had to."

In the dark, I raised my hand and groaned. The mark I'd received when I'd made a deal with Kira was no longer branded on my skin. "What did you do?"

"I did what had to be done. Just as you," she rationalized, which in my mind was a lame rationalization.

"Angel," I growled.

"You're making a mountain out of a mole hill. It's not a big deal. I traded your freedom for a deal."

"What did you promise her?" I demanded.

She shrugged. "Nothing I'm not willing to do. She asked me to destroy a demon of her choice, no questions asked."

"That's all, huh?"

She let out a small yawn. "See, I told you it was no biggie."

Yeah. We'd see about that. There was no reason to get all

huffy, because there was nothing I could do about. The deal was done. "I know I should thank you, but I'd rather be the one indebted to a demon."

Her eyes fought to stay open, and she swayed slightly. "You're welcome."

I shook my head, and before she fell asleep on her feet, I grabbed her hand and crawled back into the bed. She didn't hesitate and moved into my arms, situating her head on my chest. The scent of her warmed my mood. "I know it's a waste of breath, but I'm going to say it anyway. Don't ever do that again," I whispered.

She yawned a second time. "What? Scare the crap out of you, or have secret meetings with demons?"

"All of the above."

As she lay snuggled in my arms, I thought about hog-tying her to the bed. How else was I going to ensure she stayed put? I'd rather avoid having another heart attack, but realistically, I knew there were plenty more times ahead that were going to stop my heart.

She'd been chosen. She was the weapon.

Angel was the demon slayer.

~*~*~*~

{Angel}

REDEEMING ANGEL

A weird thought suddenly hit me as I walked through my house. There was plenty for my mind to be circling about, but all I could think was, I'm freaking engaged. To Chase Winters. My eyes got huge and my feet tangled slightly, making me stumble. I caught myself on the wall, the stones in my ring catching the light dangling from the ceiling. Then, like a crazy person, I started to giggle.

My smile was ridiculously bright as I turned the corner into the kitchen. I grabbed a bottled water from the fridge and chugged, quenching my thirst. Sweat dampened my forehead and the sides of my flushed cheeks—another grueling practice with Chase. This time Emma and Travis had joined us. Emma amped up the stakes. No mercy.

The way she could move while fighting, it was hard not to be jealous. It was like a choreographed dance routine. No amount of training was going to make me as graceful as Emma—or Lexi for that matter. I was the supernatural black sheep.

I screwed the cap back on the bottle, and as I turned to head back outside, Mom strutted into the room. Chase and Travis were each following behind her with their arms full of grocery bags. "Angel, what have you been doing? Running a marathon?" she asked, dropping her purse and keys on the counter. "Are you sick?"

I rolled my eyes. "I don't get sick anymore, remember?" It

was part of the whole healing deal. Pretty handy, not ever having to worry about the flu and puking my guts out in the toilet bowl.

She pursed her lips. "Right. I'm still adjusting to my daughter being...*special*."

I snickered at her choice of words. "What's all this?" I asked.

She started to unload items from the bags—green peppers, onions, steak. "I thought I'd make us a celebratory dinner."

Quickly, I linked my hands behind my back. *She couldn't possibly know about my engagement, could she?* "Do I dare ask? What are we celebrating?"

Her lips spread into a grin. "I sold the house."

I gripped the side of the fridge for support. Chase was suddenly beside me. "Um. What?" I shrieked. "How can that be? It's only been on the market less than a week." Okay, even though I knew someone had made an offer, I thought it was a joke.

Mom shrugged. "The buyers bought sight unseen."

And that only reinforced my theory that whoever bought this house was cray-cray. "I can't believe you actually got an offer on this dump."

Travis plucked an apple from one of the bags and took a bite. The crunch echoed over the kitchen.

"Well, it was an offer I couldn't refuse," Mom said.

"What kind of idiot would do that? Buy a house without even looking at it?" *Buy this house?*

Chase cleared his throat, shifting on his feet.

Mom raised her brows.

And I realized I'd just stuck my foot in my mouth. "Oh sorry, I wasn't implying you were an idiot when you bought this place."

Unloading a bag of groceries, she started opening cabinets. "I know you weren't. Anyway, I remember you saying something very similar the first time we pulled into the driveway."

"Sounds like Angel," Chase added.

I smashed my heel on his toes.

"I thought you liked living here?" Mom asked, looking over her shoulder as she stretched to put away a box of PopTarts.

"I do. It's *my* dump. What I really liked about this house were my neighbors." *Did I just say that out loud?*

Chase's lips twitched.

{Chase}

She looked hotter than the California sun. Who would have thought having her almost roast me like a pig would be hot? Little flames danced at her fingertips, and it turned her sexy all the way up to ten. While she was feeling damn good about herself, I made my move before she singed all the hair off my body.

I felt the heat radiate as the ball of fire whizzed past me.

Angel smiled. "You almost got incinerated."

Her aim was improving. "Almost isn't going to destroy a

demon." I probably should've been grateful her aim wasn't deadly accurate. Being burnt to toast wasn't on my bucket list.

"Hurting you would hurt me. Did you ever think that maybe I'm missing on purpose?" she asked.

"No."

Her eyes narrowed, and I thought she was going to hurl another one of her flaming missiles, but instead the white-gold fire cavorting on her fingertips brightened, growing in size. Her control was definitely improving.

"I think we're done for the day," I said, before she could change her mind and nail me.

Hard lines of concentration folded over her forehead. It took a few tries, but she finally managed to douse the flames. A faint smile crossed her lips. "You're the boss. What do you want to do tonight? Watch a movie?"

Our days and nights had slowly fallen into a routine. Training during the day and as much normalcy as we could manage at night. "Rain check? The guys are coming over for another meeting of the minds."

"Wonderful. Divisa gatherings are my favorite." Sarcasm dripped in her tone.

I snickered, knowing she would rather be doing anything else than discussing strategy. These meetings seemed to be happening more frequently, and I normally wasn't much of a tactic kind of guy. Kicking butt was the only tactical policy I employed.

She wiped the back of her hand along her forehead. "I'm going to hit the shower."

"Good idea."

"Are you implying that I stink, Winters?" she asked, a playful smile on her lips.

Drawing her close, I placed kisses all across her skin—nose, forehead, and cheeks. "Not to me. You always smell like Heaven and Hell."

She gave me a kiss on the lips. "Nice save."

My hands shot out, capturing her waist as I pulled her body against mine. "That was a pathetic kiss." I wanted to kiss her again.

"Why don't you show me what a real kiss is?" Her hands gripped the front of my sweaty T-shirt.

"My pleasure." I bent my head and kissed her damp forehead. "I love you."

Her eyes fluttered open. "You owe me a kiss."

Chapter 26

{Angel}

"Anyone else think this is the stupidest plan ever to be concocted?" Emma asked. She was reclining on one of the chairs in the Winters' family room, picking the gunk from under her fingernails with a pocketknife. I didn't even want to know why it closely resembled blood.

And so the argument began on whether to draw out Alastair or wait for the SOB who ruined my life to take us by surprise. I was all for drawing him out. Our turf. Our terms. Why wouldn't we want the advantage? There was only one giant obstacle in the way.

Chase.

He was like an iceberg, icy and immovable. "No. No way. Angel is not going to be bait. What if something goes wrong? What if he—?"

Like I said, one immovable force. I quickly interrupted before he went to a dark place. "I know the risks, Chase." He was more than afraid; he was petrified Alastair might have something up his sleeve. I wasn't sure what else the demon could possibly do to me.

Silver eyes hardened to steel. "Absolutely not. I will lock you up again if I have to."

I scowled. "You stubborn ass."

Unfazed, he lounged on the couch, throwing an arm alongside the back. "I've been called worse, sugar."

Argh. He knew how much I disliked nicknames like honey, sweetie, or sugar. "Oh, I'm not done yet. I was just starting with the As. We still have the rest of the alphabet."

"Angel," he growled.

"You're going to get us all killed," I contended. "I, at least, have regard for other people's lives."

Chase shot me a glare. Tension was high. "I have regard for their lives. Yours is just more important."

Protests died on my lips. I had nothing more to say to him, and I settled down on the couch for what was sure to be a bitch-fest.

Hayden cleared his throat. "There has to be another way to provoke him."

"I don't care how, just as long as I get a crack at him," Craig said.

No doubt Craig would feed me to the wolves if given the chance. There was no lost love between us. College hadn't made him any less scary or unapproachable. That internal warning you get when you realize someone is following you in a dark alley was exactly the feeling Craig gave me.

I shuddered.

Chase eyes meet mine in a silent question. I nodded. Yes, I was fine.

"Get in line, brother," Chase grumbled, clearly frustrated.

"Is there no way to summon him?" Colin asked.

Until he had spoken, I'd completely forgotten he was in the room. A flop of his sandy hair fell over his face, and his usual soft brown eyes were sharp. Colin was serious.

Too bad Chase wasn't going to take him seriously.

"Why is he here?" Chase snapped. All eyes moved to Colin who shifted uncomfortably in his seat.

I bristled, but kept my mouth shut.

Lexi's chin pinched. "He refuses to leave." The two of them were sitting cozily on the loveseat, Lexi's legs crossed on top of Colin's. By the look of it, they had made up.

Chase arched a brow.

I grabbed his forearm before he could stand. "You're not going to escort him out. If Lexi really didn't want him here, do you think he would be here?" I whispered in his ear.

"I want to help," Colin said, scooting forward in his chair.

I exhaled. Here we go. Colin had no clue what can of worms he'd just opened. He was earnest in his offer, but I knew Chase.

He wasn't about to put a human's life in danger, especially someone he knew Lexi cared deeply for.

"Just how exactly do you plan to help?" Chase barked. "They don't care who is calling. Hell doesn't take collect calls." His back muscles tensed.

Sometimes it was difficult to not be amused by Chase's sarcasm.

"For once in your life, do you think you could not be a dick?" Lexi spat, jumping to Colin's defense. "His intentions are good, which is more than I can say for you."

He thrust his fingers through his hair, looking ready to pounce. "He'll only be in the way."

"Look, I'm not here to start anything or get in the way," Colin replied.

The whole room erupted into unruly chatter, everyone talking over each other, throwing out a variety of ideas, all of which sucked. I sat silent with my hands on my bouncing knees. Nervous energy trickled through me. Something was wrong. More wrong than usual. I didn't know what it was, but something was coming. I felt it crawl up my spine, the marks on my hip tingling erratically.

Chase's name began to form on my lips.

Out of nowhere, Lexi shot across the room in a blur of speed and sparkle. She sat down on the coffee table, taking a firm hold of my hand. "What's that on your finger?" she squealed.

The room had gone quiet. "Umm, a ring," I replied, feeling color stain my cheeks.

"I can see that. Did you—? Are you guys—?" Lexi tongue-tied didn't happen often.

"I think this is the first time I've ever seen you at a loss for words," Chase said.

"Don't ruin this moment," she said, wiping under her eyes, which were brimming with emotion. "Oh. My. God. You're engaged?"

I nodded. "That was pretty much my reaction."

Voomphf. I found myself engulfed in a hug that almost knocked me on my ass.

"Why didn't you tell me? Why didn't either one of you tell me? How long?" And off she rattled, question after question.

"I was going to. After…" *I kill Alastair*, I finished in my head.

"I want to know everything. Every single detail." She turned my hand from side to side, studying my rock. "It's beautiful. I can't believe you picked this without me," she said, turning to Chase.

"Believe it or not, I do have taste."

"I guess you would have to. You fell in love with my best friend."

Congratulations came from all sides of the room. The guys did the guy thing—back pats, handshaking, and one shoulder hugs.

"We have so much to do, so much to plan," Lexi proclaimed.

"Ugh. Stop. You're giving me a migraine," I grumbled.

Chase laughed, amused.

"I was thinking about eloping," I muttered. "No fuss."

"No flipping way," Lexi protested. "You can't take this away from me. If you don't want to plan your wedding, then let me. I will do everything. All you have to do is show up on the day."

I pressed two fingers to my temple. "Do we really need to talk about this now?"

"I'm with Angel. The mushy stuff is over. Can we get back to killing demons?" Emma asked.

Lexi held a finger in the air, hushing Emma. "When's the wedding? Can I be your maid of honor? OMG. We have so much to do…Chapel, venue, food, invitations, guest list, dress…" She ticked off each item on her fingers, and when she ran out of fingers, she started over again.

I blacked out after dress.

"Reality check, princess. There won't be a wedding if we don't destroy Alastair," Emma interrupted in her usually boorish self.

Lexi pouted, eyes a mixture of the sea and the sun. "You take the fun out of f-u-n."

Things were getting pretty lively in the Winters' home tonight, and when you were dealing with a group eighty-nine percent supernatural, stuff was bound to get broken. Hopefully, it wouldn't be anything valuable or that couldn't be replaced.

Much to Lexi's disappointment, the conversation steered back to killing, Emma's favorite topic. "We still haven't found a way to destroy them," Emma said. "Before we start baiting demons, we should probably figure out how to terminate them. For good."

There were a lot of head nods. I tried to sound brave and confident as I shouted over the group. "It has to be me. I have to kill Alastair."

As expected, I got a bunch of crazy looks, but at least the volume in the room had gone down a few notches. Hayden with his boy-next-door good looks eyed me thoughtfully. "Angel, no one here expects you to singlehandedly take on the big bad wolf alone."

"No," Chase said, his head down, staring at the floor. "She's right. Angel is the only one who can defeat Alastair. Or any demon for that matter."

"I'm confused," Travis said. "Thirty minutes ago you completely shut down the idea of her drawing them out, and now you're endorsing the idea of Angel killing Alastair. What gives, man?"

"It's…"

"If you say complicated I'll hit you," Travis interjected.

"And then I will," Craig added.

No one was going to hit anyone if I could help it. "I'm a slayer," I blurted out.

Silence followed. And stretched.

"A slayer?" Emma broke the dead air. "There hasn't been a slayer in centuries."

Chase's eyes narrowed. "How do you know?"

"Because I attended hunter boot camp, remember?"

"What do you know?" Chase asked, inching to the edge of the couch.

The entire room was waiting on pins and needles. Emma flipped closed her pocketknife. "Only what I've read, which was very little. Most hunters believe slayers are a myth. They've been extinct for so long, most everyone has forgotten about them."

Suddenly, I felt like I was on display. "The why and how aren't important. What is imperative is whether or not my flames will really destroy the soul of a demon."

"So we don't know if she can really obliterate them?" Craig sneered.

Jerk.

"There haven't been any volunteers since I found out, which was only a few days ago." Cynicism laced my voice.

"What else have you two been hiding?" Lexi pouted.

"How did you find out?" Hayden asked.

Chase, Travis, and I all squirmed in our seats.

"Kira?" Lexi squawked. "Why would you believe anything that comes out of her mouth?"

"What choice do we have?" Chase countered. "This is our only option, because everything else we've done thus far hasn't worked."

"This plan keeps getting screwier. I'm tried of being a sitting duck, and I'm ready for some action," Emma said, flipping her knife open.

It seemed to be the consensus all around. Everyone was tired of being at Hell's mercy.

You ask and you shall receive. Emma's little call for action was answered.

Pop. Pop. Pop.

One by one the pins and screws holding the front door to the frame hit the hardwood floor. For several heartbeats, everyone in the room stood, staring at the door, immobilized by disbelief.

WTF.

With nothing securing the large wooden door, it crashed to the floor with a loud boom that shook the lower part of the house. Colin paled beside Lexi.

Hell had come knocking.

Chapter 27

{Angel}

"They're coming," I said, fumbling with my ring. The cool metal against my skin gave me strength and courage. It wasn't the ring itself, but what it represented and the guy who had given it to me.

"No," Chase said, his expression troubled. "They're already here."

It should have been no surprise, but I hadn't expected things to kick off so quickly. I wasn't ready. Not yet. I needed more time to practice, to hone my skills, but my time was up.

Emma and Travis hauled ass into the kitchen, throwing open drawers and cabinets, pulling out the secret stash of weapons. Travis tossed Hayden and Craig each a blade dipped in rubies. Lexi bent down, reaching into her boot for her own weapons.

In under a minute, everyone in the room—even Colin—was armed and loaded. Emma had her bow strapped onto her back and wicked-looking blades in each hand. Her red hair was tied into a ponytail. "How about we put this slayer theory to the test?"

Adrenaline started firing inside me, flowing through my veins.

I nodded. "Why not?"

All plans previously made were pretty much thrown out the window. This wasn't like any other demon fight, I told myself. This was bigger. The stakes were larger. My hands were shaking, fear soaked my skin, and my heart beat wildly in my chest. Yep. Just like my other encounters with demons.

With unsteady hands, I pulled out my phone and sent a text to my mom, advising her to seek a safe place and to stay there until she heard from me.

Be safe, Angel, she texted back. **I love you.**

One by one we crept over the fallen door, prepared to meet the horror that waited for us on the other side. The chill in the air was more pronounced than usual for this time of year. Chase's shoulder brushed up against mine, sharing his warmth and his steadiness. Night was in full swing, the moon a circle glowing brightly and illuminating the fields.

Travis tweaked the end of my nose, a gesture of affection. If things didn't go down the way we hoped, then this was it. I gave him a weak smile. "Even in Hell, I'll still kick your butt in CoD."

He laughed. "Go get 'em, firestarter."

It was weird having them depend on *me* for once. I'd always looked to Chase, Travis, and Lexi to keep me safe. They'd been stronger and faster. Here was to hoping I didn't crack under pressure.

Chase and I held hands for a moment, offering silent assurances, but the moment wasn't long enough. "You good?"

I wanted to say no. How could I be good? His warm hand felt strong and sturdy in mine. "Yeah. You?"

He blinked, his eyes flashing amber. "Just peachy, Angel Eyes."

Let the good times roll.

As a group, we spread out but kept our ranks close. We passed the property line, each of us on alert. Chase's expression was menacing. Craig, Hayden, and Travis bantered as we walked, easing a bit of the tension. Lexi stayed close to Colin, afraid to leave him alone in the house, but probably more afraid to have him in the middle of a war. The demons, in their true form, came out of the darkness, a sea of glowing scarlet eyes.

"Guard your loins boys. Trouble has arrived," Emma said. "Better get those flames hot and ready, Angel."

I rolled my eyes.

My body went into some sort of protective mode as I cleared my mind in preparation for a fight. I was definitely borrowing some of Chase's confidence through our bond. He gave my hand one last squeeze, and I blew him a raspberry as we turned our focus to the parade of creatures coming right at us.

The ground thundered and trembled from the immeasurable pounding of feet as demons, hellhounds, and whatever else raced across the fields. Weeks of training prompted me into action. I only hoped it was enough, and I didn't end up in tiny little pieces scattered all over the place.

I lunged forward, bracing the blade in my hand.

Emma fired her bow, the arrow slicing through the air, sprouting four ruby points at the tip, and straight into a demon's throat. Hayden and Travis tag-teamed two demons, circling around the creatures and binding them with a rope made of properties I didn't yet understand. The demons howled, and the skin touched by the red threads bubbled and oozed black goo.

"I'm going to rip out your sticky bits," Craig threatened right before he plummeted his bare fist into a demon's chest, splattering his shirt and face with demon blood.

I cringed.

Lexi was plastered to Colin. She was wielding a whip, twirling and slicing it through the air as Colin clutched her dagger. His knuckles were white, as was his face. Lexi wrapped the end of the whip around a demon. "Ooops. Sorry, not sorry," she said sweetly, staring down at a pile of ash.

Chase was in the process of shoving a row of demons and making sure each landed on his blade. Craig, Hayden, and Travis started working their way through line after line of monsters. There were a few demons in human skin. I figured they were called to join the army, but most of them came in all their ugly glory. Black skin. Long, pointed nails. Some with horns. Some without. Razor sharp teeth. Demons came in a variety of shapes and sizes, but the one thing they all had in common, besides their bloodlust eyes, was they were all skin-crawlingly grotesque.

I stopped in the thick of the fight and shook out my hands. A demon tried to grab me just as I spread my fingers, and I jumped back a step, barely missing being minced by the creature's claws. Chase was there in the next blink, sinking his knife into the demon's eye socket. It gave an unnatural howl, shriveling to the ground.

Chase held the tip of his blade skyward. There was a scarlet eyeball dangling at the end "Well, that's just disgusting." He flung the hilt, sending the eyeball sailing through the air.

"I think it's time to add a little spice to the party, don't you agree, Chase?" Travis asked, looking at me.

"Definitely." He squeezed my hip. "Light 'em up."

Now it was my time to shine, but I was suffering from a bit of performance anxiety. I held my breath, arms outstretched at my sides. If I let my nerves get to me, we were all dead. *You are not going to crumble under the pressure.* So I kept telling myself until…

Fire leapt over my fingertips, and in that instant I could have whooped for joy and done a ridiculous happy dance. *I can do this.*

Another demon made a play for me just as my hands ignited, and this time I was ready, veins filled with torrid power.

The demon's eyes bulged. "It'sssss not posssssible."

Geez, the lisp on these guys was heinous. "Believe it, atomic jerkwad." I let the romping flames loose.

I stopped breathing, waiting to see what would happen, as did everyone else. The fire traveled through the air as if it was attracted to the demon, drawn to it, and the beast was powerless to stop it. His tar skin caught. I held out my hand, flames crackling over my fingers. One second passed, two, three. I didn't know how many more. I lost track of time, and I was too enthralled with the flames that rushed over the demon's body, until it covered every inch. As the demon fell, its head detached from its body.

Boom.

The body exploded, leaving behind a black residue burned into a perfect circle on the ground.

Panting from exertion, my friends had stopped to watch me with spellbound fascination.

"Holy shit," echoed a uniformed chorus, including me.

"I think it's safe to say that Angel's a slayer." Emma said. "You're going to make a helluva hunter."

Chase scowled, his demon eyes glowing. "You okay?"

I nodded. "Yeah, I am." The flames subsided, sinking into my pores, but the heat stayed with me, just under the surface, ready and waiting to be called forth for more. "And you? Are you hurt?"

"I'll be fine. Nothing that won't heal."

In that instant, I thought about Mom, Devin, and the small town I'd grown to love. Tonight was going to be a night many would never forget. I know *I* wouldn't. Demons were popping out of every nook and cranny this town had.

The wind had picked up to alarming speeds and the sky had turned an ugly greenish-black. In the distance, the emergency alarm sounded, indicating a severe storm was headed our way. They had no idea. The storm was already here.

Looking around, I realized we were barely making a dent. At this rate, the demons would eventually overrun us. I needed to amp things up. I concentrated on the swell of energy flowing through my body, and in an instant, it spread down my arms.

Using my speed, I moved to the next demon and the next. One by one, I set their asses on fire. Just a touch and the demon promptly burned and combusted into nothingness. They had no defense against me. And soon there were no creatures left in the field.

Emma laughed behind me. "Didn't anyone teach you not to play with your kill?"

"Have you met my instructor?" I panted.

"Unfortunately, countless times."

"Is that all you got?" Travis screamed, provoking Hell as he came to stand beside Emma.

Chase shook his head. "Don't count on it." He spit blood on

the ground, and used the back of his hand to wipe his mouth.

"You guys are like the Avengers," Colin said in awe. There was black blood splattered on his cheek, but the blade still seized in his hand was clean.

"Let's get one thing straight, Rolin. We're not superheroes," Chase rumbled.

"Speak for yourself, man," Craig said before Colin could correct Chase for his deliberate blunder of his name. "I am definitely super."

Travis chuckled. "Super lame."

Hayden and Emma barked out a laugh.

We all needed a moment to relax and let the tension of fighting for our lives roll off our shoulders. I looked my friends over, taking in the cuts marring their skin, the blood soaking their clothes—mostly demon—and I was more determined than ever. "I'm going to char that son of a bitch," I growled.

"That's the plan, Angel Eyes."

A smile curled on my lips. "What are we waiting for?"

Hell didn't disappoint. My heart sank to new depths as I spotted another wave of telltale red eyes in the distance. Two, three times as many as before. My marks twitched, increasing in alarming speeds, and I heard the groans and grunts of Hell.

We all got serious in a snap.

A putrid stink of sulfur wafted in the air. I grabbed Chase's shoulder, steadying myself as the ground quaked. The demons branched off, half surrounding me, half zeroing in on Chase. The air was so thick and hot it clogged my nose and burned my throat.

I coughed, suppressing the urge to gag.

Chase's eyes meet mine for a brief few seconds, surging with a magnitude of feelings. Love. Courage. Rage. Fear.

Here we go again.

Do or die.

I summoned the fire. The flames at my fingertips sputtered before blazing beautifully. So many demons. So many monsters. It was too late to come up with a different plan.

Inhaling sharply, I watched as Alastair suddenly appeared out of the shadows. He didn't charge like the lower demons, letting them do all his dirty work, but as soon as I saw him, I couldn't take my eyes off the beast responsible for tearing my life in two.

"Angel!" Chase screamed. It was the pure panic in his voice that broke the spell.

I was fenced in by twenty or so demons. One managed to get a hand on my ankle, his claws slicing my skin. I winced, and Chase called my name again. Bending my knees, I tapped my hand on what I guess would be his shoulder. At the moment of contact, my flames licked over him.

I pushed back the sting of the pain and turned around in time to see that Colin and Lexi were in serious trouble. Chase noticed a millisecond before me and started to move. I was right behind him, but the coconut-sized pit in my stomach warned that neither one of us was going to make it in time, not with the army of demons spanning between us.

Lexi screamed.

It was a sound I'd never forget. I stumbled, my knees weakening at the sight of Colin being raised in the air by his throat. The lower-demon manhandled him like a doll, except when I played with a doll, I didn't rip out its heart and toss aside its body.

I felt sick.

Oh God. Colin was dead.

Lexi sunk to the ground, her hands covering the blood spilling from the opened wound on his chest. She shook her head. "No. No. No," she repeated over and over again, but there was nothing we could do, and our situation was looking dire.

I was dumbstruck.

Wildly, I searched through the commotion, until I focused on Chase. There were at least a dozen demons encompassing him as he fought and hacked with his blade, alternating with his fists.

I knew he needed help, and he wasn't the only one. Travis and Emma were trying to keep Lexi from being demolished as she lay over Colin's lifeless and bloodied body.

"Get her out of here!" Chase yelled.

Lexi wasn't making it easy. "I'm not leaving," she said in a tearful low growl. I don't know how she didn't fall utterly apart. My guess was she was running on rage. Lexi got to her feet and swiped at her eyes. From where I stood, they were pure gold.

Oh crap.

There wasn't time to breathe. One crisis led straight to another, and the confidence I'd been feeling before withered away. I needed to get to Chase. He was in trouble. My marks flared as his pain registered throughout my body. I raced toward him, but my worst fear came true.

No matter how many demons I touched and torched, it wasn't enough.

A hellhound barreled up behind him and took a chunk out of his calf. Chase's wounded cries filled the air as he fell to his knees.

No. God please. No!

Breathe, I told myself. *Just breathe.* I gave myself up to the heat. White-gold flames spread down my arms, over my chest, down my waist, until I was basking in nothing but fire. Empowered, I grinned and dove forward.

Demons fell. My flames licked over their torsos and faces, howling as they ruptured into dust.

Buh-bye.

Chase was limping, but at least he was back on his feet. I never should have doubted him, but I learned you couldn't be overly cautious. As much as I wanted to continue fighting alongside my friends, I needed to focus on what Chase and I really wanted.

Alastair.

The bastard must have had ESP, because he suddenly appeared just at the edge of where the fields met the forest line. Finally, he showed some balls and revealed his slimy self.

"I'm going to destroy you," I whispered.

Chapter 28

{Angel}

A gross feeling slithered through my belly, worming its way up my chest. I faced Alastair. "What took you so long?" My heart banged at my own courage. The rest of my body quivered.

"Ah, I see you brought the B-team with you," Alastair said, smiling.

I strode forward, and Chase discreetly stepped between a formidable Alastair and me without looking my way. Always trying to be my hero.

"Wow. Showing your ugly mug here takes guts. You've just issued your own demise," Chase rumbled.

"Not everything is always as it seems."

I really hated cagey replies that left me more puzzled. If his plan was to use suspicion and doubt to get inside our heads, he was going to need a better plan. "Then you know what I am," I declared.

Hidden by the dark green shadows of the ominous skies and the thick covering of the evergreens, Alastair's voice rang out over the field. There was a godly quality to the texture as he replied, "It doesn't matter what you've become. What matters is what you're not."

The winds hadn't let up; if anything, they had gotten stronger. Bits of wheat blew in the air and, in select spots, circled in a cyclone. "I'll tell you what I'm not, and that is your slave."

He grinned wryly. "Glad to see you haven't lost your spunk. It would have been a shame."

I bit my lip, trying to figure out how this was going to play out.

"I'll admit I'm seriously disappointed in you, Angel. Such potential. I gave it all to you and you threw it away, wasted such power. Now you're useless, and Chase knows all too well what I do with waste."

"I was hoping you would feel that way." I flung open my palms, the tips of my fingers glowing embers.

"Ah, someone learned a new trick. I'm quaking," he mocked, not an ounce of fear or surprise.

He made it sound like I was a dog, which pushed my buttons. "We'll see about that." I planned to have the last laugh. Raising my hand, energy crackled at my fingertips and wrapped down my arm like a snake. I hurled a bolt of fire from my palm, shooting it across the field toward Alastair.

A blur of red light flashed as it rolled and rolled. Not going to lie, I was feeling pretty good about myself, but there was a little voice in the back of my head. *This is it? This is the best Hell's got?* I wanted to tell that voice to stop bursting my bubble.

I waited for the flame to take root and spread like wildfire over his body. I felt the need to hold my breath. Out of the corner of my eye, I saw Travis and Emma inch up behind me. I lost track of everyone else, solely concentrating on the bright flame. The edges of Alastair's body started to flicker, and I thought this was it. He made an inhuman sound. And then…

Nothing. Gone. *Poof.*

The orangey-red sparks fizzled out, not a single drop of ash.

I inhaled sharply.

What the shit?

I didn't understand. If I was the slayer, why didn't he go *poof?*

Well, that just plain sucked. What was I going to do now? Everyone was depending on me, and I somehow managed to totally doof the single most important task I'd ever been given. *Only me.*

Alastair laughed. "You're going to need more than that, little slayer."

The blood drained from my face.

A cacophony of groans, gasps, and sounds of shock created this domino effect of confusion. Right then, I think we all knew it was about survival.

"Mine turn." Alastair raised a bear-sized hand.

I hadn't even noticed he had moved until he was directly in my face. My eyes went wide, and I heard Chase holler my name as Alastair's hand arched in the air. I stumbled sideways toward the ground at the force of Alastair backhanding me. Delirious, my cheekbone pounded with pain.

Chase roared, vaulting forward, but he didn't get far. A trio of demons intercepted. Chase blocked a punch to the head, only to take one in the side. He recovered like it was nothing, throwing a quick precession of hits to the culprit.

"What are you waiting for?" Alastair shouted to his subordinates. "Kill her! Kill them all!"

Demons scurried in every direction, and my gaze crawled along the field as I slowly lifted my head. My friends were out there battling for their lives while I was having a panic attack. Chase fought one after another, pure malice radiating in his eyes as he tried to get to me, even Lexi with tears of potent rage streaming down her pale face, was ferocious.

Horror settled in my gut like rocks.

Craig cracked his neck. "This stopped being awesome about five minutes ago."

"It's too late," Travis said, grabbing a demon and slamming him into the ground.

Whirling around, Chase pulled me against his chest, tightening his hold. "I got you." He twisted, bringing me with him, and drop-kicked a hellhound in the snout.

"It didn't work. I don't understand." My voice was hoarse, and my throat was dry from the dirt, dust, and wheat.

"We'll figure something out. Stay close to me," he told me.

This was one of those times when I was actually going to listen.

Things went from hopeful to craptastic in a matter of moments. War had been imminent, but I had always visualized us on the winning side. Now Colin was dead and the monsters nightmares are made of were everywhere.

Chase and the others did what came naturally to them, moving so fast I didn't think there was a measure of time available, but the demons were faster. Flying over the ground, two rushed at Chase and me. Chase leapt, slamming into both demons. The three of them collided, rolling over the ground, and my breath faltered as I watched Chase take a direct hit that was like a cannonball. And another.

My heart tripped.

His pain was undeniable. I felt it.

Feeling his agony finally snapped a thread inside me, and I conjured my best means of defense. The bolt slammed into one of the demons, spinning him around. Seconds later, he went up and blew to bits as I'd expected.

Lower-demons I apparently had no problem with.

My brain stopped processing things, and I went on demon-killing patrol. I was going to take out as many of these a-holes as I could. At least give us a fighting chance. My arms continued to glow brightly as I ripped through the demons, touching this one, touching that one, each going up into flames. The screams.

The sound was going to be in my nightmares for years to come.

It was during this rampage that I noticed something, and it gave me an idea—a stupid, risky idea Chase would have quickly shut down, which was why I didn't tell him. As I touched one of the demons, setting him ablaze, he slithered once out of my reach, so I gripped his arm. And something happened. Something different. Then the sucker detonated. But an idea was born.

I just needed to get close enough to Alastair.

Using my fire as a shield, I weaved through the maze of demons toward the commander-in-chief. He wasn't doing a whole lot, other than smirking and enjoying himself too much. I lost sight of Chase. Not necessarily a bad thing, but it would undoubtedly have repercussions later, assuming there was a later.

Alastair's smile officially creeped me out.

He stepped forward. "I guess this is it. Just you and me, *slayer*."

"Looks that way." As inconspicuously as I could manage, I

inched my way step-by-step closer to the higher demon.

"So tell me, how would you like to die? Bleeding out takes too long. Snapping your neck is too quick. How about strangulation? It's one of my personal favorites."

Oh, how nice. He was going to give me options.

"No offense, but all those choices suck. I have another idea." I appeared at his side and craned my neck, looking up. "You'll no longer have control over him, over me, or over another demon." Without further ado, I exploded into action, grabbing his arm and sending a blast of pure heat straight from my soul to Alastair's.

His blood-red eyes bulged. Jerking, he tried to pull away, but the current of energy rolling off me to him made it impossible. And unfortunately, it was a two-way street. There was no going back. I couldn't break the connection either. "What have you done?" he ranted.

"If there's a will, there's a way. And my will is strong. Payback's a bitch." This was what Kira had meant when she said killing Alastair could be potentially harmful or worse. I felt the ripple of the fire flowing from my fingers to his veins.

To rid him from both Earth and Hell, I had to fill his veins entirely with the flames of a slayer, but there was a problem. There was always a hiccup when dealing with a demon. The longer I held onto him, the more danger I put myself in. It wasn't only my energy levels, but my life source.

Alastair screamed as the flames spanned over his skin, the red of his eyes turning to coals. His entire body lit up like the Vegas strip, becoming the center of attention.

I felt a rumble deep in my chest, and I knew it was Chase. He was about two seconds away from interceding and this would have all been for nothing.

"Don't, Chase," I whispered. "Don't."

Angel.

I heard him say my name inside my head. It seemed to touch my heart, my soul, and my body. Our bond.

Even if he tried to stop me, I don't think he could, but I was more worried he would get caught in the crossfire. I didn't want to hurt him, and if he touched me now, it would be lethal. My whole body was burning from the inside out, veins pumping with fire.

Alastair's body started to convulse, and I knew the end was near.

But the longer I fueled the fire, the weaker I became. My body trembled, and little dots of blackness pranced behind my eyes. I forced my eyes to stay locked on Alastair, and it wasn't until his pupils became large and black, snuffing the scarlet color, and his head fell forward that I knew I'd won.

The sound of Alastair's soul vaporizing was reminiscent of firecrackers on Fourth of July. *Pop. Pop. Hiss.*

And in one grand finale, he exploded, the night bursting into a light so bright I went momentarily blind. Without any support, my knees buckled and I collapsed. On impact, the flames extinguished and my skin returned to normal. I fell backward, panting, trying to decide whether I was going to pass out or babble joyous nonsense. Lying against the brittle grass, staring up at the stars, I felt my first taste of victory.

It felt fan-freaking-tastic.

And exhausting.

I felt as if I could sleep for a month. *Thank you. Thank you. Thank God.* It was over. And as far as I could tell, I was still in one piece.

Face splattered with blood and black goo, Chase closed the distance between us and grinned down at me. He loomed over me, his features tortured with concern. Fear radiated from him. Gray eyes scanned every fiber of me, searching for injury. "You're okay?"

I nodded. "You're free. Do you feel it?"

"Yes, Angel Eyes, I feel it. You broke the bond connecting us to Hell."

I grinned. "But not between us."

He leaned forward and kissed my lips. "Never."

The skies opened up and torrential rain poured as if it was wiping clean the mess Hell left behind, washing away the ash that covered almost every inch of the field.

WEIL

Chapter 29

{Chase}

In the aftermath of Spring Valley's "worst storm in history," the community came together, rebuilding. The small town was crowded with people from surrounding areas, helping and comforting others. Complete strangers in the midst of chaos, removing debris, lending their services, and supporting their neighbors. Talk flew around town about the destruction and how, miraculously, the death toll was only one.

There had been no warnings, nothing to alert the people to safety. The storm had hit swiftly and violently, blowing through the small town at alarming speeds. Lightning had lit the sky like this town had never seen, striking trees and burning a barn to the ground.

Crops were destroyed, homes damaged, and people injured, and every local news station was reporting how lucky we all were that it hadn't been worse, that the whole town hadn't been swept off the map.

I didn't share their blessedness.

The life that had been lost was my cousin's boyfriend, and his death left wounds that would affect her for years.

They were all clueless about what really went down during the storm. It hadn't been Mother Nature that had torn through our small town. If they knew what was really behind the devastation, Spring Valley would be a ghost town.

As we fled the field that night, I couldn't seem to let go of Angel's hand. The rain pelted down on us, cooling not only the night's air but also washing the grime and demon blood from our bodies.

I pulled her into my room and cornered her against the wall, needing a few minutes alone. I grasped her face between my hands, and she held onto my waist. All I could do was stare at her, unsure if I should kiss her or hug her. "You did it."

"*We* did it," she whispered in disbelief. "I can't believe he's really gone."

The truth of those words did something funny inside me. It was hard to comprehend. In a way, I wasn't sure what to do next.

"It's unreal, isn't it?" she asked.

I rubbed the pad of my thumb along her chin, pressing kisses to her cheek, the tip of her nose, her forehead, and then finally her lips. It made me feel alive. I wrapped my arms around her, knowing that in another part of the house, Lexi was crying. She'd broken down.

Hearing her soft cries gripped my heart, and tears gathered in Angel's eyes. She buried her head in my shirt. "She'll get through this. She's strong."

Angel sniffed. "And we'll be there to help her."

"Always." I kissed the top of her head, running my fingers through her hair. We clung to each other, both knowing how damn lucky we were to have one another. Death was the hardest on the living.

~*~*~*~

A week had gone by and we were settling into life without the constant threat of Alastair. I was officially parentless, but my life was full and rich. No complaints.

Angel and I were just returning from a trip in town. Before we went inside, I stopped her. "Hang on, I have something for you, but first I need you to open your palm."

She gave me her what-do-you-have-up-your-sleeve look. Under normal circumstances she would argue, but after a moment or two, she rolled her eyes and opened her hand.

"No flames." I smirked.

A small smile split her lips.

I dropped a small key into the palm of her hand.

She glanced down at the single silver key. "What's this? The key to your heart?"

My lips twitched. "Hardly. You've already managed to unlock

that all on your own. This is something more tangible."

Her violet eyes went wide. "A car? Chase, did you buy me a car?"

I laughed. "Think bigger."

She wet her lips, putting on her pondering face. "You know I hate surprises."

"How about I give you a hint? Close your eyes."

"Chase," she warned. "Just tell me."

"What fun is that? Now close your eyes."

She huffed, but her lashes fluttered shut. I walked behind her, brushed the hair off her shoulder, and whispered in her ear, "Don't peek."

I felt a shudder roll through her body and smiled. Gently, I placed my hands on either side of her arms to guide her. "Okay, put one foot in front of the other."

"If I run into something, so help me…"

I chuckled. "Trust me. I'm not going to let you face-plant the grass," I assured. "This will be worth it. I promise."

"It better be," she warned, walking like a mummy across the yard. Her steps were slow and unsure. I let her set her own pace, drawing out the surprise. Plus it was kind of funny watching her fumble across the grass.

When she was right where I wanted her, I told her to stop. "Now open your eyes."

Flashing in front of her so I could see her face, I watched her long lashes lift. She stared at me a moment before her gaze flicked over my shoulder at what used to be her house. Some crazy person had bought it.

"Uh, I don't get it. What's the surprise?" She glanced down at the key dangling between her thumb and forefinger, and then back up at her house.

I rocked back on my heels, waiting for the moment when she made the connection. I didn't have to wait long.

"Holy shit. Chase, you didn't. You're the lunatic who bought my house?"

My grin was full-wattage. "It's not mine. It's ours." I smiled down at Angel who still seemed dumbstruck.

She blew out a breath. "You. Bought. A. Freaking. House."

My shoulder lifted in a slight shrug, and I shoved my hands into my pockets. "I figured we'd need a place to live after we got married."

Her cheeks flushed. "You did, did you?"

"And I know your mom selling the house tore you in two."

She linked her hands on the back of my neck. "I love you."

I twined my fingers around her waist, content to just stand there holding her and feeling happiness stir inside her, blooming. "So does that mean you like the surprise?"

She leaned down, placing the softest kiss on my lips, the kind

I'd treasure forever. "When do we move in?"

I wiggled my brows. "As soon as we say I do."

"When's the next flight to Vegas?"

I coughed. "Angel Eyes, we're not getting married in Vegas." There was no way I was ever going back there. Hell-to-the-no.

Her brows drew together. "What do you have against eloping?"

I brushed the tip of her nose with mine. "Nothing. Name the time and the place, just as long as it's not Vegas."

She rested her cheek on mine. "I think I want to get married here."

My hands flattened on the small of her back, and I pulled her close. "You mean like *here*? In Spring Valley?"

She nodded, tracing the line of my jaw. "Right where it all started. And I was thinking it might help take Lexi's mind off…things."

"I think it's perfect." And just what we all needed, something happy to look forward to for once. I brushed my lips across hers.

Giddy with joy, she laughed. "You're perfect. I don't know how, but you're absolutely perfect."

I framed her face and again kissed the girl I loved. The girl I would marry. "I'm perfect for you."

We walked hand in hand, toward our house, toward our future together. Tonight was the beginning of our happily ever after.

Epilogue

{Angel}

Ten years later…

"Mom!" yelled a little voice. "Dad's fighting again." It was coming from outside, through the screen door.

Smiling fondly, I stepped out on the porch and that smile slipped from my lips as I watched Chase deliver a killing blow. The demon went up in ash.

"Cool," said the little four-year-old at my side who was the spitting image of his father.

I glanced down, ruffling Liam's dark hair. "Chase," I said in a disapproving tone.

He sauntered over to me, a sinister smirk on his lips. The man had not aged a day—well, except for crinkles near his eyes, which only made him better looking. Beads of sweat from the summer sun dotted his temples.

Leaning my elbows on the railing, I met Chase's impish gaze. "Will you stop using Kira's demons to impress your son?"

A dark brow shot up. "What? You know he's not the only one impressed."

I folded my arms. "Is that so?"

"Come on, Angel Eyes. I can't get rusty. These skills need to be maintained."

"Mmm-hmm. You don't see me out there lighting things on fire, do you?"

A little giggle sounded behind us, and Chase's smile grew, his eyes twinkling. "Did you hear that? I think we have faeries in the garden."

It sounded again.

A little girl with faerie blue eyes peeked her head out from a bush on the side of the porch. At only three, Olivia was a glittering toddler who had an eye for pretty things, much like her aunt Lexi. Sometimes I wondered if she was my daughter, so opposite of me except in coloring.

"I think we might need to call the faerie exterminator," Chase said.

I laughed.

Chase was an exceptional father and a loving husband. I never imagined my life could be so happy. Not to say it wasn't without its problems.

I mean, whom was I kidding? He was part-demon and I was a slayer, but neither stopped us from living—from giving our two children a happy but slightly unusual childhood. They were raised knowing what existed in the world, brought up to defend themselves and their family. Lines got a little blurry when Kira came to visit, but that was another story.

Emma and Travis often brought over their little girl, Nora, who was just three months older than our daughter, Olivia—the sneaky faerie. Mischief lived on in the Winters' bloodline and our children were proof. Nora was stubborn and strong like her mother, a born leader. She was also full of life and humor like her father. Nora was going to make a great demon hunter one day. Emma, like Chase and me, chose to raise our families with a different outlook on the world.

Our families gave new meaning to the definition of blended.

The sunlight sparkled off the twirling wind chime hanging on the porch next door. Mom and Devin absolutely adored being able to spoil their grandchildren. They'd been married for seven years now.

Chase snuck around the side of the bush, and when he captured our little girl, she squealed with delight. It was music to my ears. His laughter mixed with hers.

He would always be my soul, my heart, my life.

Chase Winters was mine. His eyes took on tiny gold flecks of light when he was annoyed, upset, or ridiculously happy as he was now.

REDEEMING ANGEL

I felt sorry for all those girls who didn't have a Chase. I was never going to let mine go.

The End

In case you go through Chase and Angel withdrawals like me, check out my Wattpad, where I will randomly be posting bonus scenes from Chase and Angel's life after Redeeming Angel. This collection of bonuses is called Eternally Angel.
https://www.wattpad.com/user/jlweil

Stalk Me Online:
(I'm serious. I would love to hear from you.)
Website: http://www.jlweil.com
My Blog: http://jlweil.blogspot.com/
Twitter: https://twitter.com/#!/JLWeil
Facebook: http://www.facebook.com/#!/jenniferlweil
Goodreads: http://www.goodreads.com/author/show/5831854.J_L_Weil

REDEEMING ANGEL

Acknowledgements

First and foremost, I want to thank each and every reader who picked up this series. Without you I never would have been able to write The End on the final page of the final chapter. I never would have had the courage to continue writing. So I thank you from the bottom of my heart. I love your guts out.

It's crazy for me to wrap my head around the fact that this is the end for Chase and Angel. When I sat down a few years ago to write book one, I didn't think a single person would read it, let alone grow to love these two very cheeky characters as much as I did, and here we are, book five. I had no clue what was going to happen, but I adore how the story unfolded.

I have so many people to be grateful for.

My two ah-ma-zing boys, for knowing when to wait patiently while I finished a thought, a sentence, or a whole chapter.

All the awesome book bloggers for taking the time to post and spread the good word, as well as my rockin' beta team.

And as always, to my family for their support and inspiration. I couldn't have done any of it without them.

Made in the USA
Middletown, DE
20 October 2015